God's Forge

PATRICK DORSEY

LEGENDARY PLANET

SAINT LOUIS

Also by Patrick Dorsey
and available soon from Legendary Planet:

The Champion Sky
(expected 2014)

ISBN 978-1-939437-08-2

COVER ILLUSTRATION COPYRIGHT © 2013 BY LEGENDARY PLANET, LLC.
COVER DESIGN BY EVAN WILLNOW.
BOOK DESIGN BY EVAN WILLNOW.
TYPESET IN ALEGREYA AND YATAGHAN.

MANUFACTURED IN THE UNITED STATES OF AMERICA

LEGENDARY PLANET, LLC
PO BOX 440081
SAINT LOUIS, MISSOURI 63144-0081

LegendaryPlanet.com

CONTENTS

Non nobis Domine non nobis
Sed nomine tuo da gloriam

Not unto us, O Lord, not unto us,
But unto Thy name give the glory.

- Psalm 115:1
  The prayer of the Knights Templar

CHAPTER I

The tower had been swaying for hours. The huge, gilded lion that stared out over the desert from atop it listed, feverish, and tipped slowly forward, pulling down the surrounding wall with it as it finally crashed.

Fires rumbled, belching sooty, black smog that burned eyes and choked away air. Trumpets blared, deafening even over the crash of cymbals and drums. Shouts of pain and rage dissolved in the clamor of swords and axes chopping at armor and shields, of bones breaking and flesh rending. Blood hung thick in the air, a wet, red haze, and the Mediterranean sun blazed white and without mercy, beating down attacker and defender without favor.

Acre, vast seaport and the last Crusader stronghold in the Holy Land, was falling.

Weeks of relentless Saracen assault led by Al-Ashrafi's Mameluk army shattered the city's massive wall north of St. Anthony's Gate. The enormous stones and flaming logs hurled for days by the two great catapults *Sayaghliboona* and *Sarsaran* and the other Mameluk mangonels hammered the southeast fortress tower.

Led by the Emirs themselves, desert warriors flooded furiously through the ragged breach. Howling war cries, they scrambled over the debris, wickedly curved swords flashing.

An army a quarter-million strong followed behind them.

All that blocked the crumbling fissure were the knights of St. Lazarus and the Order of Teutonic Knights. The black-coated Knights Hospitaller charged over the dusty, sun-beaten stones street to bolster them, but outmanned ten to one by the enemy already through the wall, they, too, were swallowed in the tide of steel.

Then came the Knights Templar.

"Be glorious!" rose over the awful roar. The Templar rallying cry rippled up and down the battle line, punctuated the awful cadences of the clashing weapons and Mameluk cymbals and trumpets. Wading in with sword, mace, and shield, the Templars were ruthless in their discipline, terrifying in their craft. Scattered through the dense battle line, they dealt blow after blow. Scorning injury, they refused to yield, refused to fall, locking their formation as their devotion solely to prayer and the practice of war had prepared them.

The cleft in the great wall broadened under the Mameluks' tearing hands, widening the stream of attackers. The Crusader forces pressed the line, snaking it by inches to keep between the rift and the St. Anthony's Gate, which if seized and opened wide, Mameluk forces could flood in unchecked and unstoppable. Wave after wave of fighters crashed across Templar swords and shields, inching them back. The Mameluks could afford the losses, each fallen man replaced as he dropped, while the crusaders had no reserve.

Greek fire and arrows rained down in a terrible storm, burning and stabbing. Shoulders dug in behind shields. Steel found flesh, and man after man fell. Knees and elbows jabbed where weapons were lost, fingers rabidly clawing when there was nothing else. The stench of blood and sweat, char and terror, struck with each breath like another blow to the face. Still, they all fought on, the sun-bleached and sandy streets thick with gore.

✛ ✛ ✛

Alessandra Letizia Oliverio had come to Acre from Genoa with her father and mother, Eugenio and Donata, and younger sister, Mia, over a year before. At seventeen, the move for Alessandra had been difficult, leaving her friends and family villa—the only home she'd ever known—for a large, dusty house in the merchant quarter at the rear of the ancient walled city above the harbor. She'd resented the uprooting at the time, and now, terrified, she wished somehow she could have been more of a brat then and managed to badger her parents into letting her stay with her aunt and uncle back in Genoa.

Like everyone else, she was now fleeing for her life.

Word of the wall's collapse had torn through the merchant quarter, creating nearly as much turmoil and confusion as at the breach. The Venetians, the Pisans, and the Genoans wasted no time fleeing. Some took to their heels at once. Many hurriedly stuffed away their most salable and easily carried valuables before racing for the harbor and the ships anchored there on the cool, blue waters of the Mediterranean. Those with families dragged worried wives and scared children behind.

Acre had stood since before the time of the Romans. A center for trade and commerce made more significant by its tactical value, it had changed hands many times through the centuries. Under the Crusaders, its populace approached forty thousand. With nobles and servants, merchants and laborers, criminals, soldiers, and clergy, the port's population waxed and waned for the merchants, sailors, and pilgrims coming and going.

The Bay of Furor was living up to its name. Hundreds of ships, large and small, merchant and fisherrman fled the deepwater port beneath the city's looming wall to the safety of the sea. Snagged anchor lines and moors were cut. Crews fought to get their vessels from their slips, sabotaging others' ropes or sails to escape ahead of them. Decks thick with passengers, some were sinking as they got underway, overloaded. Bodies littered the sea, floating arms outstretched. Some couldn't swim, others were victims of frenzy.

On the piers, desperation. Craftsmen and laborers, threatening and pleading with sailors, shoved and fought to board as low-ranking nobles and well-to-do traders waved handfuls of coins and gold chains and screamed for passage. In terror, many threw themselves in the water, and whores and noblewomen alike offered themselves to sailors, stripping naked on the spot and tearfully begging refuge.

Mobs streamed from the harbor gate. Children wailed, lost and separated from parents. Alessandra lost sight of her father when the sea winds shifted and drove a sooty black cloud over the mob. Blinded with lungs burning, a desperate flight aggravated to screams and stampede.

A shove caught Alessandra between the shoulders. She pitched forward, losing her feet and crashing hard on the packed dirt. Coarse gravel raked her arms and hands. She cried out as a foot, then another, mashed down on her hand as she tried to get up. She screamed for her father, but knew it hopeless. In the crowd, he had no more chance of fighting his way upstream than would a leaf fallen in a brook. She struggled to her hands and knees and was kicked, a knee catching her in the ribs even as another foot crushed down on her ankle.

Her ribs seared with each breath. Another knee jabbed her side, someone tripping over her and crashing across her shoulders and neck before scrambling away. She fought back tears, gasping. Pain made it hard to breathe let alone scream as she was stepped on again and kicked again. She clutched her arms over her head, surrendered to the trampling, when something rough clamped on her arm and wrenched her to her feet.

She found herself staring up into the intense gray eyes of a man a few years older than herself. His lean face was burnt by the sun. A closely cropped, sandy beard edged his jaw, his hair hidden beneath the hooded chain mail coif banded above his brow by a thick, knotted helmet pad. Her eyes strayed to his armor, his white tabard marked with a scarlet cross.

A Templar.

Like a stream past a rock, the crowds flowed around him. He spun the girl, pointing her toward the docks. She craned her neck to eye him.

"Keep moving," he shouted into her face. She could barely hear him over the racket.

She started away slowly, her eyes locked on the knight who had saved her. Her mouth opened, but she glanced past him at the embattled city and the black smoke boiling above and she ran away, melting into the wild, fleeing mob.

Brother William of Barking watched her retreat. When he lost her slim form in the crowd, his eyes shifted over the desperate chaos of the harbor. Age twenty, he had been a Templar for almost two years, a soldier in God's Army on Earth, charged with his Order's founding duty to escort pilgrims on their long treks to the Holy Land and back. His mind raced for a way to meet that duty.

"William!" The voice snapped him to the moment. He spun, looking up, finding the caller. Upon the harbor wall, he spied Brother Odo le Coeur Du Sauvage. Mantle thrown back over his shoulders, he was a brawny man, middle-aged and barrel-chested. Head dangerously lacking helmet or coif, his hair was a wild, black mane with a long, thick beard to match.

From atop the wall, Odo could see through the great harbor gate and over the rooftops of Acre to the collapsed tower and the death gushing from the breach. His dark eyes took in the layout of the city out of habit, the numbers of attackers and defenders, and the positions of their forces. He cursed the results of his reckonings.

"Get the pilgrims to the boats!" he shouted at William again.

"They're already overloaded!" William shouted back.

Odo turned, and without pause sprang to a lower point on the wall. William watched as he climbed down before bounding to a lower point, to William, impossibly sure-footed and agile for a man his age and size.

One last leap and Brother Odo was on the ground. His white cloak dropped over his chain mail sleeves, hiding burly arms.

William slipped upstream through the wild flow of refugees, sometimes dodging them, sometimes pushing them aside. As he joined the elder brother, he turned back to look over the blue harbor.

"At least three ships have sunk." He pointed to another boat drawing too low, its deck completely obscured by the bodies crowded on it. Tangled arms and legs dangled over its sides, dragging in the water. "Too many are going out overloaded."

"Too many are underloaded," Odo pointed out a number of smaller craft slicing over the waters, their decks bare.

"We can use our Order's galleys, but we need time to withdraw," William said.

"The city's lost. The Saracens have breached the wall near St. Anthony's Gate." He studied the scene at the harbor below, shook his head. "The fighting will be on us soon."

"In hours, if not a full day," William began. "We can hold them off—"

"Scouts have broken through our line," Odo countered. "And we're outnumbered. Heavily."

"The streets are narrow," William pressed, "They can't all get in at once—"

"They have six companies of fifty thousand each."

William shook his head vehemently "All squeezing through one narrow, jagged hole in the wall. The breach, the streets—they eliminate the advantage of their numbers."

"Reduce," Odo corrected, "Not eliminate. The Saracens *have* taken the city, Brother. All we have left is to play it out with them."

"But if our forces can fall back to our keep, it's the most fortified section of the city, defensible, and adjacent to the harbor. Surely Grandmaster De Beaujeu will see—"

"Our defenses are shattered. That would buy us only days, maybe a week, maybe two at most, with the Saracens right at our door the entire time."

William shouted over the tumult, "Brother, these pilgrims came here to the Holy Land under *our* protection. We're responsible—"

A scream split the mob's clamor, cries multiplying. The two knights whirled, eyes frantically searching the throngs as a horrible screech pierced the air.

The crowds parted, people scattering. From the city's harbor gate, three Mameluk horsemen exploded, driving the citizenry ahead of them. The bellowing stallions waded madly through the crowd, headed for the docks. The horsemen surged forward, slashing down with their deadly curved swords, a wake of broken bodies behind them.

William's sword flashed into his hand even as Odo's leapt to his. Without as much as a glance at each other, they charged the horsemen as the crowds around them panicked.

Eyes wild from the shock of battle, the lead horseman spied William as the young Templar overtook Odo. He spurred his horse at the knights, William sprinting at him.

Odo slowed, his gaze meeting that of the next horseman. The creases around his eyes, the spidery gray in his beard—he was a veteran like himself, who had fought as much, seen as much of war as he. The veteran horseman slowed, weighing his course, when the last Mameluk horseman behind him—a boy, really, so young he appeared—pushed past. Flashing his senior a mirthless grin, he rode straight for Odo.

The wild-eyed horseman roared a war cry, somehow splitting the din. Less than a dozen feet from William, he brought his right arm high, readying his blow.

William darted away from the weapon, dashing across the horse's path. He sidestepped the pounding hooves, slicing his blade over the beast's forequarters as it hurtled past. Its flesh tore open, muscle and sinew severed. William whirled on his lead foot, spinning about and slashing down across the rider's back, finishing the move.

The horse screeched. Its front legs buckled and its long face snapped forward, spinning it heels over head. The rider flew from the saddle straight into the hard-packed dirt road. He lay unmoving.

Odo stayed his ground, noting the younger horseman's sneer and the veteran's hesitation as the two bore down on him. His sword easy in his hand, its point low, he stood and waited.

The younger horseman thundered toward him. His sword flashed high. Odo sprang forward. He drove his pommel straight at the horseman before whipping its trailing blade over his own head and across his attacker's ribs, slashing him open.

Before the rider's blade could fall from his limp hand, Odo immediately thrust his sword high to deflect the veteran horseman's oncoming weapon and gut him in a single move.

Too close, Odo realized— He'd held too long. His sword point caught the veteran's thigh. A gash erupted in a burst of blood and flesh as the point ripped its way up through the muscle before burying itself in the horseman's groin, trapping Odo's weapon.

The impact tore the sword from Odo's hands. Even as the Mameluk veteran doubled over the Templar's blade, his long, curved sword reached over the failed parry, crashing across Odo's face with a burst of blood and a horrible *crack*.

CHAPTER II

Odo snapped awake, clutching at his right eye. His heart pounding, his breathing heavy and rapid, he sat up in his simple monk's cot.

The dream again. He let out a long sigh, slowing his heart. It had been years since the dream last afflicted him, and its appearance never augured well. In the seventeen years since Acre fell, it came to him less often, and he had to consider for a moment how long ago it had been.

His hand came away from his eye. His fingertips traced the jagged white scar that started above his right brow. They trailed downward, across the smooth, black linen eye patch before finding the scar among the weathered creases upon his cheek.

A glance at the dark, shuttered window showed him it was night. A dim, metal lantern in the wall beside the window cast pale light over the rest of the room. It was a rule of the Order that Templar brothers must sleep with a light at night, a constant reminder of their struggle to hold back the darkness in the world and, more importantly, in their own hearts.

The flickering lamp threw odd, shifting shadows through its stamped and hammered surface, revealing a barracks. Odo watched the light play over the room, the warm glow advancing and retreating across a dozen more cots, each occupied by a sleeping Templar. Wearing the same plain, white habits they worked in during the day, another rule of the Order, some lay unmoving as others turned restlessly, a few snoring gently.

His gaze strayed to the door, which stood uncharacteristically ajar. Beside it, one cot was empty, taut bedding and folded blanket not slept in. His eye narrowed. He rolled from his bunk onto his feet, the rustle of his habit the only noise he made as he stood. He paused a moment, making sure all the brothers in the room were asleep, and made for the door. He paused, eyeing his sleeping brothers once more to see if he'd been noticed. Satisfied they all lay asleep, he slipped out.

The corridor was dim, the wall dotted with the same tiny metal lanterns as the sleeping quarters. He padded through the gloom, the soft shuffle of his feet on the polished stone floors loud compared to the cloister's silence. Though the feel of the passageway—the wear of the flooring, the echoes on the walls—told him where he was in the winding halls, he watched ahead. Looking both ways, each turn of his head was wide and purposeful. He proceeded cautiously, not wanting his progress checked by a chance encounter with another brother. The rules of the Order prescribed penalties for any who left their quarters after final prayers, yet Odo felt no need to answer to anyone why he chose to be out.

The scents of myrrh and frankincense spiced the air lightly, reminders of daily mass. Stationed here in the Paris Temple for over two years, he remained awestruck by the enormous place, with high, vaulted ceilings and pointed, arched doorways lining long, winding corridors. The lines of every room, every passageway, were strong and vertical, a yearning for Heaven carved in marble and granite. Buttressed walls soared upward in tribute to God, and domed ceilings rested on great, skeletal stone fingers that Odo found a reminder of his own mortal impermanence.

Built with the Order's reverential care for detail, the stonework was a tribute to the glory and good of God's creations, delicate and lively, rich in images heroic and quiet, from biblical tableaus to scenes of the saints' lives. Odo paused as he neared a row of shuttered windows flanking a stained glass pane. Exquisite even in the night, it shone black, smooth against the rough granite wall.

He closed on a steep staircase, one of dozens connecting the many levels of the Temple. Spying nothing in the gloom at the top of the stairs, he ascended them. From his own nights on watch, he knew the sentries' stations and routines, and he planned his path to keep wide of their posts and routes.

Distant and hushed voices stopped his progress. Words drifted to him from ahead. He knew where the watch would be and knew he couldn't double back here, so he pressed on.

Near the corridor's end, he made out a soft, faint glow in the intersection ahead, different from that of the ever-present metal lanterns. He drifted toward it, and where the passages met, he stopped.

Looking to his left, he saw a heavy, dark wooden door outlined in dim light from behind it. A long shadow at the bottom of the door shifted from one end to the other, someone pacing, he realized, on the other side. The whispery voices had become intelligible to him.

"There was no choice, Grandmaster."

Odo strained to listen. The youthful voice was unfamiliar to him. Probably a novitiate.

"The ship left with the tide."

"You should have been there when it sailed," came the second voice curtly. Raspy, measured words betrayed weariness. This voice Odo knew well, and it troubled him. Well past midnight, he wondered what could be so urgent as to require a meeting with this man, so long after last bell.

Shamed suddenly by his eavesdropping, Odo hurried by. War would justify such a breach of the Order's regulations, he reasoned as he climbed another dark staircase. But their Temple stood in the heart of Paris, far from any front. Yet only in war would anyone hold council here, at this hour.

For this was the Grandmaster's office.

Jacques De Molay, Grandmaster of the Knights Templar, paced his office deliberately. Clad in the same white habit as all the brothers of the Order, his pale features were thin and creased, framed by a flowing gray beard and hair, like a figure of Christ in silver. Pausing wearily before his desk, he squeezed his eyes closed. Fourteen years after succeeding Grandmaster Thoebald De Gaudin, he had been in Paris for less than a year, relocating from the Templar headquarters on the Isle of Cyprus at the request of His Holiness, Pope Clement V. After the long journey home, he found that even in the heart of Christendom, the Knights Templar, God's Army on Earth, were little better received nor understood than in Arabia or Persia. Church and crown had begun to withdraw support for crusades and Crusaders, focusing more on their own borders. They openly questioned the need for the Templars and the resources they required. Or rather, De Molay had long ago decided, the resources the crowns envied.

"Again," the Grandmaster ordered quietly, his throat scratching. Two days without sleep had begun to blur his focus, made his thoughts hazy. But forty years in His service had taught him more than a few means to stay sharp.

Before him stood a young man, his eyes forward and shoulders squared. Barely eighteen, his hair was thick and his beard thin, Brother Andre De Saint-Just stiffened and set his jaw, tightening his grip on the helmet he clutched under his arm. Like the chain mail of his hauberk and chausses, it was smooth and polished, new and unused. His mantle, though, was dusty, and his tabard streaked and splattered heavily with mud, so he was embarrassed when he had to present himself to the Grandmaster.

"We rode day and night," Brother Andre repeated. "We had a horse fall dead from exhaustion racing from L'Ormteau to La Rochelle."

"I don't understand why your Preceptor or your House Commander didn't send this out earlier." De Molay glanced at the small leather pack that lay on his desk, a tightly wrapped bundle visible inside. The young knight's seniors would face discipline when this was over.

"All the wealth this Order possesses is worth nothing compared to this single treasure," De Molay slapped his hand on the desk and regretted instantly his loss of control. The novitiate kept silent, the muscles of his cheeks and jaw flexing as his back teeth clenched.

"And on *this night*," De Molay continued, reining his voice, "you manage to bring it to Paris."

"To the great Temple," The young Templar's discipline slipped and he met the Grandmaster's eyes. "To our headquarters, the seat of our Order in France. Where could it be safer?"

"You had no way of knowing," De Molay muttered, stalking away. His mind raced for a solution. He shook his head. "No matter. You must take it from France immediately."

Andre's gaze snapped forward again. "Yes, Grandmaster."

De Molay was pacing again. He darted to his desk, snatched up a blank dispatch in one hand and dipped a pen with the other. "The Order's last galley is anchored on the Seine, downstream of the city's limits," he said as he scrawled. "It will set sail at dawn." He sanded the page, eyes skimming over it once more before he attached his signet.

He presented the orders to Andre. "Or upon my instruction."

The young knight kept his eyes forward and nodded.

De Molay took up the leather satchel from his desk and stepped in front of Andre. Eyes locking on his, he placed the pack in his hands. "This will not leave your person."

"I won't fail, Grandmaster."

De Molay was silent for a moment. He had little choice at this point.

"No, you won't." He stepped away, his back to the novitiate. "Go and awaken one of the elder brothers. Tell him I will speak with him now, and bring him to me."

De Molay continued shaping his plan. He decided he'd need a veteran, an able but level-headed fighter. Devout, blessed with instinct—

"I can—"

"Find Brother William," De Molay cut him off. "He's English— That will help."

"English?"

"Go," the Grandmaster said quietly.

Andre started for the door, then turned. Back straight, he bowed his head toward De Molay before squaring his shoulders.

"God lives, Grandmaster."

De Molay returned the bow with a deliberate nod. "God lives, Brother Andre." He watched as the young Knight Templar spun on his heel and stepped into the dark corridor, closing the door behind him.

Alone, Jacques De Molay prayed there would still be enough time.

CHAPTER III

The labor had been difficult. Kneeling in the straw beside his straining mare, Brother William prayed the delivery would go easier.

After the evening meal, William had gone to check on the gray mare, finding her pacing in the stall. Restless, she pitched from one side to the other, tail switching nervously. Calming her with a hand on her neck, he peered beneath her and spied the waxy colostrum, a hard covering on her teats for weeks, now soft and stringy, sliding off in melting drips. Her body temperature was up and labor was imminent. For hours, she strained, alternately pacing, rolling, and lying down until she got down and stayed.

The mare's body was rigid, all four legs stiff and straining at each contraction. Knelt in the straw beside her, William stroked his gray mare's neck, his gaze even and watching her haunches, waiting.

In the shadows outside the stable door, Odo paused. Suspecting it was the labor of his old friend's mare that kept him from his bunk, he'd made his way outside. The warm lamp glowing in the stables confirmed his speculation as he crossed the dark courtyard.

No more the novitiate he'd met in Acre and seen again in his dream, the excited boy had been tempered into the quiet, confident man patiently delivering the foal. His frame was lean, his beard remained cropped short. Brother William appeared to have changed little. The years had weathered him, hardened him. His features were more rugged, his eyes wearied.

"Easy, girl," William murmured to the mare. "You're almost there." He continued watching, cooing, his tone with the beast soothing. The floor was wet, the animal's water breaking when the foal's forelegs first made it through. The air thickened with the fluid's almost sweet smell. William had been relieved to see the foal's hooves pointed down, which meant he wouldn't have to turn it. He shifted closer to the grunting mare's hindquarters. Squinting against the uneven light, he spied what he was waiting to see, and shifted again, directly behind her.

A tiny nose had emerged from inside the mare, joining the spindly forelegs that jutted limply from her. William waited, watching her, counting the rhythm of her contractions, noting the signs of them in her body.

He gathered the bottom of his habit in his hands and wrapped it around the foal's legs. In time with the mare's contractions, he pulled gently, slowly inching the newborn into the world, guiding the forefeet and head, careful to keep one hoof lower than the other, angling the foal's shoulders so they wouldn't lock in the mother's pelvis.

"One more push, and you can see your baby," he said under his breath.

With the next contraction, William gently pulled the foal down toward the mare's hocks, its hindquarters emerging from the mother with a gush of more thick fluid that splashed on the floor, washing into the straw.

"There you are," William said to them.

The exhausted mare craned her neck, eyes wide. William grabbed up a handful of straw, briskly wiping off the coughing foal with it. Making soft, soothing sounds to the newborn, he wiped its muzzle, noting the fading blue of its nostrils and mouth as he cleared them. With a soft hand over the foal's left chest, he counted its heartbeats, and satisfied, he backed away from the stall on his knees.

On her side, the mare wriggled, angling to lick the foal, cleaning it herself. William stopped, pausing to watch the mother and child. She continued, her foal dazedly nuzzling her back and connected by the umbilical. William would wait until she passed the afterbirth to cut and tie it.

He climbed to his feet and withdrew from the stall, closing it behind him. He wiped at the birthing stains that streaked and smudged the front of his white habit.

"You could have helped." he announced without even looking up at the stable door.

Odo cocked an eyebrow and stepped into the stable. "I would have been in your way."

"Probably," William agreed, suppressing a smile. "What brings you out here after last bell?"

"I couldn't sleep," Odo began. "There's something—" He searched for the words and shrugged as he found none. "Something's in the air. I saw your bed empty, knew your mare was due to foal." He stepped up to the stall, leaning in to see with his good eye. "It looks healthy."

"She's bleeding," William stated flatly. Then softer, "More than she should." Odo noticed the bright red rivulets on the mare's hind, the red staining in the straw. "She started right before sunset. I've done what I can, but—" William's words trailed off. "It's in God's hands."

"It always is," Odo reminded him. "That mare's a strong one, Brother. Smart, too. A fine palfrey. She got you here all the way from Cyprus."

William nodded. "I'll miss her."

Odo looked into the stall again. The gray mare was licking her foal vigorously, cleaning away the caul. "Don't count her out yet."

"No. I'm giving them to the Order."

Odo turned, his eye meeting William's. "The last I knew, William, even with a vow of poverty a knight needs horses. It's difficult to ride to battle without them."

"I'm leaving the Order, Brother. Tomorrow."

He'd noticed Brother William was quieter as of late, more than the Order's rules of silence required, spending more time in prayer and meditation than usual. He'd thought nothing of it though, chalking it up to one of the dark periods of reflection all men pass through as they begin to need to define their place in the world. But to resign.

"I spoke with the Grandmaster," William continued, "Sunday, after mass. I asked to be released from my vows."

Odo stooped down to sit. "What did he say?"

"He was surprised."

"I can understand."

"And he seemed somehow ... relieved," William added.

"He said nothing?"

"He said I'd chosen the right time to go and that my instincts always had been good." William recalled his own surprise at the Grandmaster's unexpected emotion. "Therewith, he shook my hand and told me I should leave immediately."

"Then why are you still here?"

"I informed him my mare was due, and that I intended to leave her and the foal with the Order. I wanted to be sure they were healthy before I went. I agreed to leave as soon as I could afterward."

"I'm sorry to hear this. You'll be missed, Brother William."

The two remained for a while, neither meeting nor avoiding the other's gaze.

Odo at last spoke up. "What will you do?"

Eyes on the stable floor, William sank to his haunches. "I joined the Order when I was sixteen after my father died. My brother Hal—as eldest son—had inherited the entire barony. Everything. All the titles. All the properties. I had nothing."

"And that nothing's calling you now?"

"With the unrest back home and the troubles in Scotland, King Edward's going to be requiring more support from the nobles. I think Hal may need an experienced military man to oversee his troops."

Odo eyed William, unconvinced. "You are that. But a baron's seneschal is a far cry from a knight in God's Army on Earth."

"Perhaps," William said.

"Perhaps?"

William again looked to the floor. "I've prayed over this for months," he began slowly. "The Order isn't the same as when I joined, Odo. Back then, we fought to hold the Holy Land. We protected pilgrims on their long treks through the Seljuk lands to the sites of our Lord's passion." He met Odo's gaze. "For two years, we've been stationed in Paris— *Paris*. The most we've done here is escort funds from one city to another."

"It's dangerous work, William. There's highwaymen, rogues—"

"It's not what I joined for." He stopped. "We're bankers now, Odo, financing skirmishes between rival kings."

Odo had to agree. The Order was changing, as it seemed was all in the world around it. "I've heard talk of a new crusade," Odo prompted, "to recapture—"

"You and I were there when we lost Acre. Even if we could retake the Holy Land, we couldn't hold it. Not for long, anyway."

"Perhaps."

"Perhaps," William deferred to his old mentor. "You know, I will miss these talks."

Odo nodded.

"You should head back to quarters." William warned. "You know the penalties for being out without permission after evening prayers."

"So, I eat a few meals alone," Odo's fingers brushed his eye patch. "I've had worse done to me." The men paused. Odo listened to the mare and foal, the lapping sounds of the bathing tongue and the scrape of hooves as the two scrabbled closer together.

"Everything did change after Acre, didn't it?" Odo asked.

"I survived it when I shouldn't."

In his years with the Order, Odo had heard the same from others who'd lived through lost battles. His brother was striving to define his place, his role, in God's design.

"Tens of thousands were slaughtered," William continued, "including all our brothers who stayed and fought, while I—"

Odo shook his head. "God wasn't finished with you."

William shrugged, unconvinced.

"It's all part of His plan, William. You survived for a reason."

"Perhaps." His voice conceded, but his soul did not.

Odo chuckled suddenly, squeezing his eye shut. "You should have seen your face when Grandmaster Guillaume De Beaujeu ordered you onto the boat."

"As if you could remember, dazed as you were."

"I remember your expression." Mouth and eye wide as his brow furrowed, Odo's jaw dropped open, like a fish gasping on the shore. He laughed.

"I was there to fight," William defended, "Knights Templar battle to the last man. We don't retreat."

"No, we do our duty. The battle was lost. Someone had to go with the casualties and those pilgrims."

William shrugged a halfhearted agreement. He squinted at a dark corner, as if searching for something in the distance. "You know," he began, "of all we saw there, it's Grandmaster De Beaujeu's face that's stayed with me through the years. He'd been warning the city's nobles for weeks that the signs were there, that an assault was coming."

"I remember," Odo said, letting William speak.

"They were too busy planning the season's social events to listen. They mocked him, called him a coward. And then, when Al-Ashrafi's army appeared on the horizon, marching from the east, they begged for the Grandmaster's help." William replayed the day in his mind. "When we left... His expression as he stood on the shore, bloodied, the smoking city behind him, watching us sail away. His eyes... He knew he was going to die."

"He knew he was going to die *well*, William," Odo said. "All men die; a great man creates purpose through his death."

"Brother William?" a small voice interrupted.

In the doorway stood a skinny boy of twelve. Small for his age, his hair was fair and short. His features were those of a child, with large, pale eyes that seemed to fear most of what they took in. He wore a brown habit, marked with the same eight-pointed red cross as all other Templars—an initiate's robes, the garb of a Templar who had not taken his vows. With long, slender hands on rawboned wrists, he struggled to lug in an oversized bucket, water splashing over its sides with each swaying step.

"Etienne was here when the labor started," William said in a low voice to Odo "I asked him to stay up and help with the mare."

"Brother," Etienne continued, "the trough was empty, so I had to go all the way to—"

"She just delivered the foal, Etienne. Come look."

The boy inhaled sharply with excitement. He practically dropped the bucket water splattering over its rim when it struck the floor.

Rushing across the stable, Etienne's foot caught on the hem of his robe. Spilling forward, he righted himself, feet stamping awkwardly as his hand clawed at a stall gate. Accustomed to the embarrassment, he neither spoke nor looked to either of the knights. He peeked into the stall and his eyes widened at the sight of the newborn, its mother still cleaning and nuzzling it.

A smile warmed William's face as he watched Etienne become entranced, wondering over the pair in the stall. Crossing the stable, William bent down at the bucket the boy had dropped, dipping his hands and rubbing them together before dipping them again to rinse. He stopped and looked up, listening. A glance at Odo showed him the other veteran heard it too: a distant, rhythmic shuffling.

"Marching?" Odo said finally.

Both knights listened for another moment, the two-beat pounding of hundreds of boots on packed dirt and stone unmistakable to them.

"Double time," William added, standing up. He turned to the boy. "Etienne, stay here."

The two Knights Templar left the stable. Dark storm clouds obscured the waning moon, making the night darker. The marching sound grew louder.

If the inside of the Temple was built as the Order's tribute to the glory and good of God's creations, the outside of it represented their intent to defend it. Imposing, it was part monastery, part military keep. The structure reflected the contrast of its builders: barracks and cloisters, storehouses and gardens, courtyards, chapels, and armories, a labyrinth of plaster and timber buildings two and three stories high, all surrounding a sailing church spire of stone. All enclosed by a fortified, twenty-foot wall, the entire facility was situated in the heart of Paris.

Near the top of the Temple wall, a narrow catwalk edged inside the ramparts. Finding a ladder for the stable's hayloft nearby, William and Odo clambered up to the stable's roof, making their way to its peak. The catwalk lay above it. Springing up, William caught hold of the walk and pulled himself onto it. Crouching low, he peered past the battlements. His blood ran cold at what he beheld in the gloom.

In the street below, and stretching into the murky dark of the adjoining avenues, marched an army. A great dragon of armored men snaking its way through the winding streets, their polished helmets glinted from the light of the occasional torch or lantern. They looked as if they were heading to defend the borders of France.

Huddled next to William, Odo peered into the gloom. "That's not the Night Watch," he whispered.

William shook his head, studying the troops as they began breaking into companies and smaller units, fanning out around the Temple. Torch-bearing sergeants hissed orders. Between the gloom and the cloaks most wore against the impending weather, he couldn't make out colors or livery.

"There must be two thousand men out there," Odo whispered.

"More like three."

The clopping of hooves drifted up from the street. Mounted officers, William knew, presented a better chance to identify the force below. Common troops had to obtain their uniforms by saving for them from their own wages or having them issued by the king in lieu of pay. The cloaks they wore would be whatever they had on hand. The officers, though, would be aristocrats. Always eager to show off the finery of their expensive uniforms, they'd have compensated their tailors well for creating with the uniforms cloaks and mantles to match.

He picked out one of the torch-bearing sergeants, and was rewarded when a mounted officer, his hair long and flowing, rode into the glow of sergeant's torch. As he'd suspected, the cape matched perfectly the uniform beneath it. The blue and white were unmistakable.

"The king's colors," William pointed out. Odo exhaled sharply, squinting into the gloom.

William looked down the catwalk, first one way, then the other. He gazed out over the Temple.

No one else was on the wall.

No guards stood inside the gates. No one at all was on the compound grounds outside the Temple except for Odo and himself.

"Where are our sentries?" he asked Odo, pointing to the tower points along the wall. "Our lookouts?" A knot in his stomach pulled tight. He slipped from the edge of the walk, dropping back to the stable roof. "Come on."

The pool of blood had grown in the minutes since Brother William had left with Brother Odo, and Etienne was troubled by it. Though the gray mare's strength seemed to be returning, evidenced by her vigorous caressing and cleaning of her foal, he worried the bleeding was something he should check. He feared for the mare and the foal, knowing well the life of a child without a mother.

William and Odo appeared in the doorway, lost in urgent conversation. Startled, Etienne leapt to his feet, the wild action of his arm knocking over a rake propped near the stall. The knights barely noticed the flustered boy as they strode in, finishing their plan.

"I'll find Grandmaster De Molay and inform him." William said. "You keep an eye on the troops' movements from here. They're the king's army, and this is Paris. They may be on their way to some new campaign of his."

Odo shook his head as William hastened from the stable. "They were readying," he countered. "Taking up positions."

"I know." William said at before disappearing into the night.

Odo stared at the darkened doorway, weighing action.

"Is something happening, Brother Odo?" Etienne asked.

Odo bit the inside of his lip absently, "Go inside," he said to the boy. "Go to my quarters, and fetch my arms and armor. And Brother William's."

Etienne said nothing. He turned and faltered, stuttering words falling from his mouth. Odo realized the boy's fear of breaking any of the Temple rules.

"If anyone asks," he told him firmly, "you're following my instructions, proceeding under a senior brother's authority." He waited for a response from the boy. "Is that understood?"

Etienne snapped back to the moment and nodded. "Yes, Brother Odo," he said, "Right away." and he darted out the door.

Left alone with is thoughts, Odo again considered the scene outside the Temple walls. Three thousand men, all armed, were rapidly surrounding the Templar stronghold. Yet they were setting back. They had no engines, catapults, nor ballistas for attacking the Temple's fortified outer walls, and they stood little chance of winning a siege without them. He hadn't seen but a simple battering ram for even a direct assault on the doors. They were positioning to control the streets.

They wanted to contain the Temple, not attack it.

A dozen scenarios flashed through his mind, none of which he liked. Provisioned and armed as they were, the Templars could sustain and defend themselves under siege for weeks, but the sight of the torches made him uneasy. The wood and plaster of so much of the Temple was a far cry from the hewn stone of their keeps in the Holy Land.

He stepped outside the stable, listening to the dark, ears straining for some clue. Aside from the sounds of marching, he found no clues. With a glance at the top of the wall, he decided he would watch and see what he could discern of their plans.

He started up the ladder, going over the night in his mind. He stopped, recalling his detour near the Grandmaster's office.

Only war would be reason for a meeting there at such an hour.

Yet if war was impending, why were the brother knights not roused and made ready? Hunkered down on the catwalk to keep watch, he prayed Brother William would have words with the Grandmaster soon.

CHAPTER IV

"They're taking too long," King Philip IV of France complained to his chancellor. Watching from horseback in the Rue des Fountaines as the royal troops swarmed through the Rue du Temple and around the Templar fortress, the king sank back in his saddle, eyes narrowed. Broad-shouldered and slim, with cool blue eyes and blonde hair the color of gold, he was a handsome man and knew it, his fine features early on gaining the appellation "Philip the Fair." Dressed for battle, the steel of his mail coat was polished to a bright luster, trimmed in gold, and decorated with precious stones. His surcoat was of fine silk, smooth and blue, dotted with golden fleurs-de-lis, as was the mantle wrapped over his shoulders. His irritation grew over the plodding operation he saw unfolding in the streets before him.

"It's nighttime, my king," excused the chancellor, Guillaume De Nogaret. "The clouds cover the moon, making the night darker still." He was a smaller man than his king, but his ambitions were as large. Coiled and calculating, he preferred the skirmishes of courtly intrigue to the messy engagement unfolding in the street. He, too, sank back in his saddle, a rich, expensive piece that would pay a full year's wages for an entire company. "To move any faster would risk discovery."

"Any slower and the Templars may have time to respond."

De Nogaret shook his head. "Preparations for your plan were put into motion six weeks ago." Disagreeing or correcting the monarch without him taking insult was an art, and De Nogaret was quite the artist. "The men are ready. They know their orders and will carry them out."

The king glowered. "For their own sakes, they'd better."

"The battles to the north will be funded," De Nogaret encouraged. "By morning, two hundred years of Templar treasure will pay for a great deal, I reckon."

King Philip sat up, turning his head in slow menace. "Do you mock me, Nogaret?"

De Nogaret said nothing. King Philip's attention was unsettling.

"You continue to disbelieve what they've amassed," the king hissed. "I've seen the riches they hold there."

During the uprising the year before, when his recall and diluting of France's currency sparked riots and revolt, even in Paris, the Templars took him. In spite of their offer of refuge, protection if it came to it, Philip had been annoyed by his stay in the Temple. A place for hermits who'd sworn vows of poverty, it lacked the essentials for a royal monarch and sovereign. After a few days, he found the knightly monks mostly kept to their own, offering him the rare chance to explore their rambling keep unaccompanied. He took particular delight in the carvings that adorned the walls, and on one of his excursions following a particular series of tableaus, one of them depicting the exploits of his grandfather, the great King Louis IX, that he came across a group of Templars packing away two cases of gold and a smaller case of jewels, readying a fund exchange for one of their outlying preceptories.

Like all the Templars he'd met, they paid him only the slightest consideration, a habit he blamed on the Order's insistence that they answer only to the Pope. But as he made his way past the laboring Templars, he spied inside the vault.

"You can't *imagine*," he said to De Nogaret, words failing him. "No *king* has that kind of wealth at hand. No Order of monks should." He tugged absently at the corners of his gloves. "Not when my France needs it."

"We will correct that shortly, highness."

From the direction of the Temple, a pair of horses trotted toward them, carrying an officer and his sergeant. Waiting to address the two until they rode close enough for him to make them out, the king silently cursed the dark that made his weak eyes seem weaker.

The two stopped a few paces away, lowering their heads in obsequious bows. The officer, a young man barely older than the king, sported a full head of thick, silver hair. "Your majesty," Captain Renier De Ronsoi intoned.

"*Comte*," acknowledged the king. He knew this one, a regular in his court and in his father's court before him.

De Ronsoi looked up. His commoner sergeant kept his eyes averted. "I hope to please his majesty with a report that all is ready."

King Philip glanced coldly at the chancellor. "Excellent," he said to De Ronsoi. "You, then, will lead this?"

"If it pleases your majesty, my nephew, Captain Érard De Valery, has gained his commission in His Majesty's Royal Army."

De Nogaret noted how this De Ronsoi managed to correct the king without saying "no" and then to ask his permission without asking favor, seizing the opportunity to secure more position for himself and his family.

"He's able?" King Philip inquired.

"Our family has served the crown of France for generations. It's in the blood, majesty. My nephew stands at the fore of your troops, awaiting only your command."

Things were taking too long, and Philip's patience had worn thin. "Have him commence," the king ordered.

De Nogaret choked back an objection. For weeks, he and the king had planned over long nights and days. Furtive dispatches sent to the farthest provinces of France. Troops moved only at night and under pretense, their clandestine orders kept sealed until sunset today. He would have preferred further reports, with confirmations from the other captains, but the king was distracted, and in spite of his military experience, his mind was set and he was making his opening move.

De Ronsoi bowed from his saddle, quietly pleased, and moved off, his sergeant in tow.

King Philip turned to De Nogaret. "You will see," he said.

+ + +

William crept through the dark Temple corridors. Something was definitely amiss, as outside, no guards were at their stations or patrolling.

As he rounded the corner near the Grandmaster's office, he paused, padding toward the door. As he drew nearer, he found it open slightly, troubling him further. In the time he had called the Paris Temple home, Grandmaster De Molay never let his door stand open.

William edged the heavy wooden door further open with cautious fingertips, turning his head enough to peer through.

The room was empty and dark. More strangely, the shelves that held volumes of the Order's rules and records, stood bare. A whiff of bitter smoke burned his nostrils and on the floor, he spied the faint red glow of embers, thin and curling, like the remains of burnt leaves. Or burnt papers.

His eyes narrowed and he backed away from the office, leaving the door open as he'd found it. He disappeared into the dark Temple hallways.

+ + +

Without a doubt, they were being surrounded. What troubled Odo was the purpose in it.

As he clambered down the ladder again, he thought about every battle he'd faced, every battle he'd been taught. From the wall top, he had watched the darkened streets, counting men, noting the positions of the companies and smaller parties and the cover they took. Concentrated too heavily to the front of the Temple and without as much as a ladder in sight among them, Odo knew they had no intention of attacking the Temple. A siege seemed more likely. He spied archers moving into hidden positions, possibly to provide cover for the foot soldiers from the arrows of the Temple's own bowmen. But their lines were too thin and offered little support to one another. Should the Temple launch a focused attack, they could punch right through at almost any point.

The French army's strategies were better than that.

Perhaps, he considered, his problem was of perspective. Thinking as a man of war, he was examining the objective of warfare: control. Take a position, secure it, and use it as a base to launch the next move. This city, however, was under the dominion of the king of France even though the Temple was considered sovereign ground. Yes, what he saw outside the wall was a demonstration of strength, certainly to be followed by a demand.

But for what? An enemy of the crown? As far as Odo was aware, they'd offered no one sanctuary since the king stayed a year ago. Tribute? The Knights Templar answered only to the Pope. The Temple vault did store a sizeable share of the Order's treasury.

In the stable, Odo looked to the gray mare's stall. Opposite it, he spied Etienne backed up against another stall gate. The boy's breathing was rapid, uneven. His eyes were wide and came near to near tears when they met Odo's. He looked cornered, or caught.

Odo's brow knit. "Etienne, where are my—"

The boy's eyes darted nervously, looking past Odo. The veteran stopped, and with his good eye he followed Etienne's gaze and froze as his mouth dropped open, wordless.

✚ ✚ ✚

The entrance hall to the Paris Temple was a grand space, designed to intimidate and awe those who entered. Like a cathedral, its arched ceiling was high and vaulted, ringed by a lofty gallery that emphasized its enormous scale and made it defensible by bow.

In the middle of the vestibule, an immense staircase of polished marble and wood rose, flanked by darkened corridors. Adorned in splendid carvings, the stair flowed up and split, the resulting halves curling off before each joined the shadows above.

A dozen paces from the foot of the stairs stood a pair of enormous doors. Carved of oak, trimmed in black iron, a heavy crossbar stretched across to secure them. Two young Templars stood guard over the doors, shoulders square, backs stiff, weapons at the ready— Night watch was a serious assignment, which most of the brothers welcomed the privilege to safeguard the Temple, and to make the personal sacrifice of a night's sleep to better serve God.

A dull, pounding hammered the Temple's silence, a heavy fist on the dense door timbers.

"Open up," a voice commanded, muffled by the hick doors. "Open up in the name of the King."

The door guards looked to each other. Neither had been in the Order more than a year, but guard duty had always been uneventful. One drew his sword, steel hissing free of its scabbard.

The pounding continued, echoing. The second door guard drew his weapon.

In their white habits, more brothers of the Order filtered into the entry hall from the hallways and down the majestic staircase, men of all ages, all nationalities, all wearing the same scarlet cross, most with drawn weapons.

"Report," demanded one senior brother with a bushy red beard and shaven skull. The confused door guards shook their heads. Before they could answer, Brother Robert asked, "Has the Grandmaster been alerted?"

"Not yet, Brother," answered one guard. "This has only just begun."

Again, the pounding upon the door and the barked, muffled order. "Open this door in the name of the King."

The bushy-bearded elder turned to the brother nearest him. "Go to the Grandmaster. Inform him and ask his directive." His voice trailed off as he glanced up at the staircase and saw the thin figure of Grandmaster Jacques De Molay descending, head up, shoulders square.

"Open the doors," the Grandmaster commanded. The door guards could only stare back. The cloistered hush of the Temple magnified the expectance of the Grandmaster's next words. All eyes on him, Jacques De Molay descended the stairs without hesitation.

"Open the doors," he repeated.

Together, the two door guards hoisted the massive bar from across the doors. De Molay seemed to brace himself.

"Grandmaster?" one of the elder brothers began with concern. De Molay waved him to silence.

In the gallery above, Brother William lingered, out of sight. Flattening himself against the wall, he hid among the shadows of the ornate stone tracery that edged the archways. His eyes narrowed on the scene below him.

The bar removed, the door guards slid back the latches with a hollow thud and together pulled open one of the heavy doors.

It swung wide, pushed from outside by a dozen hands. Imperious and arrogant, Captain Érard De Valery shoved past the two Templar door guards, his entire company at his back. He was a young man, barely older than the Templar initiates, with a face that was handsome to the point of pretty and long, blond hair that spilled over his shoulders and the expensive blue fabric of his cloak. His nose wrinkled as his dark eyes fell over the assembled Templars.

Boot heels and the jangle of weapons echoed loudly in the great hall. At the sight of the invaders' swords, axes, and spears, the assembled Templars raised their weapons. De Valery immediately picked De Molay out at the foot of the staircase, his silver hair and beard unmistakable. He strode straight for him, his troops hanging back at the perimeter of the room.

Grandmaster De Molay's eyes met the young officer's as he neared. "What do you want of these humble soldiers of God?" he asked.

Without missing a step, Captain De Valery backhanded De Molay.

CHAPTER V

The Grandmaster staggered back a pace, caught unawares. The knight brothers started forward, swords raised.

De Molay waved them back harshly. Eyes burning, he faced the youthful captain, hands at his sides, refusing even to acknowledge the blow.

With all the disdain he could show, De Valery shouted, "For heresy and immorality, you and all your men are under arrest, in the name of His Royal Highness, King Philip the Fourth of France."

Glances were exchanged among the Knights Templar and hands tightened on the hilts of swords still sheathed.

De Molay kept his eye on De Valery, "Remember your oaths," the Templar Grandmaster barked to his men. "Any one of you spills a drop of Christian blood, and you'll answer to *me* right before you explain yourself to God."

No one moved.

In the gallery above, William had heard enough. Whirling, he stole through the gloomy passageways, mind racing. As it was, the details didn't fit. The Temple had been unguarded when sentries were always posted along the walls. The Order was besieged, but as the French crown held no jurisdiction over them, the siege was unlawful. The Grandmaster permitted the troops into the Temple, when at most he should have agreed to a parley with their commander. To allow that whelp to strike him... Grandmaster De Molay was too experienced, too adept for such errors. Even more, the Grandmaster had reached the entry hall before the guards could send him word of the hostile troops, meaning he was on his way in the middle of the night.

Movement in the shadows ahead of him caught William's eye. Head down, he hurried past, then whirled and grabbed the figure out of the shadows, twisting limbs into compliance as he pinned it to the wall.

"Who are you?" William demanded through clenched teeth. As he spat out the words, he noticed his captive's garb, the muddy white tabard and rustling iron mail. Another Templar. In armor.

William freed him.

"Brother Andre De Saint-Just," said the younger knight. "Just arrived from La Rochelle."

William's gaze shifted from one end of the corridor to the other. His voice was a harsh whisper. "We have to leave."

Rubbing the circulation back into his wrist, Brother Andre shook his head. "I heard the King's men at the door," he whispered back. "We have to do something."

William nodded. "Except we have to leave."

For a moment, Andre considered his senior's direction. He paused, looking back and then ahead, torn. Jaw set, he whispered, "Knights Templar never retreat."

"We do retreat," William corrected, "when circumstances dictate. But one has to engage an opponent before it can be called a retreat. Think of this as maneuvering to take up a better position before the fight." He glanced back the way he'd come, searching the dark corridor for signs of pursuers, listening for booted footfalls on the stair.

"I can't go," Andre began, whispering, "I was instructed by Grandmaster De Molay to find Brother William."

"And you have."

Andre stared at him, blinking, uncomprehending at first. William pondered why the Grandmaster would send for him. Another detail to puzzle over. Later.

"Let's go," William ordered.

Taking Andre by the elbow, he strongarmed him into the gloom, into the maze of passageways and rooms of the Temple. As they crept through the darkness, William briefed Andre on what he and Odo had discovered, adding, "I haven't seen you before."

The young knight hesitated, "I've arrived this night," he said haltingly "I was sent here as a courier."

"They certainly chose the wrong night," William said, surveying the next intersection. Andre checked the tiny pack Grandmaster De Molay had given him, hidden on his back beneath his mantle. Its presence reassured him.

Growing more certain they could proceed undiscovered, William picked up the pace, leading Andre to a flight of stairs. At the bottom of them was a low door that opened onto the compound outside the Temple.

Dark storm clouds had blown in, blanketing the sky, blotting the moon and stars. The deep, edging shadows to scurry through had disappeared. All was equally inky. William dashed directly across the courtyard, Brother Andre in tow. Halting under the eaves of a storehouse, he scouted the dark before angling for the stables. "Brother Odo's there," he explained to Andre. "Three of us have a better chance of resolving this than two."

They'd managed to proceed without incident, confirming William's estimation of the royal troops' strategy: to seize the main entrance to the Temple and then sweep back through the compound to apprehend all Templars they encountered. The forces in the surrounding streets were positioned to capture any attempting escape.

"On what grounds can they arrest us?" Andre interrupted William's musings.

An answer would better quiet him than an order, William thought. "I heard the officer say heresy."

The stable was ahead.

"Heresy? But we're a Holy Order," Andre whispered as William led him into the stable. "We answer only to the Pope himself. The king has no authority over us."

William stopped short, eyes darting over the stable's interior. The mare and foal were unattended. Odo hadn't been on the wall as they approached.

William heard a rustle at his back. He shoved Andre behind him and whirled, arms out like swords, ready. His eyes went wide, as did Andre's.

At the other end of the stable stood Brother Odo, flanked by five more knights. All in full armor, the crosses above their hearts were vivid and red on their white tabards. The mail of their hauberks and coifs was dark, seasoned by battle. Helmets in hand, swords and shields at their sides, they stood, eyes hard but uncruel, bodies tense like coiled steel. They were a terrifying sight in battle, yet in that moment, William was heartened. They were his brothers.

They were Knights Templar.

Andre fell back a step and William stood down, confusion playing over his face. "Brothers?" he began but turned to his old friend. "Odo?"

"For once," began Odo, cocking an eyebrow, "be glad for Etienne's stumblings."

Beside Odo, the boy stood with a thick bundle of leather and folded, white cloth pressed to his chest. His chin dropped from embarrassment. With his heavy, gauntleted hand, Odo tousled the boy's hair roughly, ending with an affectionate shove.

"I sent him to our quarters to bring our armor," Odo continued. "It seemed we might need it. In my haste, it didn't occur to me it would all be too heavy for a boy to carry."

"He woke us when he dropped Brother Odo's mail coat and tripped over it as he carried your arms from the room," explained Brother Francesco Di Orsini. Younger and thinner than William, his eyes were as black as his hair and beard. Gauntlets tucked into the sword belt at his waist, his hands were hidden in a pair of soft, white gloves indicating his rank as a chaplain.

William smiled slightly, warmly at Etienne. "It's a wonder you didn't wake the whole Temple."

"I asked what he was doing," added another. The dark eyes of Brother Ramon De Los Dos Rios eyes sparkled with humor that some in the Order found inappropriate in a monk. "He said Brother Odo and Brother William needed their things."

"We knew it meant trouble," finished another, surprising William with his words, as Brother Nicolas De Gauthier was a taciturn young man, whose sad eyes William always felt belonged in the face of a veteran twice his age.

"Brother, was there fighting inside?" interrupted Brother Armande De Vichiers, upon spying the gory stains smearing William's tabard. An old comrade of Odo's from the battles of Palestine and Lattakioh before the fall of Acre, he pushed past the others. Hand on his hilt, the flames of his usually smoldering anger fanned brighter at the suggestion of an attack.

"No," William assured, indicating his mare's stall. "This is from the foal."

"Make ready, Brother," said Brother Bernard De Montbard. William nodded to him. Though initiated at the same time at the Temple of England, the two had never served together before Paris. William studied him a moment, wondering as he did sometimes what sadness it was Brother Bernard always carried inside.

William looked them over, relief tempering his concern. Unknotting the cord at his waist, he stripped off his stained habit, and held out his hand. Etienne handed the bundle in his arms to Brother Odo. To William he passed the leather sack containing his mail coat and his white tabard, folded in a tight square, on top the scarlet Templar cross.

✝ ✝ ✝

Captain De Valery stepped forward, taking up the ground Jacques De Molay yielded when he staggered backward from his blow. De Molay pulled himself to his full height and faced the young officer. His face still stinging, his cheek swelling and throbbing, the Grandmaster's gaze burned into the royal captain.

The criminal's insolence, his arrogance, his brazen disrespect for the crown and its authority angered Captain De Valery. He dared too much, and De Valery wouldn't stand for it. His hand flashed up to strike De Molay once more.

De Molay caught it this time, snatching the younger man's hand out of the air. The pretty, young captain's eyes bulged in shock before De Molay torqued his trapped wrist, the pressure buckling the royal officer's knees and forcing a gasp from him.

De Molay leaned in close. "You get one, boy," he said, his voice low. "No more." He released him with a shove. De Valery tripped backward, stumbling over his own heels, barely staying on his feet. He wobbled to a stop, outraged at the humiliation.

De Molay gathered himself, his men ready behind him. He stared at the young officer and his soldiers. Behind the Grandmaster, the gathered knights stood coiled and ready to strike. He had no doubt they could clear the room and recover control of their position in minutes. The muscles of his neck pained him, and he realized it was from the tightness he held in his jaw. If only there were another way. Too much was at stake. Praying and planning for months, he knew this was their best and only option.

"Lay down your arms," he commanded his Knights Templar loudly. "Cooperate with the king's men."

The Templars doubted their own ears, positive they misheard the Grandmaster's command. Swords came up in reflex, ready to lay into the intruders.

"Lay down your arms," their Grandmaster commanded again.

De Valery ordered his troops to seize the thunderstruck Templars. "Pile their weapons here," he pointed to the base of the great staircase. A few of the Templars struggled at first against the crowding soldiers, giving in as orders settled upon their souls.

Surrendered swords and axes clanked to the floor alongside maces and knives behind De Molay. He eyed De Valery coldly. "We surrender to your custody," he said, voice nearly failing him as his head sank.

De Valery directed more men through the Temple's wide front doorway and up the grand staircase.

"Arrest anyone you find," he ordered.

Led by Brother Francesco, William, Odo, and the company of knights knelt in the stable, heads bowed in prayer. Each held his sword by the blade, point down, the handle and guard forming a cross before him.

"*Non nobis Domine non nobis*," Francesco intoned quietly. "*Sed nomine tuo da gloriam.*"

The knights remained quiet, meditating on the task they faced.

"*Procedamus in pace,*" Francesco spoke up. "*In nomine Patris, et Filii, et Spiritus Sancti.* Amen."

"Amen," the others intoned.

The knights rose to their feet. William buckled his sword to his hip and flung his white cloak back over his shoulder, exposing his weapon's hilt. Armored now, with his brothers at his back, if he didn't feel safer, he was at least ready to face what awaited them.

"I don't yet understand what's going on," he addressed them all, "But we can do nothing to aid our brothers if we are taken into custody."

"What will we do?" asked Ramon. His eyes burned like dark coals, concern displacing the customary sparkle.

"Avoid capture. Beyond that—" William shrugged. "There's no time for planning. The king's bailiffs are no doubt sweeping through the barracks and halls, arresting all the brothers in the main buildings. We must escape the Temple."

Andre spoke up. "Then we'll leave France?"

William studied the initiate. "Paris, at least. We can decide on a course of action once we've bought some space to breathe."

"I don't see why they were let in," interrupted Armande. With bony features and cheeks hollow and creased, the gray stripe at the center of his dark beard bobbed as he spoke. "We could defend the Temple from attack for weeks.

"I know what I saw." William replied. Andre looked away too quickly, and William noticed.

"And now we run away." Armande's repulsion was clear.

"We're *surrounded,*" Odo retorted. "You haven't seen the forces they've assembled at our door."

"It's not our way—" Armande began.

"Stay and fight then." Odo turned away.

Armande chose not to let it rest. "I never said we should make a stand, just that as—"

"Enough." William cut them off. He positioned himself between the two elder brothers, addressing them and the others. "We'll do our captured brothers no good if we're in the king's dungeons with them, that much is certain."

The stable grew silent. All eyes fell upon William. He knew his next words would decide the night for the others. He could quarrel with them or challenge them.

"This is far from a retreat," he stated, glancing from man to man, eyes hard. "I'm going. Stay or don't." He slung a light pack over his shoulder and started out the stable door.

With a harsh, one-eyed glance at the others, Odo fell in behind him. Francesco followed, with Ramon, Bernard, and Nicolas following.

As he marched from the stable, William noticed Etienne, small and pressed in the shadows near the stable door. Eyes averted, he squatted on the floor, chewing his lip with fright.

"Etienne," William said without stopping. "You're with us."

The boy's teeth stopped working over his lip. He looked up, unbelieving.

Nicolas spoke. "The boy, too, Brother William?"

William stopped but did not turn. "I'll not leave him to the hands of the King's men." He continued out the door.

Etienne rushed into the formation of knights. Nicolas said no more, but Armande paused, watching the others set out, the boy in tow. They weren't handling this like Templars, he thought. Their present circumstance offered little room for mistakes. Breaking the disciplines of the Order, not following its tenets and directives would lead to trouble.

His eyes strayed into the stall where the gray mare lay still, the newborn foal suckling loudly beneath her. The animal was exhausted, her breathing hard and uneven. When the foal shifted, the mare struggled to stay close to it, finding the strength she needed to wriggle nearer.

The last of their group had almost exited. Brother Armande glanced over his shoulder, out of routine, and fell in, following up the rear.

✝ ✝ ✝

Different from their fortresses in the Holy Lands, the Templar architects made concessions in their designs since the stronghold was to stand at the heart of the most prosperous city in Europe.

The Temple's walls were not as tall or thick as those meant for a true fortress. Many of the structures were of plaster and timbers rather than the heavy, solid stone used throughout their keeps close to hostile lands. Some elements, though, took advantage of the city location. Tunnels beneath the grounds joined the catacombs under Paris to provide stealthy ingress and egress. Other hidden exits existed.

With royal forces focused on the Temple's forward wall, William decided their band should head for the rear wall, along the wide Rue De Baujolais, where the smaller Rue De Foren dead-ended into it.

"The angle of the two streets there makes for a kill-box," Odo warned.

William agreed. "It's also most distant from the point of their attack, and the farthest from the main buildings." He spied a ladder propped against the walk's edge and hastened for it. "They'll have themselves extended and thinnest back here."

He ascended the wall, Odo, Bernard, and Nicolas climbing behind him.

In the Rue De Baujolais, royal soldiers fidgeted beneath the broad, blank walls. In spite of the orders from their captain to maintain watch, they peered only occasionally at the Temple, intimidated as much by its dark walls as its dwellers.

Their aversion allowed the brothers to watch them.

Hidden behind the parapets at the top of the wall, Ramon stole a look at the street below. He ducked back, crouching down with Bernard and Nicolas, out of sight of the surrounding force.

Ramon shook his head. "They may have the entire Temple outnumbered."

"Brother William is counting on their thinking it's enough," Odo whispered.

"Unless it's more than three-to-one, it won't be," Bernard injected soberly, sad eyes hardening. All knights of the Temple were required to be capable of fighting at those odds.

Ramon leaned past the parapet again, taking in a second look at what they faced in the boulevard below. "The arrangement of the streets doesn't leave them much room to hide archers."

"Doesn't mean there aren't any," Odo said.

"It means they're few, if any," Nicolas stated flatly. "They'll have ineffective cover." He laid a pair of hatchets against the wall before him and pulled a pair of long daggers from his belt. He hefted each in his hand, feeling the weight and balance. He nodded to himself, reassured, satisfied with their feel.

Beneath them, William and the remaining bothers assembled near a wide door in the wall. After several minutes, they had used their daggers to remove the bolts and pins that secured it, and they waited. William stepped out from beneath the catwalk, staring up at the detachment that watched and waited above.

Ramon glanced at Nicolas, who raised the pair of daggers in his hands, and then at Bernard, who returned his gaze. Odo looked over the three once more, and giving them a nod of approval, leaned over the walk. Extending his arm and fingers, he made a tight ball of his hand and waved his arm twice.

William returned the wave and rejoined his group, braced behind the door.

"They're ready," he said.

CHAPTER VI

William rebound Brother Odo's wound, pulling the bandages tight over his eye. The Bay of Furor was worse now, with more fighting among the desperate, more sunken boats blocking escape, and more bodies littering the sea.

Brother Odo groaned as William reapplied pressure to his face. The blow to his head left Odo groggy, probably a blessing given the state of his eye. The bleeding had soaked through the first dressing, but William knew that was the way with head wounds. Even the simplest cut spilled what appeared to be a frightening amount of blood. He was fortunate, as far as William could discern, that there was no fracture in the bone surrounding his eye. In binding the wound, it would have been like fitting broken fragments of a clay bowl together, the jagged edges beneath his skin scraping against one another and Brother Odo's enflamed nerves. The eye itself, though, was beyond remedy. Hacked open by the Mameluk's curved blade, it looked like damaged meat, no longer lit with the intensity his other dark eye still held.

William managed to get Odo to his feet. Supporting him, he lurched with the dazed brother through the fleeing crowds to the city's Templar keep. Crossing the Pisan Quarter, he found the throngs thicker and more panicked. Dire word of the city's situation, he guessed, was spreading through Acre's quarters, evacuees reaching the merchant quarters and the harbor below. Looking up to fix his position, William kept to his left as he pressed through the panicked mob, bearing for the Templar fortress in the city's southwest corner.

At the breach, the fighting in the streets was fierce and one-sided. Despite the scenes unfolding at the harbor, able-bodied civilians—nobles and servants, craftsman, and traders—were taking up whatever arms they could against the Mameluks,

The Mameluks were widening the breach, using their powerful mangonels to fire huge stones directly through the fissure, providing cover for their engineers as they tore the gap wider. Larger with each passing hour, more attackers swarmed through it, swelling their forces. Braced behind their shields, the defenders were thrown back with each surge of fresh attackers, feet sliding in the slick, sandy gore in the streets. The battle line collapsed by inches, and the Templars were forced to plan withdrawal and making for their keep before they were outflanked, the ranks at either side of them folding.

With Brother Odo heavy on his shoulders, William made his way through the crowded courtyard of the Templar keep. Black-robed Knights Hospitaller tended the injured, their own stronghold overrun and under Mameluk control. Moans melted into the terrible chorus of sobbing women and wailing children who'd begged sanctuary from the Templars when they found no passage at the docks. Mameluk drums throbbed in the distance under the blare of their trumpets and the jarring clash of their cymbals. Had his hands been free, William would have clapped them over his ears.

Two Hospitaller brothers eased Brother Odo's great frame from the young Templar's shoulders. Working the knots from his neck, William watched them conduct Odo to the courtyard surrounding the barracks, billeted only for the Knights Templar. Even in this carnage, he noted grimly, Templars kept to their own.

He searched for a commander or marshal or a senior brother he could report to. Except among the casualties, he saw no white tabards, no scarlet crosses. Only the black-robed Hospitallers walked among the refugees, the injured, and the dead.

He closed his eyes in silent prayer. Brother Odo was right. The fighting was going to be on them soon, sooner than he thought. William knew though, with all the certainty he held in his heart, that things would not have to play out the way he was told. The streets were narrow and winding, the buildings tall and close-set. Just as the breach was keeping the Mameluk army from descending upon them in full, so would the city itself. With the right strategy.

At last he spied a figure in white pacing through the injured and displaced. In full Templar armor, helmet tucked under one arm, he was a great, brawny man with a stiff, white beard, eyebrows black and expressive. His head was wrapped in the local fashion, a long, checked *kafiyya* cloth draping to his shoulders, protecting his smooth, bald pate from the burns and blisters of the unforgiving Mediterranean sun. Streaked in the gore of the day's fighting, he was making his way to the injured Templars, silence falling around him as he passed.

William stopped before him, eyes front, shoulders square. "God lives."

"God lives, Brother," Grandmaster Guillaume De Beaujeu replied.

CHAPTER VII

Odo, Bernard, and Ramon climbed from the Temple's second-story parapet. Lowering themselves as far as they could until their feet and hands could find no purchase on the wall, they dropped to the street, rolling as they hit the ground.

Odo came to his feet first, surveying the dark intersection with a broad sweep of his head, his one eye taking in the terrain. Bernard came down next, backing against Odo so they looked opposite each other. Ramon regained his feet but stayed crouched, low to the ground, his hand behind him and on the hilt of his dagger.

As in all cities, the streets were filthy. Dung and other refuse muddied together in dark patches and streaks on the lane, the garbage of the city dwellers rotting in grimy piles strewn across the hard-packed dirt. A shallow, narrow trench split the street for its length, a clogged gutter to channel the worst of the filth off the road and away from the houses and buildings that lined the street.

"Halt!" boomed a voice from the dark. "In the name of the King!" The knights outside the wall froze and looked in the direction of the voice.

Captain Charles Le Brun was a bear of a man, heavyset and imposing, with a neatly trimmed moustache that curled past the edges of his mouth. Like most of the aristocratic officers, his uniform and armor, bought at personal expense, were as much an example of the finery he could afford as a mark of his rank. Across the street from the Templars, he sat astride a solid-looking steed whose saddle and accessories matched the captain's in style and cost. Behind him stood a full company of the king's soldiers.

Brother Ramon stood up slowly, keeping his hand on his hilt. Odo and Bernard lifted their arms away from their bodies and weapons.

"Stand where you are," the captain commanded. The snared Templars looked to one another doubtfully, then back toward the captain and his men.

"Arrest those three," barked Le Brun to his men. "Strip them of their weapons and bind them." The officer leaned forward in his saddle, squinting against the gloom. Distant lightning lit up faraway clouds, rumbling thunder following softly a few moments later.

Five of the captain's company pushed forward, one soldier taking the lead. With thick, shaggy eyebrows that made his too round eyes stand out more, his mouth was tight with contempt. He closed on Brother Odo, identifying him as the leader of the group. He seized Odo roughly, bunching the Templar's white tabard in his hand.

Odo eyed him calmly. Grabbing the soldier's wrist, he reached across with his other arm, locking the soldier in a painful arm-bar as his foot snapped out in a kick to the stomach. The soldier slumped forward, only the pressure of Odo's hold keeping him on his feet.

Bernard smashed an armored forearm into the face of the soldier nearest him even as Ramon's dagger flashed into his hand to parry the slash of another soldier who'd found enough presence of mind to draw his sword when Odo moved.

A shriek split the air. Ramon turned, and found Bernard sinking to the ground, clawing slowly at the shaft buried in his chest.

From his cover in a window across the street from the Temple, the archer nodded, proud of his shot, and notched another arrow. With practiced speed, he drew back the bowstring, unfocusing one eye as he took aim at the wild-maned one.

The bow went suddenly slack in his hands, and his eyes sprang wide at the sight of a long Templar dagger handle jutting from his chest. The wooden bow clattered to the floor, and the archer fell backward. Behind the parapet on the Temple wall, Brother Nicolas scanned the darkened streets with hawk's eyes, another dagger in his hand.

Brother William was braced at the door. The sounds of the fight in the street were clear to them all, the arrow's shriek distressing. Ready to move for some time, Armande stared at William, eyes darting from the Templar brother to the door and back. William ignored his silent urging and looked up at the catwalk. Watchful Nicolas, blade in hand, concentrated on the street below.

"Not yet," William ruled, speaking as much to himself as the others.

In the street, Odo yanked his captured soldier up closer to him, wrenching his arm to make him move. Another arrow shriek, and the soldier went slack in Odo's grasp, a shaft driven below his shoulder.

Before the soldier slumped, Nicolas's eyes raced to retrace the arrow's path, finding a second archer across the street, hidden around the corner of a house. Nicolas took his dagger in hand like a dart and hurled it down toward the dark corner.

The archer let his second shaft fly just before the Templar dagger tore open his throat. The arrow leapt into the darkness, hurtling into the fight, striking Ramon.

As it was designed to, the flat, steel ailette that armored his shoulder deflected the shaft. Glancing off the plate, the arrow dove into Ramon's left arm, burrowing between the chain links and into his bicep. The impact slammed his arm back, spun him around and away from his attackers as his shield thumped to the street.

Eyes vacant and body limp, the soldier's corpse in Odo's hands slowed him, cut his mobility. Timing his move to the press of the next two attackers, he let go of the body and slid back, throwing the dead soldier into the dirty street to trip the pair as they were almost on him.

Odo glided to Ramon's side. Even with an arrow in his arm, Ramon held his own, stabbing one soldier with his dagger and leaving it in the man's ribs, freeing his hand to draw his sword and cut down the next. Odo kicked at one of the fallen soldiers as he blocked the blade of another.

William watched the catwalk above him anxiously. Through the wall, he could hear the crashing and cries of the melee in the street. The sounds nearly drove Armande mad, so ready he was to go to his brother's side. From the catwalk, Nicolas lowered himself, dropping close to the others. He landed on his feet, heavily, nodding quickly to William.

"Now!" William cried. As in a shield rush, they dug in their feet and threw their weight against the door.

Back to back, Odo and Ramon fought on. Their attackers' numbers growing as Le Brun set more on them. The injured Templar's breathing was ragged, the arrow in his arm stabbing and twisting within his flesh with every attack, every turn and twist he made.

Behind them, the broad, blank Temple wall exploded, the band of Templars bursting through the bolt-hole door hidden under its surface.

Another concession to the Temple's location in the city, such doors were scattered over the walls to provide escape if brothers were cornered inside the Temple. With the door reinforced and pinned in place, it was weaker perhaps than the surrounding wall but still solid. Plastered over skillfully, it was invisible from the outside and accessible only from the inside.

The soldiers fell back, uncertain about what happened or might happen next. Captain Le Brun, shouted orders, waving his company on. He wheeled his horse around, damning his archers in a loud bellow.

"Fire!" he roared, unaware neither was breathing any more.

The Templars were on the soldiers nearest Odo and Ramon first. Shoving the wavering troops aside, they darted past their two brothers, Odo and Ramon falling in behind them. The entire group charged through the remaining soldiers like cavalry. Their boots pounding, their arms and armor jangling menacingly, they dashed across the dark street. Rounding a murky corner, they disappeared into the night.

A dozen chased after them, dogs on their heels. More started after, but Le Brun waved them back.

"Hold your positions!" he shouted, waving them off. Most of the men stopped, with only two more disappearing into the dark streets after the fleeing Templars.

"Hold your positions," he repeated. "Let the others take them. This could be a diversion or some other trick." The first three that went over the wall had been a ruse to get his company to betray its positions. The second group, he reasoned, may have been to draw them all away and leave the hidden gate unattended for more to escape. He turned to his sergeant. "See to the archers," he said. "I want to know why they stopped firing."

As Le Brun's company regrouped at an angle to the bolt hole, the sergeant dashed down the street to the bowman's post. He disappeared into the covering shadows of the dark intersection, only to return a moment later shaking his head, a bow held high for Le Brun to see. Le Brun glanced over his shoulder, eyes tilted up at the darkened window, realizing why their cover fire had failed. The Templars were some type of devils, he decided in that moment. The gloom at the corner and in the window was almost impenetrable, and each man had taken fewer than three shots. His archers should have been safe.

Le Brun turned to another of his men. "You," he said to a young, lightly armored soldier with a neck too long for the rest of him. The soldier pushed his cap back and clapped his arms at his sides. "Find Captain De Ronsoi, and report to him what's happened."

"Yes, lord." The messenger bowed and took off along the shallow trench dividing the street, up the Rue De Baujolais at a full run.

Le Brun's sergeant signaled for help with the archer's body. Another small detachment of Le Brun's troops began moving their injured and dead from in front of the exposed secret door in the Temple wall. They prodded cautiously at the lifeless Templar with a spear, then drove its point home through the soft flesh of the throat to ensure no further deception. Le Brun watched. They'd gotten one at least.

Leaving a smear of blood on the ground behind them, the soldiers dragged the body of Brother Bernard to their Captain's feet and dropped it like a full sack of grain on the packed dirt. The dead brother's mouth was agape, his eyes open and rolled back in their sockets. The arrow jutted from Bernard's chest, and blood stained his white tabard, a seeping red circle consuming the scarlet cross over his heart.

CHAPTER VIII

The side streets, lanes, and back alleys of Paris were a labyrinth, a web of stone-cobbled cart paths and planked tracks and packed dirt footways. Snaking turns yielded to steep hills, and all was pressed in and confined by the tall, narrow houses and shops that crowded at their sides. William at the point, the Templars raced, maneuvering the dark maze of narrow, twisting avenues and alleys, Le Brun's soldiers a turn behind them.

Dodging right, they scrambled up a steep hill. Ramon worked to concentrate, his breathing growing more ragged. Each time his left foot came down, the arrow buried in his arm bounced, its sharp, steel head raking and twisting in the wound. He clutched at it, whispering the *Ave Maria* in desperate repetition to direct his thoughts. His fingers dug more tightly into the muscle, as if enough pressure might crush the pain out. His lungs burned, the sting of his arm stealing his wind and the focus he needed to control it. He fell to the back of his troop as they ran on but managed to keep pace.

Shielded in the center of the knights, Etienne ran as only a boy can, with speed and abandon not of fear, but exhilaration. His eyes were bright with excitement, as his skinny legs flashed out almost twice as fast as the men's, making up in speed what he lacked in stride.

Beside Brother Ramon, Andre glanced over his shoulder as he ran. He could just glimpse their pursuers behind them, before turns or on a long straightaway. Brother William led them to another turn, and the royal soldiers disappeared behind the last bend.

A jog through an opening to their left brought them through a tangle of merchant's stalls. Empty of their day's wares, William hoped the awnings and tent poles and deserted stands might buy them some time, obstacles to trip the careless among their pursuers and give pause to the cautious.

William strove to balance their need for swiftness and their need for stealth, fast enough to get away but slow enough that their arms and armor weren't a rattling and ringing giveaway of their location. He ducked suddenly to the left, leading them through a planked passage between two low buildings so narrow they were forced to run single file. Over the hollow clomps of their feet on the timbers, he heard a crash in the distance behind him, and then another as the soldiers overturned the merchant's stands one by one. William allowed a smile when he realized they'd gained a greater lead as the soldiers took time to check the stands for any men hiding among them.

The narrow path gave way to a wide alley and the Templars spread out into two columns, Ramon following up the rear. William's arm flashed out, his fist held high for the others to see. His hand then opened flat, fingers together, and flicked twice to the left. Confused, Andre watched as Ramon peeled away from the group, followed by Armande. As the two disappeared into a nook darker than the rest of the alley, the remaining brothers raced on.

They turned another corner, and William's hand again went up, flicking twice this time to the right. Nicolas broke off, disappearing into the shadows. Huffing, Brother Odo leaned down to Etienne.

"Stay behind Brother William," he instructed soberly before fading away into the darkness, joining Nicolas out of sight.

As the alleyway straightened out again, William broke into an all out run, the remaining Templar brothers in line behind him. Le Brun's soldiers, a dozen strong, caught sight of fleeing Templars and raced after them.

At the head of the pursuers, soldier Arnoul Le Gore's eyes were bright with the thrill of the hunt. Though moments before, his cheeks had burned hot over the time he and the others had wasted kicking their way through the market space, his face lit at the prospect of distinguishing himself to his captain, and the rewards that could follow from the noble.

Though he'd served his term with pride, he joined the king's army six years before for only one reason: to escape his family's life and seize the spoils of battle that were every soldier's right to take. As dyers, his parents toiled all day in the mills over hot vats of color, tinting fabrics they could never afford for themselves to just the right hue for aristocrats. The work was sweltering in the winter, blistering in the summer, and always left them with a damp, earthy smell that never went away. When a captain of King Philip's army came one day to their block seeking conscripts, Arnoul sought him out, pleading with the royal officer and his sergeant for a place in the king's service, the chance for a life away from the vats and wool sheep irresistible.

The riches of war, however, had so far eluded him. Stationed in the city, he'd had to rely on his livery and the bribes he could extort from the Parisians. The only chance he'd ever had to fight was in Gascony, and there, the officers had been strict, claiming every scrap of loot in the king's name.

This night's campaign had been serious and unusual. He'd learned who they were to arrest as they were ordered into position at the rear of the Temple. Arnoul saw opportunity to serve king and country and for reward in bringing in the Templars. Although they usually kept to themselves, hidden away in their temple, Arnoul had encountered many over the years on the roads or at the city's gates. He'd never cared for the ones he'd met as they transferred from one Templar installation to the next or conveyed funds in some un-Christian arrangement. Stubbornly silent, the Templars seldom spoke with His Majesty's soldiers, answering only direct questions that pertained to their immediate task. They never laughed at the soldiers' jests and banter, a sign to Arnoul of their arrogance, like so many of the aristocrats that filled the officers' ranks for the king. If the Templars all wasted in the royal dungeons, he wouldn't miss them, especially if there were a boon in it for him.

Shouting threats of arrest and harm, Arnoul plunged headlong down the alley, dashing ahead as he saw their quarry disappear around another corner. "Move your feet!" he shouted to the other soldiers. "The king wants them, and we'll have them for him!"

The men behind him, Arnoul rounded the corner.

And stopped suddenly.

The soldiers immediately behind him nearly ran into Arnoul's back. Skidding on their heels, the remaining dozen stopped. Swords and axes in hand, they fanned out from the alley's mouth to see past Arnoul.

Ahead of them stood Brothers William and Andre, Etienne behind them. The three stood in front of the broad, dark wall of the cul-de-sac.

A dead end.

Rags and rubbish, sticks, old bones and waste of all kinds littered the ground. Deep shadows hid the corners where the two tall walls met the third. The Templars had yet to draw any weapon. They simply stood, the two men in their white tabards and armor, the boy in his dark robes, hands empty and at their sides. The boy drew behind the elder of the two Templars, eyes cast down, uneasy. Arnoul realized that the mouth he and his men blocked was the only exit from the alley. The Templars must have realized they were trapped. Yet the elder one's gaze was even and cool, not at all the look of a cornered man. When they started after them behind the Temple in the Rue De Foren, there were more than three.

"Stand down," William said in a low voice, interrupting Arnoul's thoughts. "Turn back. Just go. Tell them you lost us in the night."

The royal soldiers looked to one another. The Templars were only three, two men and a child. They stood no chance against a nearly dozen soldiers, yet the Templar who spoke seemed unconcerned.

Arnoul shook off his apprehension. He'd earned a cast-off sword in his service to Captain Le Brun, allowing him to replace the axe he'd carried in the king's name with a true weapon. For bringing back the Templars, helping the captain curry favor with the king, his reward would be as valuable.

"Stand down," William repeated quietly.

That Templar arrogance. Outnumbered six to one, and the bastard was threatening *them*, giving *him* orders. Arnoul stepped forward and drew his prized sword. Its hilt of curving, polished brass, the blade was bright, a single notch marring its edge, a chipped tooth in an otherwise unblemished smile. The other soldiers raised their axes and spears.

"In the name of His Majesty King Philip," Arnoul said loudly, repeating the words he recalled the captain used, "You are arrested and ordered—"

"I'm giving you a chance to live another day," William said through clenched teeth. "Go."

A few soldiers glanced nervously about. Arnoul was certain more were afoot when they started after them. In fact, one was wounded. Neither of the two men before him showed any hint of injury. Arnoul's doubts scratched at his thoughts with cat's claws, but he couldn't let them escape and couldn't return to the captain empty-handed.

"Take them," he ordered the other soldiers, deciding on the spoils he might be allowed to keep from the fugitives or their bodies.

The soldiers started forward. Arnoul noticed what he could only call disappointment flicker over the Templar's face as he drew his sword.

At that signal, the other Templars burst from the shadows.

Too fast for the soldiers to comprehend, the outermost of their group found gloved hands across their faces, and a heartbeat later, cold steel slicing their throats. The remaining soldiers were oblivious to the Templar snare until they heard the heavy sounds of their comrades' bodies thud on the dirty ground.

Their number was halved, and they were surrounded.

The Templars were upon the remaining soldiers, slashing and stabbing. One soldier managed to sidestep the killing blow meant for him, the blade instead glancing across his armor's hard, boiled leather and linen. He dashed for the mouth of the alley and shouted for help. Nicolas slid from the shadows, clamping a hand over his mouth and dragging him into the deep shadows. The soldier's struggles stopped.

Nearly mad with panic, Arnoul charged William, to run the Templar bastard through. William's blade flashed, its edge catching the soldier's flawed blade and winding the weapon away from him, binding it as the Templar's point pierced his chest.

The Knights Templars stood unmoving over the corpses, their faces narrow-eyed masks. The silence was terrible. It pressed on them all as their ears strained against the darkness, listening for any more pursuers.

Ramon sagged against a wall, his face slick with perspiration. Francesco was immediately at his side, tending to the arrow still embedded in Ramon's bicep. Francesco unlaced the ailette from Ramon's shoulder, stripping the plate from his mail and tucking it into his own belt. Gingerly, he turned Ramon's arm. The arrow pierced the mail of his sleeve at a steep angle. Entering below the muscle of the shoulder, it plunged almost straight down to his forearm. Francesco stripped off his gauntlets and white gloves, and slipped his hand up into his brother's sleeve. Above Ramon's elbow, his fingertips traced skin pulled taut and over something hard and pointed within the muscle, a metal point barely pushing through, the arrow's tip jutting out from inside.

"It didn't make it through," he whispered to Ramon. Ramon nodded, closing his eyes. Keeping his finger on the arrow head, Francesco studied the shaft, the angle it penetrated Ramon's arm. It had missed the bone, and most likely, the artery. The damage was minimal, but the barbs on the back of the arrowhead made it impossible to withdraw without tearing the muscle more and widening the wound.

Turning up the palm of Ramon's injured arm, Francesco placed the back of Ramon's wrist upon his left shoulder, stretching Ramon's arm diagonally between the two of them.

"*Pater noster, qui es in caelis, sanctificetur nomen tuum,*" Ramon began to pray. He met Francesco's eyes briefly as the young chaplain joined him.

"*Adveniat regnum tuum. Fiat voluntas tua,*" they intoned together. Again Ramon closed his eyes as Francesco gripped the arrow and shoved down, driving the shaft further into his arm.

Ramon choked back a cry as his skin split and the arrowhead emerged, bloody, from his arm. He swallowed his last few words as Francesco continued praying for them both. *"Sicut in caelo et in terra."* The fletched shaft protruding from one side of Ramon's arm, the gruesome head from the other, Francesco could now set about removing it.

With his back to the wall, William surveyed the blind alley. At its mouth, Nicolas and Armande had taken up watch. Behind him, Andre and Etienne stood motionless, trying to take in all that had elapsed.

"Strip them of their cloaks," William ordered, indicating the bodies of the dead soldiers littering the ground.

Andre looked to him, bewildered, hesitant.

"We need something to hide our Templar garb," William explained. "Right now, it's as if every one of us was wearing a target."

Etienne didn't move. Avoiding Brother William's gaze, he breathed hard, his small shoulders heaving. His wide eyes darted over the slain soldiers, occasionally turning to the Templars.

Andre started forward then stopped, turning to William. "This is wrong," he said.

William stepped in closer to Andre. "We're not robbing them, Brother," he explained in a low voice. "But we do need those cloaks to disappear."

"We've each taken an oath to protect all Christians."

Etienne's breathing slowed to long, even draughts as he watched William closely.

William noticed. "Sometimes, Brother, it's the intentions of an oath, not merely the words."

Francesco rolled back Ramon's bloody mail sleeve, revealing the gory, steel head of the arrow. Long and flat, its edges were like razors. On it, Ramon's blood stood out in distinct, beaded drops, an effect of the wax applied to help the broadhead slip through chain mail armor. Braced against the wall, gulping air, Ramon's lips prayed where his voice failed.

Francesco slipped his long dagger from its sheath, still praying with Ramon.

"Et nos dimittimus debitoribus nostris—"

He pressed the dagger's edge on the shaft where it stabbed into Ramon. The flat of the blade grated softly on his bloodied chain mail.

"*Et ne nos inducas in tentationem—*"

He sliced through the arrow, clipping it close to Ramon's arm. The fletched shaft fell away. The wood sounded hollow and innocuous as a stick as it bounced on the dirty street.

"*Sed libera nos a malo.*"

"Amen," Ramon managed to whisper.

"Don't rationalize," Andre hissed to William. His eyes were clear in their anger and sincerity. "We've all taken sacred oaths never to spill even a drop of Christian blood—"

"Strange," Odo rasped, "In this light, they looked like Saracens to me."

William stepped between them. Brother Odo's wit, he knew, more often aggravated even when he intended it to ease. "Christianity's better judged by action than baptism."

At the alley's mouth, Armande looked suddenly into the gloom beyond. His body tensing, he was certain he heard footsteps.

Andre persisted. "You make jests," he said to Odo. "And you," he looked at William, "spout platitudes, when we can be expelled from the Order us for this. Those men—"

"Were here to kill us," Odo finished for him.

"Were here to kill us as we fled an unlawful arrest," William clarified.

"They weren't foreigners or heretics," Andre went on. "They were soldiers of the king's army. Citizens. Christians."

With one hand, Francesco grasped the arrow, bracing his other hand against Ramon's arm where the arrow's point emerged. He felt his wounded brother tense, heard his soft, guttural groan as he yanked the shaft down, wrenching it the rest of the way through his arm. Ramon strangled another cry, his wail escaping as a tortured hiss.

Francesco dropped the bloody point to the ground. No longer stoppered by the shaft, blood poured freely from the wound, splattering the cast-off halves of the arrow. Ramon sagged, shaping his choked cries into hushed, urgent prayer as Francesco bound his arm.

William decided on another tack. He locked his eyes on Andre's. "The Order was founded to escort pilgrims to the Holy Land."

"To protect them from cutthroats and robbers on their holy journeys," Andre finished impatiently. That was their most basic history, the origins of the Order. Every novitiate, everyone who knew anything about the Order, knew that. "Defending pilgrims on the road from ambush isn't the same thing."

"Isn't it?" William challenged. "Do you think no bandit between here and Jerusalem was ever baptized a Christian?"

The young Templar took almost a full *Pater Noster* to recover his senses. "That's—" He stopped. "That's not the same."

"Get their cloaks," William ordered again, voice firm. "Before more men come and we're trapped in this dead end for real."

Andre hesitated. Then he bent down and started unwrapping the cloak from one of the dead soldiers. When he looked again to Brother William, he found him walking away toward Etienne.

The boy had not moved. With his back to the wall as it had been when the soldiers first appeared at the mouth of the alley, he stood, overwhelmed and terrified and desperate not to show it. His breath was rapid and sharp. He bit at his lip and stared with glittering eyes at the dark beyond the alley's mouth.

At his lookout, Armande eased, relaxing his guard, satisfied there was no immediate threat out in the shadowy streets. They'd been fortunate that only one company of men had been positioned at the rear of the Temple.

Their situation was graver than he'd thought, and he credited Brother William for his estimate of it. Had the royal troops managed to reinforce their positions, they might have all ended as Brother Bernard.

His mind drifted back to Tripoli and Lattakioh before it, and he choked back the bile the memories of those losses stirred at the back of his throat. Somehow, he was stationed in Cyprus when Acre was besieged, and rather than facing their enemies there, he tended casualties and their escorting knights as they limped into port. He'd seen the Order suffer some of its worst losses, and a loss here in Paris could be more dire. Coldly, he realized that his own redemption could depend on their success. They had no room for failure, no room for error or weakness. He turned a cold eye on Etienne as William came up alongside the boy.

William sidled up to Etienne without meeting his eyes. He said nothing. He stood nearby, watching the other knights as they carried out the tasks they'd each taken up.

Andre had freed a cloak from one dead soldier's body, and with it tucked under his arm, he set about taking another. The sleeve of his hauberk no longer pinned to his arm by the arrow, Brother Ramon leaned upon the wall, chain mail rolled up to his shoulder. Brother Francesco wrapped Ramon's wound, pressing it closed, binding it tight in strips of white fabric cut from the hem of his own white tabard. With eyes closed, Ramon continued whispering his prayer.

For a few more moments, William remained silent, watching the scene with the boy. Without shifting his gaze, he said quietly, "You're frightened."

"No, Brother," Etienne said suddenly. He looked to William. "No, it's just—"

William resisted meeting his eyes, looking out over the others. "Fear distinguishes the wise from the foolhardy," he said. "It shows you know when you're in over your head." His gray eyes narrowed, staring out at something past the men and the alleyways. "Now, overcoming fear. *That* is what makes a man courageous."

"Yes, Brother," Etienne said, turning his gaze to match William's and staring, too, into the dark.

"Battle is like fire, Etienne," William went on. "It's God's forge. If you're steel, it makes you harder. Stronger. If you're anything else," he paused, lending weight to his words. "It consumes you."

The sparkle in Etienne's eyes danced and grew brighter, tears welling up. "Then I've already failed," he said and bit down on his lip.

"If that's what you decide," William said, keeping his eyes forward as another long silence passed. "Or you can choose to be steel."

He allowed himself a glance at the boy before he walked away. Etienne hurried to Brother Andre's side, helping him roll over another of the dead soldiers.

CHAPTER IX

William joined Armande and Nicolas at the alley's mouth. "No sign they've sent any more after us," Armande said.

William expected as much. "They're too busy guarding against more escapes. For now, anyway."

Brother Nicolas kept his gaze fixed on the gloom ahead. "We need to get moving."

"Yes," Odo agreed as he joined them. "At once."

Armande turned from his lookout to face William. "But first, we need to discuss thinning our ranks." Following Armande's glare, William saw Etienne at the far end of the alley. Taking the wrist of the dead soldier William had tried to warn off, the boy helped Andre drag the warm corpse to the shadows of the alley's corner. They shoved it in among the litter, strewing more over it for camouflage.

He turned back to Armande. "I'm not leaving him."

"He's all liability." Armande explained, soldier to soldier. "He's small, untrained. He can't protect himself in a fight."

"All the more reason he should stay with us."

Armande had made up his mind. "He's a distraction," he said. "A vulnerability. Something else to shield besides our own backs."

"He's a child."

Nicolas' eyes slid from the dark alleys. He watched the two coolly.

Armande shook his head sharply. "He's dead weight, slowing us down." In his agitation, his voice drifted above a whisper. "We've made it clear of the Temple. He's safe from arrest."

William dropped his voice purposefully, speaking through clenched teeth. "Until some street urchin finds a bailiff and turns him in for a turnip or crust of bread. He'd be alone."

"He's not even one of us."

"He hasn't taken his vows, but he's served the Order and earned its protection."

"And I haven't?" It was more accusation than question.

"We fight as one, Brother Armande," William reminded him. "Shoulder to shoulder, back to back."

Nicolas returned to his watch. The argument would change their options in no real way.

"We can be no stronger than our weakest member, "Armande pressed. "Odo, when we fought at Tripoli—"

"At Tripoli, we fought together," Odo said quietly. "Not amongst ourselves."

Keeping watch, Nicolas closed out the hisses of their whispered arguing. The wind had changed direction, blowing cold from the west now, with a damp smell. Along with the dark clouds that shrouded the moon and helped hide their flight, it was a sure sign of storm. Absently, he checked for the daggers at his belt, finding the leather-wrapped scabbards empty. Facing battle with less than a full kit of steel at his waist left him uneasy. He made note to check over their pursuers' corpses before moving on.

"For the moment, avoiding capture is our best option for protecting the Order." Armande looked to William and to Odo. "That requires fighting ability and stealth. The boy has neither."

William shook his head.

"Every battle requires hard decisions."

"No."

Armande's voice rose. "He'd understand. If it was explained to him, he'd *volunteer*."

William's voice dropped. "Which is why you will say nothing to him."

"Think like a soldier, William, not—"

"Like a knight of God?"

Armande clenched his teeth, balled up his fists.

"He continues with us," William stated.

Armande cut himself off as he spied Brother Francesco making his way toward them. Brother Ramon trod weary beside him. Except for the blood smeared on the mail of his sleeve and streaking his mantle.

Ramon winced as he flexed his tightly bound arm. "Problem, Brothers?"

William shook his head, turning the corners of his mouth down. He glanced at Armande.

"We're eliminating our least likely course of action."

Armande clenched his jaw and turned back to the alley's mouth.

"Your arm?" William asked Ramon.

"Strong enough to fight on," Ramon smiled.

"The arrow pierced the muscle," Francesco explained, tugging on his white gloves. His tabard was ragged at the bottom, draggled in loose threads. "God must have been smiling on him."

Ramon beamed. "He always has." His words came slowly, and he forced a smile. He was holding off the pain William was sure, concealing the sharp aches that he knew from experience the wound would cause for days.

"Just the same," William joked, "I say we tighten your brases and tie your shield to your arm, so I won't have to keep picking it up when it slips from your hand."

"I've fought on worse," Odo pronounced.

"Probably your sword arm," Ramon said, "hanging by a few tendons?"

"I've told you that story?" Odo asked innocently.

Ramon clapped a hand on Odo's shoulder. The one-eyed veteran flashed a grin behind his dark beard.

Francesco turned to William, his face more serious, questioning. "Since you've—" he paused to cast a glance at Armande's back, "—eliminated our least likely actions, what *is* our plan?"

Thunder rumbled, low and distant. The Templars squinted at the sky before Nicolas spoke up, "We'd best effect it shortly. They'll soon realize their men haven't reported back."

"He's right," Odo said. "We've tarried here long enough."

Andre and Etienne approached the group, arms full of the dead soldiers' cloaks. The alley behind them showed no sign of the brief and terrible clash. Bodies were hidden among the trash, and in the dark, the blood on the ground became more dark spots among the filth of the street.

Odo turned to Etienne and tugged at a dusty brown wrap. The boy's grip slipped and he nearly dropped the entire stack as the Templar pulled the cloak free. Odo wound it over his shoulders and pulled its hood up over his head. William took one that was nearly black and shrugged it over his white Templar tabard. The rest of the group followed, wrapping themselves in the dark, nondescript cloaks, adjusting the folds to hide their weapons and armor. Hoods hid their faces and beards, distinctive in the city where few wore them. The white-robed soldiers of God were gone from the alley, replaced by six dark, faceless travelers.

William turned to Nicolas, "Is the way still clear?"

"For the moment."

Too small for any of the dead soldiers' wraps, Etienne stood in his brown initiate's habit. The boy reached under his robes and produced a small dagger, then set to work on the stitches holding the red Templar cross over his heart.

"Good thinking, Etienne," William said. He looked to the others. "I'll take point. Armande will cover the rear."

Odo started for William, his objection obvious. He had more experience at patrol than any of them—

"One eye and a blind side make you a poor lookout, Brother."

Odo nodded, reluctant to agree.

Etienne snipped the last thread holding the appliqué over his chest. He folded it and tucked it into his robe as Brother Francesco spoke up.

"Then we're leaving Paris?"

"If we follow the Seine west," Ramon suggested, "we can rally at Rouen. It's not too far."

"Yes," Andre spoke up quickly. "The Seine would be—"

"Too obvious," William cut him off. "Whatever is happening has been closely planned. Our ports at Rouen and Le Havre are well known. They may expect us to make for them. Even if they haven't been seized, the routes will be blocked or at least watched."

All eyes were on William. All but Andre's, which searched the ground distractedly.

"We should leave France altogether," William continued. He nodded back toward the Temple. "Those were the king's own soldiers."

A chill crept along Francesco's spine though the cold wind had stopped. "Meaning the whole country's turned against us."

"We'll head north," William said, "through Champagne, and cross into Luxembourg."

Odo nodded approval. The march would be long, fraught with peril if they failed to get far enough ahead of the royal troops, but it would put them outside King Philip's domain, and among their own.

"We could join up with our brothers at the Temple in Echternach," Odo added.

William started out of the alley again. Time was their only ally at this point, and it would only aid them if they kept moving.

"We don't need to leave Paris to avoid arrest," Francesco proposed slowly, thinking it through.

"With the city teeming with the king's troops, that would be a pretty trick," Odo said.

Thunder crashed louder and nearer. Etienne looked to the inky sky, dreading the soaking the skies threatened.

"The Cathedral of Notre Dame is within easy distance," Francesco shared at last.

William stepped nearer "Sanctuary?"

Francesco nodded. "It's every Christian's right," he reminded. "The Church takes us in, and we avoid arrest while petitioning His Holiness the Pope to intervene on our behalf and stop this assault on our Order."

"Then we'd need to make for the Seine," Andre injected, ready to move out.

William blocked his way. "It *is* where the Cathedral stands," he said, eyeing him.

"It's not far," Francesco continued. "Assuming we're reduced to but a crawl evading the king's soldiers, we could still reach the cathedral under cover of dark, well before daybreak."

"You're also assuming His Holiness will hear out plea and act," William said.

"We're the Church's soldiers," Francesco began. "Why wouldn't he?"

A soft, distant tapping cut him off. William felt a drip upon his head. A larger drop splattered on Odo's shoulder.

"Sanctuary isn't an option," William said.

"Because?" Francesco asked.

"With all that's passed this night," William hesitated, "Like Brother Odo, I'm uncomfortable placing our fates in anyone else's hands. Call it epiphany. Call it instinct."

Two heavy raindrops splattered across Etienne's neck, cold as the drizzle at a funeral. The boy's shoulders jerked up, and a chill raced down his spine. Shaking his head to chase it away, he snatched from the pile a brown cloak, wrapping its extra length over his shoulders like an old woman's shawl. He tugged it over his head into an uneven, makeshift hood.

"Sanctuary is putting ourselves in God's hands," Francesco pressed. "Besides, as Brother Nicolas said, making for the cathedral gives us options. If sanctuary seems a poor choice, we can follow the river west and still make for Luxembourg."

"Or East," added Andre. "For Britain."

William glanced over the group as the large, cold raindrops pelted them all. His trust was short, but they were men of faith.

William conceded. "We make for the cathedral."

CHAPTER X

Pulling their dark cloaks close against the coming storm, the Templars fell in behind Brother William as he led them again into the twisting darkness of the Paris streets. Their pace was deliberate, slow, each intersection they crossed thick with potential to end their flight.

The rain hit their cloaks like heavy beads lobbed from the heavens thudding loud where they struck the packed dirt or houses. The air was thick with the smell of the coming storm, the pollen and dust blown ahead of the ozone. The wind was uneven, gusting cold over the fugitives, picking at the dark cloaks they hid themselves in.

The rapid shuffle of marching echoed to them through the empty, black avenues. William stopped and flashed his raised fist.

The Templars froze.

Against the wind and the dull thud of the raindrops, they strained to listen, eyes darting at the dark, cautious of even breathing too loudly for fear of missing the slightest sound.

Faint voices drifted to them, distant orders terse and unintelligible. The dripping rain was like a drum in their ears, pounding, blocking the sounds, the clues they strove to hear.

The Templars waited in the rain as the storm swelled. Water trickled more heavily from their cloaks. They waited, watching the darkness, listening with all that was in them.

Odo's hand tightened on his sword, squeezing the rainwater from the leather wrapping on its grip. He could hear nothing above the confounded rain, praying that the storm would either cease enough that they could hear, or grow full enough to provide cover.

The distant voices grew louder but remained indistinct, shouted orders unclear. Etienne inhaled sharply and held his breath. His heart pounded so hard in his chest he feared the others could hear it. He pulled his cloak tighter, smaller, about him.

Armande's eyes darted, searching the gloom for any sign, for any shadow cast in the wrong place. Nicolas gazed impassively into the dark, waiting for whatever the night hid to come to him.

Ramon flexed his injured arm, the sharp ache like being stabbed again each time he moved. He curled his arm again absently. The pain was something he could focus on. The muscles of his neck strained and the salty taste of blood seeped into his mouth from where he'd bitten his cheek. Rain splattered on his hood, spraying cold and sharp into his eye. He shook his head and wiped his face with his gloved hand, blinking hard. Letting his eyes close, Francesco concentrated on the dark and its sounds.

The voices returned, louder, nearer, accompanied by marching boots and clopping hooves. William's eyes narrowed, the snapped orders the wind carried plainer, just intelligible, as they directed the search nearby.

The incessant dripping of the rain hid the sounds. It teased them, droplets falling at the all wrong times. It confused the direction of voices, shrouded street names and intersections as they were called out in the search. Yet it was obvious they were drawing closer.

Andre reached under his cloak and checked the pack the Grandmaster gave him at the Temple. Comforted by its weight in his hand, he closed his eyes, a silent plea on his lips.

The footfalls and hoofbeats and shouted orders off in the darkness grew fainter. Francesco opened his eyes and gazed into the glom as Andre's eyes popped open, amazed. The young Templar rehid his pack.

They waited, unmoving and listening, until all they heard was the gentle, inconstant tapping of the rain.

William raised his hand and continued forward, a brusque wave signaling his brothers to follow. Andre slipped forward through the group as they fell in behind William.

"What if the way is blocked?" Andre asked.

William glanced at him over his shoulder.

"We're a religious Order," Andre pressed, voice hushed. "They'll expect us to seek the Church's help."

William didn't slow, as if he'd heard nothing. "There's a good chance they've made their arrests and withdrawn with their prisoners," he answered.

"Unless they're looking for any who've escaped."

Eyes forward, William nodded, "So, they sweep the surrounding streets and alleys for fugitives. Which they're doing."

At the rear of their squad, Ramon leaned down close to Etienne. "Quite the adventure, isn't it?"

"I guess, Brother." Aside from this Brother Andre, whom he'd never met before, Brother Ramon was probably closest to him in age. He noticed the flecks of blood at the corner of Ramon's mouth.

Ramon spoke quickly, "This is the exciting part, Etienne, the part that makes all the cleaning and stable sweeping worthwhile. Your chance to prove yourself in the face of—"

His words stopped short as he felt Odo's massive hand press firm on his shoulder. Shrinking away, Etienne turned his eyes forward. Ramon glanced backward and saw Odo staring at him with his one, dark eye, a finger before his lips.

William tested his patience with the novitiate. "They can't communicate any faster than they can move, correct?"

"Yes," Andre agreed.

"As long as we stay ahead of them and their messengers, no troops we may encounter will be warned."

William cut off, signaled a stop. The others froze. He listened to the night. He'd heard something.

He heard it again. A groan, a woman's pained groan. William turned his head one way, then the other to find it as she moaned once more, out of sight but near.

This time, a pained cry, a scream, followed by a shrieked "No!"

Nicolas' arm snaked past Andre, his hand clamping on William's arm. "Brother, we don't have time."

"Stop it," the woman's voice came from the dark. "Don't!" Her voice cut off as William made out the alley it rose from.

William shrugged away Nicolas' hand and raced for the alley's mouth.

"Brother!" Armande called after him.

"William!" Odo bellowed, his teeth grinding. *Impulsive* was something he'd never have called his brother, but through the years in the field, he found his judgment ruled by his own codes more than any mission. Armande's hand lashed out, punched a near wall as Ramon took off after William.

The man in the alley was huge and burly, a blacksmith by the size of his arms. Thick and gnarled as tree limbs, they were just as hard as oaken branches from his day's work with hammer and anvil. With one arm, he held a slight, wriggling girl to the wall of the dirty alley without difficulty. A meaty hand crushed her shoulder, his forearm and elbow pinning her to the grimy wall. His hips ground into hers, and with his free hand, he fumbled to loosen his belt.

Barely able to breathe for his weight on her, the girl writhed and twisted. Her skirt was torn, as was as was the *cotte* underdress beneath it, the long rip exposing her leg up well past her thigh. The laces that held the top of her dress closed over her chest were torn too, laying bare one of her breasts, pale and flattened under the blacksmith's crushing weight.

She pulled her face away from his. Her left eye was swollen, the purpling bruise around it fresh and marring her face as far as her cheek. Her lower lip bled where it was split, her own blood smeared on her chin. She started to cry out again, but the big man covered her mouth with his, suffocating her.

A few paces away, his four friends watched hungrily. One, with crooked, yellowing teeth edged brown where they met his gums, elbowed another who had a jagged scar that scrawled from his cheek and tugged at his upper lip, distorting his mouth. Bored with drinking in the smithy, they'd chanced going out after curfew to find some other amusement when the girl happened by. She'd been coy with them at first, but once she realized they'd all been drinking and the smith had made his intentions known, she laughed, wanted to slip away. With the rain blowing cold, the five had decided they would have something warm and sweet-smelling before heading back.

Bricks dug into her back, and her head crashed into one poorly set and sticking out from the wall. Whipping her head from side to side, the girl somehow managed to shake her face free of his, her tangled hair falling across her eyes. Gasping, she gulped in air, wincing as each breath burned in her side.

The smith cursed his own shoddy workmanship as the belt leather snagged on his buckle, keeping him from pushing his own garments out of the way. He yanked at his belt when stars lit up before his eyes and pain burst sharp across the back of his skull. His grip on the girl loosened. Rough hands took him by the collar and his legs were kicked out from under him, pitching him backward into the muddy street.

He landed hard and made his way to all fours, shaking his head to clear it, anger welling up hot from his belly. A glance at his friends showed him they'd done nothing. Still back in the alley, they were too far away to interfere or prank him so. They were staring, and following their surprised and confused gazes, his eyes fell upon the girl.

And the man that stood between them.

"Leave," the stranger ordered, face hidden under the dark hood of his cloak.

The stars in his head fading, the blacksmith climbed to his feet and scowled.

William stared up at him, his face impassive. Cloaked as he was, in the drizzle and gloom, he could have been anyone, any traveller or peddler who had found his way to Paris and stumbled onto this scene. He stood unmoving, hands at his sides, rainwater dripping from his sleeves.

"Go to hell," the blacksmith bellowed, inflating his chest, "and go now if you know what's good for you."

"I said 'Leave,'" William repeated.

The girl forgot how she was exposed. With tentative eyes, she looked to the stranger's back and over his shoulder at the towering smith. To her, they appeared a defiant child staring down a full-grown man.

The blacksmith's friends looked to one another, and the one with the yellow and brown teeth snickered. He'd seen Obert, the smith, dispense more than a few good beatings in the years he'd known him. Whether it was the look on their faces after the first time Obert's tree-like arms came down or the hollow sounds their heads made when he thumped them, it was always a good for laugh.

Adjusting his belt, the smith closed in. "You don't know a warning when you hear one, do you?" His massive forearms twitched as he closed in on the unmoving Templar, his fist balling up tight. "Too bad for you."

The girl flattened herself against the wall, hemmed in by the standoff she was certain was about to become a beating. Her eyes darted first over the two men in front of her, and then over the four who had watched her attack, waiting their turn. All eyes on the cloaked stranger, she shifted the waist of her dress, adjusting and tucking the fabric, smoothing it over a small bulge at her hip.

William's features hid in the shadows of his hood, and his eyes met the giant blacksmith's, cold and unyielding. He had to end this quickly. Time was precious and fleeting, and as big as this one was, he knew it wouldn't go quickly. With only the slightest movement of his hand along his waist, William slid open his cloak.

The big man spotted the stranger's arms shift, held his breath, and readied for a knife to flash out from beneath the dripping cloak. But the shine he glimpsed wasn't a blade; but the dazzling white of a surcoat, and an eight-pointed red cross stitched in place above the stranger's heart.

He'd done some smithing for some Templars, shoeing a horse, re-riveting a helmet, or repairing the loosened head of a mace. The ones he'd met were hard, quiet men. Unimposing, really, they were back from the Holy Land, part of a merchant caravan returning from Cyprus. This was in his old shop, his smithy off the road on the outskirts of Paris. Until then, he'd never believed the stories he'd heard about the ferocity of the Knights Templar. They seemed to him little different from the Benedictines he'd met.

Until the caravan left.

It was dusk. They'd gone perhaps only a hundred paces down the road, when bandits sprang from the brush lining the roadside. A queasy-looking merchant in an oversized cap was their first victim. Tackled from his horse, his throat was cut as he scrambled to get back on his feet.

Another bandit tried to unhorse a black-bearded Templar as his cohort had the merchant. He was dead before the two of them struck the ground, the Templar rolling to his feet, sword in hand. The Templar riding at the point wheeled his horse around and lowered his lance. At a charge, he pinned another of the robbers to a tree, the lance through his chest bouncing as the knight let it go. They were fast, he recalled, ungodly fast. And brutal, something he was to discover more about after the bandits had been cleared off.

At his old smithy, he'd learned the importance of discretion. Robberies were part of travel, one of the risks assumed when taking to the road. Experience had shown Obert his best response was to retreat to his shop, start working with his biggest and sharpest tools, and make sure he saw nothing and said less.

He was keeping his head down so when the lead Templar burst into his shop. Grabbing him by the nape, the knight slammed the blacksmith's head onto the anvil, demanding what he knew of the highwaymen, what part he played in the ambush. The big smith clutched at his skull and denied everything. It took the better part of an hour for him to convince the Templar.

Facing another Templar in this alley, the blood drained from his face. The sight of the red cross made his heart pound. He inhaled sharply. Sweat beaded on his upper lip. He stepped back, unsure, as the stranger allowed his cloak to fall closed.

The girl's eyes sprang wide. Seeing only the big man backing down from the smaller, she stared, more impressed than unbelieving.

The big smith's friends were incredulous. None had ever seen a fight Obert didn't finish, and none saw what the stranger did to back him away. Squinting against the gloom, the one with the scar tugging at his lip made out the shape of a sword under the stranger's cloak. "He needs more than a sword," he called out, "There's five of us!"

The one with bad teeth noticed the sword's outline. He stooped down and picked a makeshift cudgel from some cut branches stacked in the alley's corner.

"Sword makes no difference when you all alone." He brandished the knotty piece of firewood, lips twisting in a mean smile that merely bared his stained, yellow teeth.

Realizing his friends were still behind him, Obert was suddenly less intimidated. He stomped forward, making a show of his newfound courage for his friends. The stranger stood where he was. His expression verged on boredom.

The one with the bad teeth started to call out another threat when a sound caught his attention: the scraping of a boot on cobblestone. He glanced over his shoulder and felt a cold quiver in his gut.

Behind him, three dark strangers blocked the alleyway.

In dark hoods like the one confronting Obert, they stood unmoving. Rainwater running off their cloaks, they were like cathedral gargoyles posed on the ground.

He turned to his friend with the scar, touching his shoulder softly, then urgently, trying to get him to turn and see. His scarred friend ignored him. His eyes transfixed, the scarred man gazed behind Obert and the stranger before him. At the other end of the alley, three more dark, hooded figures had appeared, one larger than the others, one much smaller, all silent, menacing, and still.

The rain dripped down, cold drops spraying where they struck. William watched as the big blacksmith and his friends glanced from one end of the alley back to the other, as they saw they had lost the advantage. Calmly, William looked back to the big man. To end this, he had to be careful not to press him nor make it a matter of pride or survival.

Without a word, the tallest hooded figure stepped aside, offering the big blacksmith and his friends a path to escape.

They didn't need to be told. The one with bad teeth ran first, and they all scrambled after him for the opening, scurrying nervously past the dark figures. The smith looked to William with burning, eyes, forearms still twitching. William stood ready, considering for a moment that the big man might be too proud to take advantage of the chance he'd been extended. With a bullish snort, the smith turned.

William took the moment to glance over his shoulder at the girl. Eyes darting, she was pressed against the wall, uncertain about what would come next. William's eyes fell across her nakedness. The pale, bare flesh of her breast and thigh made her only more vulnerable and cornered.

He turned to her, and reaching out with a solid hand, William stopped the big blacksmith. He grabbed at his shirt and tore down, stripping it away and leaving the brawny man half-naked.

The blacksmith bolted like a startled bull, but he was so broad that, as he squeezed between Ramon and Armande, he clipped Etienne with a meaty hip, bowling him over as he dashed by. The boy crashed to the ground, stifling a cry as his arm smashed awkwardly on the damp earth and twisted under his weight. Ramon rushed to his side.

William turned back to the girl. He stared into her eyes, averting his from her bareness, holding out the shirt.

"Cover yourself."

The girl took the tattered garment from his hand, neither self-conscious nor ashamed. Wrapping it across her shoulder, she draped it over her breast, knotting the fabric crudely near her waist.

"I'm all right," she stammered.

Armande stepped up to William as the others neared, the girl pushed aside as they closed around him. "Of all the undisciplined—"

"Not now," William said.

"Not now?"

The rain picked up, the occasional drips turning heavy, cold and wet and blown all about by the wind.

Kneeling in the mire next to Etienne, Ramon called to William. "He's all right, Brother." His eyes were on Armande. "It's but a sprain."

William looked past Armande to see the boy sitting in the mud, wincing as Brother Ramon tended his arm. "Take care of him, Brother," he called back. Ignoring Brother Armande would do nothing to salve his arguments. He needed to make clear their priorities.

Perhaps they were to be decided for him. He turned back and saw the girl. With the big blacksmith's shirt now wrapped like a sling from her shoulder to her hip, she was boldly pushing through the knights, her eyes set upon him. The girl shoved past Armande, whose words failed him. A dark twinkle shone in Brother Odo's eye.

"Thank you," the girl said more with irritation than gratitude. She stopped in front of William. "But what am I to do when they come back?"

"They won't." William turned away.

"How do you know?"

William turned back to her, stepped in close. "I know their type," he said softly, firmly. Perhaps he'd been too long in the cloister, but it had been since the Crusades that he'd met a woman so unabashed.

"Well, I know *them*," the girl said. "I live here and I work here. They'll just wait until you're gone."

William studied her face as she spoke. He recognized the bruising on her eye and the blood drying on her lip were the marks of a fist. Her eyes were lively and bright, a pale blue that made her bruises all the worse for the way her eye stood out among the dark marks. Her neck was long and pale, in contrast to her hair, which spilled thick and black over her shoulders. He realized then that her hair was uncovered. Immodest, perhaps, but not improper for an unmarried woman her age. He guessed her to be nineteen, for she was pretty in the way only nineteen-year-old girls are.

"Once you leave," she went on, "they'll be back."

Her words were lost on William as his brow knit, his eyes trailing over her clothes, the black ribbons tied at her shoulders, the torn gloves on her hands.

"Then, "she finished, "they'll take it all out on me."

Before William could answer, Odo's hand hooked under his arm, pulling him aside. Francesco and Armande rushed in behind him, their backs to the girl. She gritted her teeth and stamped a foot on the wet street.

CHAPTER XI

"We can't stay," Odo said in William's ear, his voice low and hushed.

Nicolas pushed past the two and stationed himself at the mouth of the alley, closest to the street. He stood, staring into the darkness.

With Andre's help, Ramon, wrapped Etienne's injured arm, using the boy's oversized cloak to fashion a sling. Ramon angled his own bandaged arm next to the boy's.

"Hey," he said with a grin, "Now we match. Mementos of our adventure."

The boy nodded, rolling his eyes away from Ramon, completely unmoved.

Odo pressed William, his breath hot in the rainy night air, "If those men you chased off run into one of the patrols—"

"I know," William agreed. "We need to move."

Armande grabbed William's shoulder. "What were you playing at back there?" he demanded.

William shrugged Armande's hand away and narrowed his eyes on him. "She needed help."

The girl's ears pricked up. She listened to their whispered arguments, concealing her eavesdropping by pretending to tend to the long rip in her skirt. She tugged off her thin, ragged gloves, and began examining the tear. She spread the torn sides apart, exposing her thigh, nearly up to the curve of her hip. Helping with Etienne's injury, Ramon glanced up and the girl's pale, bare flesh captured his eye. He watched as her nimble fingers pulled and bunched the cloth on each side of the tear and tied the two sides together in a small knot. She did this again, leaving a gap perhaps the length of her thumb between the knots. Ramon noticed the way her skin flashed into view between the knots as the girl repeated this, listening surreptitiously to the others.

"You were rash," Armande hissed, "Impulsive. You put every one of us at risk, chasing off on your own like that. What did you think you were doing? More's at stake here than some—"

"Woman who required our help," finished William.

The raven-haired girl paused at her knotting.

"Whore," Armande corrected. "No upstanding woman would be out unescorted at this hour. Look at her—the black ribbons, the gloves. It's what the law requires them to wear."

William cast a glance at the girl, who feigned inattention, making a point of keeping her eyes on her work repairing her dress.

"He's right, Brother. We may be the Order's only hope," Francesco added. "When we act, there's more to consider."

"More to consider than what?" William asked, "More than our responsibilities as Christians?"

Odo spoke quietly, without the others' reproach. "We have to be careful, Brother."

"We're wasting time," said Armande.

"We cannot stay and watch over her," Odo pointed out.

"She can travel with us," William said.

The girl felt an unfamiliar chill sweep along her spine and through her belly at the hooded stranger's words. She nearly looked up at him but kept to her knotting, which had nearly reached the hem.

Armande's teeth clenched. "You're going soft. The boy was one thing, but I'll not have a harlot along."

Shifting behind William and Armande, Odo placed one of his large hands on each of their backs and began walking forward, guiding them to the mouth of the alley as they quarreled.

"Didn't our Lord Jesus choose a fallen woman as one of his closest disciples?" William asked. Behind them, Francesco cast his eyes toward the ground as Odo herded them forward.

"You can't be comparing taking her along to—"

Francesco interrupted him, his head down.

"'Inasmuch as ye have done it unto one of the least of my brethren, ye have done it unto me,'" he quoted almost reluctantly, ashamed by his arrogance in not seeing it earlier. "We are not here to judge her."

As Odo led the others past her, the girl looked up and followed. "Hey! You can't leave me here."

Her words and sudden movement shattered Ramon's reverie, and he looked away from her. Seeing the elder brothers making for Brother Nicolas and the alley's mouth, he helped Etienne to his feet. Together with Brother Andre, they joined the others at the entrance to the street. Intent on his watch, Nicolas paid them no heed as they all came up behind him.

Armande whirled upon the girl. "Lower your voice. This is not for you to decide."

"My choice would be no different were she a noblewoman," William pressed.

Odo turned to the girl. Her pale eyes met his single dark one, and in it she saw none of the scorn she'd seen in so many others. "If what you say is true," he said, "you're only delaying the inevitable. If they don't find you this night, they will find you another."

She shook her head, confident. "They had too much to drink and didn't want to pay."

Odo recognized the feral bravado. He'd seen it in the largest and most besieged cities: the loud bluster of the young—even children—who managed to endure the unforgiving life of the streets after being orphaned or turned out from their homes.

"They'll cool off in a day or two," the girl went on. "But if they come back tonight..." She looked past Odo, singling William out. "You got me into this trouble."

"We saved you," William said.

"From drunken men who didn't want to pay," she replied. "There's a lot of men like that."

With a glance at her cheek, William met her accusing gaze. "It looks like they did more than refuse to pay."

"I could have handled them," the girl boasted. A slim poniard flashed from her sleeve into her hand, the square, stabbing dagger waving in the air between them. Odo tensed, even as Armande's hand when to his hilt.

William stared at her coolly. "Then why didn't you?"

The sky opened up at that moment. Rain streamed down from the heavens in thick, pounding sheets that grew to a downpour. The torrent gushed, miring the streets, soaking the knight brothers and the girl. She slipped the knife away, scampering to join the knights along the edges of the alley. Backs pressed against the walls, they tried for what little cover any overhang above provided.

"We can't stay out in this," Odo shouted to William over the rain. "None of us has proper rain gear."

"We should press on," Nicolas countered. "The weather will provide us cover. The king's troops won't look for us in this."

Ramon agreed, "Nor will they be likely to resume their searches when the storm abates."

"We need shelter," William said.

Odo studied the men as they pulled their cloaks about themselves, adjusting the hoods and folds as they shifted against the walls, searching out the spots where the rain was best blocked. "We need shelter for a while, at least," he said. "March too long in this, then head into the field, and we'll all catch our death of fever."

The girl spoke up, "I know a place you can go and take cover from the rain." Her eyelids fluttered against the downpour, her lashes clumping together thick and wet. Her long, black hair plastered flat along her skull and neck, the rainwater stood in thick beads on her cheeks and lips. She was soaked to the skin, the sleeves of her underdress and her makeshift top wet and almost transparent against her skin.

"Quiet, girl," Armande ordered.

"No," Andre said, looking to William.

William turned to the girl, studying her face again. Water spattered from in front of her mouth as she breathed and she stared back with her pale, blue eyes.

"We can't afford to be seen," Armande warned.

"It's a place where they notice nothing and say even less," the girl offered. She met William's even gaze. "Especially if I bring you."

William looked over his men. They were drenched. He'd seen illness and disease kill more in the Crusades than fighting, and if he had to pick a death for any, it wouldn't be a lingering, consumptive one.

"What's your name, girl?" he asked.

"I'm called Solange," she answered, "Solange Parisien."

William shook his head. "I didn't ask what they call you on the streets. I asked for your name."

The girl stared at him a moment, mouth open, questioning as the rain continued beating down on them all.

"It's Lisette," she said finally.

William gestured for her to proceed. "Lead us, then, Lisette."

The girl pushed past the other knights and through the mouth of the alley. Armande glared under his hood as she led William into the darkness of the avenue. Each brother fell in behind. With a glance over his shoulder, Armande joined them, following up the rear.

✝ ✝ ✝

Storm water poured from the black sky over the Paris Temple, leaving its walls dark and slick. Huddled against the walls, the dark-cloaked soldiers of the King's Royal Army stood watch. They shifted uneasily in their wet clothing, feet cold and soggy in their boots, slowly sinking into the muddy ooze of the street. The soldiers who lined the corridors inside the Temple were thankful that they'd drawn the inside duty, the rattling of the rain on the windows and doors a steady reminder of the misery of the outside watch.

Not a white habit was in sight. Since arrest and the removal of the prisoners, only men in dark uniforms prowled the Temple halls. Officers directed men here and there, sending them up stairs and down, searching out any Templars straggling or perhaps hiding. It was an intimidating, even frightening place for a soldier, full of large, dark spaces that stood too quiet and many smaller nooks and dark corners that could conceal an armed, desperate fugitive. Statuary and carvings were scattered throughout, the flickering lantern and torch lights tricked the eye, creating a prowling intruder at almost every turn.

A heavy foot kicked open the massive door to the Grandmaster's office, shattering the cloister's silence. A pair of brawny soldiers shoved a struggling Jacques De Molay stumbling into the room. He'd cooperated with the soldiers and their officers, but they treated him as hostile, never missing an opportunity to strike, trip, shove, or manhandle him like a common felon. Free of their clamping hands, he pushed back a tangle of silver hair from his face, smoothing it against his skull. He considered turning and instructing the two on how a truly hostile prisoner behaves, when a soft, dry voice behind him commanded,

"Sit."

He knew this voice. He turned defiantly, scanning the darkness for the throat issuing orders in his offices. At the far end of the room, a single candle flickered, and in the gloom he could make out a form near it. He saw, too, his furnishings had been moved, his desk shoved aside and a low, wooden stool sat in the center of the space. The soldiers seized him roughly, forcing him to sit.

He fought back the urge to get up and deal with the two, remembering his plan. Instead, he relaxed on the stool, playing along. The figure at the far end of the room was close enough to the candle to be visible in the pale light. Thin, pale fingers tenderly touched a taper to the flame, using it to light a small brazier.

The room brightened to where it was dim, revealing a man, thin and wiry. Head shaven, his features were pronounced, a strong nose jutting from beneath a heavy brow, with thin lips above a bony chin. He wore robes of black, the light from the brazier dancing over the elaborately bejewelled gold crucifix he wore over his black habit. With a soft puff, he blew out the taper and let it fall to the floor.

"Imbert," Grandmaster De Molay called out in a low voice.

So, the Inquisition was involved.

Guillaume Imbert, Chief Inquisitor of France, ignored Jacques De Molay. Instead, he reached into his long, loose sleeve and withdrew a parchment, slowly unrolling it.

"Jacques De Molay," he intoned without looking up from the paper, "Grandmaster of the Order of Poor Fellow Knights of Christ and the Temple of Solomon, known also as the Knights Templar."

De Molay had not foreseen the involvement of the Inquisition. Less an order than a procedure, the Inquisition drew from the ranks of the Dominicans and the Franciscans. It convened when necessary to confront evil in the world. But where the Knights Templar fought to defend the faith in distant lands with lance and sword, the Inquisition fought its evils at home, empowered as judges and rooting out heresy through inquiry and interrogation. De Molay's mind raced to gauge the implications of Imbert's appearance. The arrival of France's Chief Inquisitor neither surprised nor concerned him.

"You and the Inquisition have no authority over me, Imbert," the Grandmaster interrupted. "Our Order answers only to the Pope himself."

Imbert ignored his words, continued reading the charges. "You stand accused of the most vile and obscene heresies—"

One of the soldiers still had his hand clamped on the Grandmaster's shoulder. He shrugged free of it.

"What are you after?" he demanded.

Imbert stopped reading but kept his eyes on the parchment.

De Molay pressed him. "What power do you hope to grab through this?"

Imbert set his jaw, refusing to look up. He began again to drone on, ignoring the Templar's accusations and putting forth his own. "Supremely abominable crimes, including denial of our Lord, desecration of His presence, worship of false idols, sodomy—"

"Is this some scheme hatched by your king?" De Molay pushed. He allowed a smile to tug at one corner of his mouth. "Pulling on your strings again, is he? You *are* his confessor. Is he still upset over our refusal to name him *Rex Bellator?*" Philip had put forward the proposal to Rome that all the fighting Orders be combined into one vast Order, and recommended that he—and all future kings of France—hold automatic authority over this Order as War King. Jacques De Molay had stood personally against it.

The Templar Grandmaster rose to his feet, the action challenging and disrespectful toward the inquisitor and his position. Perhaps it made him insolent, arrogant, but he had to goad Imbert. If he could draw him out, spur the inquisitor into some error, it would help him find pieces to complete the picture.

As quickly as De Molay had stood, the guards were upon him, seizing him by the shoulders and arms. Struggling with the old Templar, they tried to force him back down into his seat, but his strength was surprising, and his twisting limbs proved difficult to keep hold. They were shocked that a wiry, silver-haired old man was holding his own against them.

Imbert looked up from his parchment, unconcerned. He watched the two guards wrestle the powerful Grandmaster back to the stool. This, Imbert knew, was necessary. The Templars were too long left to their own. He had only to look to Jacques De Molay to see it. Their Order's rule was Cistercian, and the Templars were to adhere to the strictest laws of appearance, of manner and conduct, keeping to the humblest and holiest standards. Yet before him was a man with the flowing hair of a noble and the beard of an infidel, his strength evidence of full diet and time spent at practice other than prayer. He showed neither obedience nor humility, struggling mightily. His open contempt galled Imbert, the duplicity and hypocrisy almost unbearable.

These were the times that made his work most rewarding.

The inquisitor locked his cold eyes on De Molay's as the Templar was forced back onto the stool.

"Confess your sins," Imbert ordered gravely, his voice sinking. "And accept your penance, so that you may be forgiven. And spared."

CHAPTER XII

The rain pounded at Brother William and the Templars. The oiled, woolen cloaks kept them mostly dry from the water the heavens poured down. Their feet took the worst of the soaking, the streets a sodden, mired mess. Though some places were slick with mud and dung wet and slippery underfoot, other spots flooded, with deep, puddles filling the ruts and hollows of the streets. Trash floated in the dirty runnels.

Lisette walked as stoically as any of the Templars, drenched as she was, neither complaining nor shrinking from the rain's beating. Without hesitation or consideration, she guided them up one street and down another, each turn taking them on a narrower avenue and more out of the way than the last, less kept than the last, and somehow darker than the last.

The rain slowed, no longer pouring but beating down hard. The girl waited at the intersection of two streets so narrow they could pass for alleys in other parts of the city. She stopped before a large townhouse that faced directly onto the corner.

A tall building for this quarter, it was attached on either side to the walls of the townhouse next to it. Its chipped and uneven walls were pockmarked like a face given to too much indulgence. Its shuttered windows had splintered boards tacked unevenly over them yet somehow obscuring them completely. High above, the roof was patched poorly, and the chimney was crumbling, pale smoke billowing from all around it into the dark, rainy sky.

Uneven steps that tilted down at one side led up to a small door. Beside it, rainwater ran from the roof in a thick, steady stream. As Lisette mounted the steps, the knights paused, looking up at the sign above the door.

The wooden plaque was battered, its corners ragged and chewed. Carved at its center was the image of a lizard crawling into the mouth of a wide goblet. Its pointed head poised inside the rim, its tail curled around the vessel's stem. The paint on the sign was long faded, the colors streaked and scrubbed from the wood by weather and neglect. Curving letters were stenciled around the image with too much flourish:

Le Basilisk et Chalice

William, studied it a moment. Behind him, Andre looked over the image, his expression betraying confusion tinged with wonder.

"The Basilisk and Chalice?" William read aloud, over the rain.

"A tavern," Francesco pronounced, his lip curled.

Andre took his eyes from the sign. "This can be no place for godly men."

Lisette spoke up, "It's dry, and they'll have a fire."

"Templars don't crave comfort," Andre said. William prayed he had never sounded like that when he was a novitiate.

Brother Armande studied the place with slitted eyes before speaking up. "Any reputable place should be closed by now," he said. "It's hours past the city curfew." His voice held the same tone as Francesco's.

Lisette batted her eyes, her fingertips brushing against her throat in mock horror. "You mean, people could be in there *breaking the law?*" She went on with the exaggerated display, feigning a swoon at Armande's expense and to his annoyance. He glowered at the girl as she mocked him.

"What better place to hide a band of monks?" she said finally, snapping out of her display.

"You have a big mouth, girl," Armande warned.

Still on the stair, Lisette bent at the waist, lowering her head toward Armande with a pout. "All the better to—"

"Brother," Francesco said to William, "we'll find someplace else."

"We need to get out of this. Wait out the storm until it passes," William replied.

Francesco shook his head. "To enter there is to invite sin into our hearts."

"Sin can't go where it's not welcome, Brother," William replied.

"It's wrong to enter such a place," said Andre. "Nothing good can come of it."

Brother Ramon spoke up. "Purity comes from within. Perhaps this is a challenge. Something for us to overcome. Something to test our souls."

Francesco ignored the others, speaking only to William. He held his hands palms out, his white gloves plainly in view. "I can't in good conscience set foot in there, Brother."

The rain poured its hardest yet. It beat them down, most pulling their hoods closer about their faces to shield them from the cold, pummeling blast. Andre watched the others closely, deliberating. On his back, the pack hidden by his mantle and cloak weighed heavily on his shoulder.

"Nor I," he announced, agreeing with Francesco.

"I'd prefer not to catch my death out here," Ramon said over the rain, eyeing the door behind Lisette.

William turned to Francesco and Andre. "We need shelter," he insisted. His patience was running thin. "In the Crusades, sickness and the elements killed men most."

"Aye," Odo joined in. "More than the Saracens."

William watched the two holdouts. Brother Andre was thickheaded, certain of things in the way those with only shallow understanding are certain. But he could be persuaded if properly directed.

Brother Francesco was another matter. A Templar almost as long as William, he was a chaplain as well. Learned and gifted by God with insight and intellect, his certainty came from his scholarship, grounded in his conviction. He had to speak to that.

"Brother," he said to Francesco as the rain continued to batter them. "Anyone can be a monk in a monastery."

"Meaning what?"

"Meaning that, without temptation, what need is there for strength? What reason for discipline? You cannot prove yourself to God without it."

"We give God glory when we triumph in His name," he explained, tired of the cold and wet. "Avoid a struggle, and you deny Him glory." He indicated the tavern door behind the girl as the rain came down still harder. "Staying out here proves naught."

The other men said nothing, suffering the cold rain's lashing. Francesco and Andre cast their eyes from the tavern door, looking instead at the ground, at the rain drops as they pitted the runny mud in the street.

"Keep watch out here, then," William said. He pointed to a corner of the townhouse where the rainwater poured thickly to one side, blocked and channeled from above by some high overhang invisible in the dark. "Try to stay dry."

He turned to Lisette and nodded. The girl stepped to the door, and knocked: three quick raps, two slower, a pause, and two more quick.

His eyes darting from the girl to Brother William, Armande leaned close to Odo. "He dares too much," he said. "He strains our standards."

"He's kept everyone here free and alive so far."

"He taints us. First, he brings us to the whore, then he lets her lead us *here*. He gives orders, but no one's given him command."

"You did."

"I never acknowledged his authority in this."

"Back in the stable," Odo told him. "You did. You accepted his leadership the moment you chose to follow him out of the Temple." He locked his eye on him. "Now let him lead."

A quick, trilling squeak like a small bird being wrung cut them off. They cast their gaze toward the tavern door. A small panel in the door swung open, and a face appeared in the shadowed opening. Eyes, dark and sharp like a predator's, peered out, glittering in pale, pinched features that were too delicate to be a man's yet too pronounced and furrowed to be a woman's. The eyes were suspicious at first. But the instant they fell upon Lisette, they lit brightly.

"Solange," the word spilled over thin red lips. "My *darling*."

William noticed the way Lisette smiled back at the face in the door, mouth closed, lovely, enticing.

The door swung open and the reedy, androgynous figure darted out to her side. "You're soaked to the skin," he continued, taking her hand. "Chilled to the bone." His dark eyes caught sight of the hooded men in the rain and grew wary again. "You've brought—" He looked at them one at a time. "*Visitors*," he said slowly, his arm snaking around the girl's tiny waist. He pulled her close. Her torn, wet dress pressed against his thigh as he angled her between himself and the strangers. His smile twitched at his mouth.

Lisette brought her face in close to his. "They want to come in, Jean-Marie," she explained. Her voice was low, flirting. Her fingertips traced over his neck and collar. "I *promised* them a roof and a warm fire." She teased him with a light kiss on the cheek.

Jean-Marie chuckled and pulled her to him, squeezing against her. He nuzzled his nose behind her ear. Letting his tongue fall from his mouth, he dragged it lazily from her neck up to her jaw, licking the side of her face slowly.

William's eyes narrowed.

Lisette let her head loll back, her eyes drifting shut as if she were enjoying it, the corners of her mouth turning up as her lips parted with a sigh.

Francesco squared himself, his decision made.

As his tongue lapped into the girl's hair, Jean-Marie's dark eyes remained distrustful, watching for a reaction. With the rain, the dark night, and the shadowy hoods, he could see none. His gaze still fixed on them, he loosened his grip on the girl, assessing the men.

"If my precious jewel promised you," he began, voice guarded, "who am I to turn you away?"

Releasing Lisette, he went back to the door and pushed it open. The darkness beyond it was impenetrable, and from inside came the faint strains of lute music, distant and hidden. Jean-Marie took Lisette and led her in, the girl disappearing within. He waited, a guarded stance, for the others obligingly inside the doorway and cast his wary eyes back toward the soaked, hooded group.

William climbed the steps and walked past Jean-Marie, following the girl without even a glance at the cagey doorman.

As he crossed the threshold, William heard Ramon, Etienne, and Armande behind him, taking to the stairs, their footsteps cautious as if stealing into an enemy camp.

Hanging back, Odo watched them all disappear through the doorway, lost to his view in the shadows beyond. Behind Francesco and Andre, Odo bent in close. His voice low, so the doorman Jean-Marie wouldn't hear, he said, "Don't confuse discipline for pride."

Francesco looked up at him.

"Or fear of failing," Odo added. Andre started to respond, but Odo cut him off, focusing on Brother Francesco. "Go in, and prove to God the stuff you're made from." He took to the stairs, and with a turn of his broad shoulders, vanished into the darkness beyond the threshold.

Beside the door, Jean-Marie looked askance at the two stragglers, tugging absently at one ear with long, thin fingers.

The rain tapped down on the two as they stood, water running in thick rivulets from their cloaks. Francesco watched the mud at his feet, the rain cratering and filling the ground repeatedly as it fell. Francesco inhaled sharply and looked to the door. "We'd best go in," he said at last.

"But you said—"

Francesco shook his head. "Staying out here shows God we doubt the strength of our devotion, that we fear what may lurk inside." He lowered his eyes once more, ashamed. "It's cowardly."

"It's a tavern."

"It's a test," Francesco corrected. "A test we almost failed." Shaking his right hand free of his cloak, he crossed himself, intoning a prayer under his breath as he marched forward.

This was something Jean-Marie had never witnessed in the years he had manned to door of *Le Basilisk et Chalice*. He had heard many call to God once inside, but never before coming in. He tried to peer past their hoods but saw nothing as the strange, monkish figure climbed the stair.

"It's a test we may yet fail," Andre said to himself as the elder brother disappeared into the darkness beyond the door. Swallowing hard, Brother Andre lifted his head, checked the pack hidden at his back, and hurried to catch up. Taking the stairs in two wide bounds, he scurried past the doorman, who cocked a bemused eyebrow before retreating inside himself, sealing the door behind them all.

CHAPTER XIII

The place was dark, with a low ceiling and rough-plaster walls framed by exposed, sooty timbers. Odo had to duck as he stepped into the tavern's hall, so low was the beam near the door. The smell of old ale hung in the air, tinged with the crude odors of more human fluids. Too many voices in too small a place droned in their ears, and the untuned plinking of a poorly played lute drifted through the room, the musician nowhere in sight. Hammered metal lanterns dotted the walls, flickering candles inside casting a sickly light over the long tables that stretched the length of the room and over the people crowded around them

The disguised Templars were again all together in a close knot at the end of the room. In their dark cloaks, they stood, taking in the place. They were, perhaps, monks, but unlike others in monastic Orders, they were all the sons of aristocrats. Even in the Order, only nobles could earn knighthood. They were surprised to find themselves surrounded by others of their position.

Men and women alike, they were conspicuous for their fine clothes and lace and for the gold and silver coins they doled out for drink and attention. Most were drunk, wobbling even as they sat, too loud for such close quarters. Some were gambling, tossing downdice and coins in games of Hazard and Lucky Pig to eruptions of laughter or disappointment. Among them were a few who were masked, not quite as drunk nor quite as loud. Elaborate creations of leather, silk, or feathers hid their faces as they slummed in a quarter of the city they would otherwise shun.

Common people were scattered among them. Though some drank and gambled as if equals of the higher-stationed, many were servants, dressed well and waiting attentively at the sides of their masters, eyes practiced at taking in much but seeing little. Others worked at the tavern, refilling mugs, replacing pitchers and goblets, and waiting on those with coin. Women, dressed as Lisette, had ribbons tied at their shoulders and gloves on their hands. They cozied up next to the drunkest and winningest, laughing loudest, watching the most.

None paid any attention at all to the band of cloaked strangers.

As rainwater ran from his cloak and puddled at his feet, William surveyed the room. Lisette slid down one of the narrow aisles between the long tables. An aristocrat, by the cut of his surcoat and shoes, swayed to his feet from one of the tables, a mask of fine red silk hiding his face. Tied crookedly around his head, it obscured one of his eyes, the tailored triangle of fabric wet and pushed to one side of his mouth. He turned and started past William when he teetered to one side and fell to the floor, wriggling like a beached seal.

A burst of laughter to their right drew Ramon's attention. Tugging his hood back enough to clear his field of vision, he turned and caught sight of a large group packed around one end of a long table. A portly man joyfully swept the coins from a Backgammon board. Ramon's brow furrowed and a smile tugged at the corner of his mouth as he saw the man stop a passing serving girl. He jammed a few of the coins into her apron and slapped her on the rump. With a little cry of surprise, she dropped a pair of sloshing cups on the table, splashing the wooden board and the gold and silver coins upon it.

Francesco took in the scene with a resigned shake of his head. Hidden beneath his cloak and hood, Etienne crossed his arms tightly, eyes darting over the chaos of the dark room, the unfamiliar noise so unlike the Temple. He looked to Brother William and Brother Odo.

Though William's disdain was apparent, Brother Odo seemed unmoved by the place and the people. He looked over the crowded space before turning his eye upon Lisette and leaning in closer to the girl.

"I see a roof," he said to her. "But no fire."

"There are more *private* places to sit," she said. "Some near a hearth." Lisette's eyes set on a small doorway at the far end of the room, little more than a large, unmoving shadow among the flickering shadows on the rough plaster walls. "I'll arrange things," she said. "Wait here."

Before Odo or William could object, she was off. Tossing back her wet hair, Lisette made her way through the long room, gliding between the skinny tables and the patrons crowded around them. Her fingertips teased and touched the patrons as she went by. She paused a moment to caress the gray, stubbled cheek of a well-to-do merchant, then tousle the oily hair of a well-dressed aristocrat. The pleased men cooed "Solange" after her appreciatively before she vanished through the shadowy doorway.

The huddling and the laughter, the smell and the noise made Brother Andre anxious. His hidden pack felt heavy. He leaned in close to Brother Francesco.

"Are you certain we should stay in this place?"

"More certain than I was outside."

Lisette leaned out of the dark doorway, beckoning William. He made his way toward her, the others in tow. Up close, he could see the doorway was little more than a ragged, rectangular hole carved and cut to approximate the size and shape of a door.

Armande watched as the girl stepped through the door, cozying too close to Brother William. "It's in the back," she said to him, "This way."

William and the knights followed.

Inside the doorway was a woman. Small and thin, her neck was sinewy and corded, jutting straight out from a sharp collarbone and a knotty spine. She was bent over at the waist, her eyes shut. Her scrawny hands were out and braced against one of the dark timbers supporting the low ceiling. With her skirt bunched up over her hips, a doughy aristocrat ground into her from behind, sweat beading on his forehead, flabby legs jiggling against her bony thighs. Neither paid attention as William and the others walked past.

William turned forward, concentrating on following Lisette through the dark back rooms of *Le Basilisk et Chalice*. The layout of the place was more evident. Twisting and sprawling, it was a rabbit's warren of passageways and rooms. One was tacked onto the next, as if the keeper kept taking over space in the townhouse and the buildings adjacent, cutting doorways where they were needed and moving tables and chairs in. A mix of candles, fireplaces, and metal lanterns lit the halls poorly. The pale, flickering light, William realized, was meant to hide as much it illumined.

With the Templars in tow, Lisette wound her way through the rambling tavern. Tables were tucked here and there, in large spaces and nooks, with groups of revelers quiet or boisterous.

As the gloomy hallway narrowed, an aristocratic woman pushed past them, headed the opposite way. In finery that indicated she was a court regular, her skirts trailed for several steps around her—the gown of a woman who did not work. A mask of brightly colored feathers hid her features, the delicate pheasant plumes curving from her face like long, striped whiskers. With practiced grace, she held the front of her skirts, lifting them above the floor with one hand so she didn't trip. In her other hand, she held a gilded chain. The fine links rattled softly, stretching back behind her, a leash connecting to a leather collar around the neck of a young girl. Feathers obscured her face, too. She could have been no more than nine years old. Except for the collar and mask, she wore nothing else.

The little girl's leash had stretched tight as the woman in the feathered mask had continued on. Reaching the end of the leash, the woman jerked at the chain, tugging the child toward her. Tearing her eyes from the passing strangers, the girl scampered to her place at the feathered woman's heel, matching her pace, head lowered.

A wave of warm air and a scent of smoke caught Odo's attention as they turned a corner, the soft popping of wet firewood inviting to him as he began to notice the chill of his wet wool cloak and cold iron mail.

Ahead of the Templars, a pair of well-dressed men wobbled into view, stumbling across the adjoining corridor. More confident or less caring than the other aristocrats in the tavern, the fat men wore no disguises, their pale features almost aglow in the dark hallway. Spotting Lisette, one swerved.

"So-*lange*," he called and stopped short, waving to the girl. William watched as the second noble blundered blindly into his friend's back, bouncing the pair of them off a wall before they crashed to the floor.

Lisette rolled her eyes, amused and exasperated, and hurried to the side of the two. Bending to one knee, she helped up one, then the other. "Oh, *Comte*," she said as she assisted the second one to his feet.

"*Viscomte*," he slurred, correcting.

"*Viscomte*," Lisette chided herself with a smile. "One must be careful in these halls. They are far too narrow for gentlemen of—" she paused dramatically, eyebrows arched, "your noble proportions."

The two men laughed, one coughing as the other slapped her rump. Her smile stayed dazzling, tempting. Smirking, the two drunks nodded and mumbled thanks as they moved on. Lisette went back to William, taking his hand absentmindedly before turning to lead them further.

The rules of the Order were clear, and even this slightest contact with the girl violated his vow of chastity. He allowed it, her fingers rough against his own calloused hands. At his first chance, when the girl's grip relaxed as she peered into a darkened room, William withdrew his hand, hiding it among the folds of his cloak. His action did not escape Brother Odo, who watched over his old friend, or Brother Armande, whose jaw clenched.

Last in their line, Ramon lingered to peer through a gauzy curtain. His brothers proceeded without him, unaware. In the dim lighting, he spied a party of nobles socializing. Some were masked, others not. They chatted politely, voices hushed, the quiet gathering reminding Ramon of his father's estates and of the feasts his parents hosted for the neighboring *hidalgos* when he was a boy.

Until he spied the sideboard in the corner of the room, and the soft curves of a nude woman upon it.

Her face was turned away from his view, the long black hair spilled down from her head. Smooth and shining, it spread neatly on the table behind her shoulders. She lay unnaturally still, plates of eggs, sweetbreads, and pastries arranged upon her hair, hip, and thigh, and on the table all around her unmoving body. The aristocrats in the room mingled casually over her, plucking hors d'oeuvres and honeyed fruits from the plates, their offhanded manners and nonchalance making Ramon sick rather than homesick. He stared, searching for even the slightest movement of the woman on the table, the shift of a limb held still too long or the shallow rise of ribs in respiration.

Ramon hurried to catch up with his brothers. Heading toward them was an auburn-haired girl in a simple dress, carrying clay mugs and a pitcher looped through her fingers. Lisette turned and looked down, lowering her head and brushing her wet, black hair over the left side of her face.

"Felicité," Lisette called out softly, waving for the serving girl's attention. Lisette hurried ahead of the Templars, stopping the other girl. William watched Lisette whisper in the serving girl's ear and gesturing toward the hooded band behind her. The serving girl eyed them, and her full, curling hair bobbed on her head as she nodded and whispered back into Lisette's ear before hastening away down another dark hallway.

Armande trusted neither the common girls nor their whispering. He started for Brother William when something rattled across the floor nearby. A pair of bone dice tumbled over the floorboards and bounced against the heel of Brother Odo's boot.

Odo looked down to see an old man stooped on the floor, grabbing for the errant dice. His hair wispy and white, lesions pocked his nose, cheeks, and chin, crisscrossing his face. His disease was unforgiving in the marks it left. The price of excess, Odo thought, and he knew the painful death the old man's affliction was leading to.

The old man's watery eyes fell across the metal tip of the scabbard poking from beneath Odo's hem. Clutching the dice, he scurried back to the long table and the joyless game that held him.

William froze as he recognized a nearby sound, muffled by intervening walls more than distance. The thump of a thrashing fist and the smack of a hand meeting flesh, mingled with pained gasps and hushed cries. The sounds of a beating.

He strode for a dark doorway ahead, the sounds growing, becoming more distinct, joined by sharp sighs. Inside the doorway, he paused, eyes searching the gloom, finding two forms. One was a woman, perhaps his own age, sprawled against the rough plaster of the wall. Half out of her dress, even in the dim lantern light of the room, William could make out the ruddy outline of a man's hand upon her cheek as well as blotchy purples and yellows of bruises on her ribs and arms. Over her stood a young, muscular man, stripped to the waist, his eyes lost to William in the flickering shadows falling over his face. The young man closed in on the woman, and William started into the room, until a small, firm hand caught his arm. He glanced down to find Lisette holding him back, shaking her head.

"It's what she's paid for," she whispered.

William looked again into the room, and saw the beaten woman climbing back to her feet, unafraid but anxious to get back to the half-naked man. Lisette indicated the farther end of the room to William with a nod. "Just as she's paid for that."

William looked past the battered girl and her client and saw another couple. So still in the gloom, William hadn't noticed them at first. William could not describe the man, his face covered with a cloth that puffed slightly and quickly above his mouth as he breathed. Otherwise, he was naked and bound to a hard wooden chair. A young woman straddled his legs. Sitting close and concentrating like a scribe illuminating a manuscript, she was drawing the point of a long, sharp dagger over the bound man's quivering skin. Blood dripped in fine drops from scores of tiny wounds etched in his flesh.

None in the room noticed William or Lisette. Quietly, Lisette withdrew, pulling William after her.

Studying the gamblers, Odo glanced back up in time to see Lisette ducking under a particularly low and rough hewn doorway, leading his brothers into a small room. A fire danced in the hearth at its far end, casting a flickering glow over a pair of long tables that stretched toward it from the door.

The girl beckoned them in. "Here," she said. Water dripped into her face, tickling her cheek and eye. "Sit."

William led them in to the fire's warmth. He could feel the heated air taking the chill from his wet cloak. Lisette had started toward William when Odo and Armande strode to the front of the group, and past her, settling on stools in front of the fire. After taking in the room, William nodded, and he and the others sat down stiffly, uncomfortable. Nicolas moved apart from the group, taking a seat to the side of the door, his back to the wall and his attention on the hallway outside.

As he sat down with the others, Brother Francesco crossed himself. Ramon leaned in close.

"You were right, Brother," he whispered, eyes on the doorway. "More than you knew. This is no simple tavern."

Andre overheard the comment. "This is no place for pious men."

"Much is wrong here," Francesco agreed as he sat.

"So, we shouldn't stay," said Andre, starting up from his seat on the bench. "Let's speak to Brother William—"

Francesco caught his shoulder, guiding him back down. Andre looked to him, confused, and saw certainty in Francesco's eyes.

"We're Templars," Francesco pronounced. "We don't leave battles. We finish them."

CHAPTER XIV

"Battle?" Andre asked, leaning across the table. "Brother, this is a tavern."

"And a brothel," Ramon added. His eyes drifted to the doorway as his mind wandered back to the corridors. "Among other things."

The room was smoky, biting at their nostrils as it stung their eyes, the chimney behind the hearth suffering some obstruction, no doubt in need of cleaning. The smokiness made the murky room hazy, light cutting though it in dim shafts. Yet Francesco felt he was seeing more sharply than ever before.

He shook his head, disagreeing with the two across from him. He tapped a white-gloved finger on the table. "It's a battlefield," he said. "You saw what I did as we were led back here."

"Sin," said Ramon. He rubbed tenderly at his wound upon his arm, finding it suddenly sore. "Depravity, indulgence—"

"No battle," Andre interrupted. "Not even a brawl."

"Then you weren't looking," Francesco fixed his eyes on the two. "It's a battle almost lost out there. A battle against evil. Evil of the heart." He paused, looking for the right description. "A battle for souls, Brothers."

"Souls?" asked Andre.

"These patrons' souls," Ramon clarified. His mind returned to the feast behind the gauzy curtain.

"I almost failed to see it," Francesco continued. "It's no accident we've come to this place."

"You believe God's led us here?" he asked, voice hushed.

Before Francesco could answer, Félicité burst in, a pitcher in each hand, and mugs looped over her fingers.

"Ale for the good men?" Felicité announced with a laugh, then stopped as she found all eyes intent on her. "But we'll see how good you are by how much silver's left on the table for Felicité when you leave." She smacked her hip, laughing, looking for a response from the stiff, hooded strangers. The serving girl slapped Armande across the shoulder, too friendly.

She stopped laughing. Her hand stung, and she shook it as the pain faded. She'd felt the shoulders of some hard muscled men before, but this one had to be made of iron. Spying Lisette across the room, she hurried to her side.

"Solange," Felicité whispered as Lisette took her arm and led her to the door. "These aren't your usual friends. They're a lifeless bunch."

Lisette shrugged, putting on her smile. "They're shy," she tried to explain.

"Are they anxious for you to get to work?" Felicité giggled.

"Yes, so get out if I'm ever to get started."

Felicité slipped a small, lopsided pear into Lisette's hand. "To help you keep your strength up." She tittered again. "I'll need to bring something to get you tight again after so many." Lisette rolled her eyes.

Felicité's laughter stopped as Lisette's unguarded movement revealed the fresh bruises on her face. The serving girl's smile dropped.

"Your *eye*," she breathed, leaning closer for a better look. She jabbed an accusing thumb toward the silent strangers at the tables behind them. "Did these ones do that?"

Lisette's hand covered her cheek as she turned away to hide it. "No," she quickly assured her friend. "No, no. It was some cheap no-goods by the square." She inhaled, puffing out her chest while shrugging in nonchalance. "But I took care of it."

Felicité suspiciously eyed the ill-tempered one she'd hurt her hand on. The streets, she knew, were dangerous, especially after curfew, and she was grateful for the husband she'd found in Jean-Marie. She tried once more to get a peek at her friend's injuries, but Lisette turned away. "Thank you for the pear."

"Oh, Solange," Felicité chided. "I'll bring you some cold water for your bruises. And a cloth." Lisette managed a nod as Felicité scurried from the room.

A sharp cry cut the air from the darkness outside the room. Andre leapt to his feet as the shriek faded to a pleasured moan. Unnerved and embarrassed, he returned to his bench.

Brother Armande remained on edge. He turned to Brother Odo at the other side of the fire.

"I don't like this place," Armande said.

"What isn't to like?" Odo replied. "We're beside a fire. And the room's dry."

Beside him, a slow, drip from the ceiling grew steadier, turning to an intermittent stream. He scooted his stool closer to the fire, toward Armande and away from the water.

"The room's dry over here," he continued.

Armande ignored his humor. "We're hiding," he muttered.

"We're shielding ourselves from the elements," Odo corrected. "We're planning our next move. You, more than any of the others here, know the value of rallying before a charge."

Armande turned to him. "This is no place for us," he said. "Immersed in this, this corruption."

"Brother, you fought at Tripoli," Odo began, "In battles that left the streets so thick in gore it came up over our boots as we rode through it. What have you to fear from being near these people's failings?"

"This is not our way," Armande replied. Odo studied him, recognizing something more in the veteran's voice. Before his assignment to Paris, he had not laid eyes upon Brother Armande since escorting the marshal and the royal brother.

Armande shifted his eyes, indicating the younger knights huddled and whispering around the first of the long tables.

"The others concern me."

✝ ✝ ✝

Lisette sat down close to William. He cut her off before she could speak to him. "That ale the girl brought. We can't afford—"

"This is a tavern," she countered. "People drink here."

"We don't."

"If you can afford to have these people become suspicious or question you, by all means then, order nothing."

He looked at her coolly.

"Not paying will draw more attention," she prodded. Lisette studied him a moment. She decided he was handsome, with his even features, cool, pale eyes, and his beard that made him seem so exotic here in the city. "The ale's not costly." She bit into the pear, chewing noisily as she spoke. "It's not even good. You're knights, noblemen. Surely you can afford a bit of silver for drink."

William kept his voice low. "We're of noble birth perhaps, but we live as monks. Each man's sworn to poverty."

Lisette blinked, unbelieving at first. In her trade, she had met nobles, knights, and clergy.

"You have no money?" she sputtered at last.

"What we carry is all we own. We give up everything to the Temple when we join."

Lisette shook her head. "This tavern keeper doesn't believe in charity, trust me. If you don't pay, he won't take it lightly."

"Then we'll leave," William offered, "before the keeper realizes."

The girl snorted. "You don't think he's had others skip out on their tab?

William's expression hardened in a way that frightened her. "I don't think anyone here will trouble us."

Her mouth dropped open, worried, chewed pear upon her tongue. She leaned back and her concern melted. She smiled, swallowed, and laughed.

"Not to worry," she reassured. Reaching behind the laces that pulled her dress to form around her waist and hips, her hands searched for a moment before producing a small, pigskin pouch. Coins clinked inside it, muffled by the leather as she hefted it in her hand.

Her eyes danced as they met William's. "I was teasing," she said. "It's paid for."

"You shouldn't," was all William could manage.

"I can afford it," Lisette said. "Tonight, anyway." She placed a foot up on the table and pushed herself back, tilting on the stool's back legs. Rocking gently, she smiled.

William studied the girl and the pouch in her hand. It was small, the leather stained by oily spots, smudged with soot. Not the kind of stains likely to mark the purse of a woman of the streets.

His heart sank. "That's the real reason you were afraid those men would return."

Lisette shrugged, casual, without any shame or regret.

"Did you take it before or after your assault?" William asked.

"During," she said. She seemed pleased with herself. Her poniard appeared in her hand again, picking at the pear's skin and seeds with its point. William studied the dagger. The wrong weapon for the girl, it was for stabbing, with no edge. She'd have been better protected by a dagger that she could slash with as well. He noted the fine brass wire wrapping the grip and the silvering in the blade, the metal blackening from lack of care. He knew it, too, was stolen.

"He was distracted," Lisette continued. "He wasn't paying much attention to my hands." Her eyes on William, she watched his reaction closely. "After all that, he owed me."

William shrugged, disappointed. "It *is* how you make your living."

✝ ✝ ✝

Andre shook his head at Brother Francesco, unbelieving. His voice a harsh whisper, his gloved fingers stabbed toward the door. "We were led by a harlot through that maze of, of *that*." His voice fell. "I cannot believe God would ever call His faithful to the presence of such sin."

"We're God's soldiers," Francesco answered. "He calls us to fight His battles in the world."

"Which is why we should be out rescuing our brethren."

"And what of our brethren here? We *need* to be in this place. To help the weak."

"There's no fighting here," Andre began.

Ramon cut him off, intrigued by Brother Francesco's reasoning. "Not all battles are fought with shield and sword."

"Exactly," Francesco said. He closed his eyes, put his head back, and prayed for the strength to bring together all that raced through his mind. He struggled for the words. "Perhaps, perhaps our losses in the Holy Land, perhaps all else that's happened to us tonight were meant bring *us here*. To redirect us. To point us to the evils to be met at home."

"To do what?" Andre asked.

"Save these souls?" Ramon put forth.

Francesco nodded, relieved and joyous to see one of his brothers understood.

"The people here, they've lost their way. Lost sight of God and His place in their lives." With a wave, he indicated the dark passageway outside the room "They've turned to *this* to fill the void it's left in their hearts. They need help. From us."

✝ ✝ ✝

Insulted, Lisette held her chin high. "I earn what I can the only way I can."

"You talk as if you're all alone," said William.

"Since I was fourteen. When my family turned me out."

"That's little more than a child," William said. She noticed his eyes drift toward Etienne. "Why would they do that to you?"

"I'd been attacked," Lisette explained without emotion. "By a soldier. And of course, I was to blame."

"You were—"

"They called me *damaged*. Said no good man would ever have me as a wife."

"There are laws," William said, turning back to the girl, "and reparations that soldier should have been forced to make."

"You're not French," she pronounced, mimicking his accent.

"I'm English."

"Maybe I should have been assaulted in England. Here in France, there are no such laws."

"So you chose this."

She stared at him, struck by the lack of sympathy she saw. "I had no reputation," she said. "No prospects for marriage. No family to support me." Her outrage grew with each word. Who was this knight, this monk, to question her and what she had to do to make her way in the world? "No *choice*," she finished.

"And now no future."

Lisette began to rise from her stool. "How dare you."

If anything, he seemed even calmer as she rose. "You tell me: How much longer can that pretty face of yours support you?" William pointed to the mottled purples and yellows marring her cheek and eye. "Especially taking punishment like that?"

Her hand flashed to her face, fingers covering the bruises. "It doesn't happen often," she said, sinking back to her stool. "Besides, I'm saving money."

"You are?"

✝ ✝ ✝

Armande didn't look at Odo as he spoke. "Outside of battle, the Order is cloistered for a reason. You and I, we're old soldiers. Old men. The allure of wine and the charms of women are long behind us." He'd noticed the way the Spaniard, Brother Ramon, had looked at the girl and kept close to her.

"Speak for yourself," said Odo. Groaning, he reached for the pitcher on the table and poured himself a cup. "I find there's nothing like a good ale." He tilted back the clay cup and he winced. "And this, Brother, is nothing like a good ale."

"Don't jest," Armande warned. "The temptations of a place like this have undone many young men."

Odo stopped. This was more than the chafing he expected from Brother Armande.

"You think them weak?"

"I think they're young," Armande said. "Young, and vulnerable to the excesses young men are vulnerable to. And the boy," he indicated Etienne, "he shouldn't even be *with* us"

"They're good men," Odo countered. "Strong. Even the boy is. None will yield to sin here."

Armande shook his head. "The devil works subtly, Brother. In a place like this, I fear for a man's salvation, for his soul."

"You've served God well," Odo said. "Bravely. Gloriously. Faithfully."

"*You* cannot decide that. The rules of the Order are clear. We all risk expulsion here."

Odo's voice dropped. "Which bears greater consequence for you."

"I haven't spent half my life fighting on two continents and living in monasteries to risk here the salvation I've earned."

"That was a lifetime ago."

"You have no son, and never took vengeance on high-ranking clergy." Armande sounded tired. "This path is a narrow one. And the only one I have to avoid damnation."

Francesco's eyes lit with his passion, and he could barely keep his voice hushed as he spoke to Ramon and Andre. "What greater glory can we bring God than by restoring the ranks of His faithful?"

Ramon understood. "We must set our own house in order first. Battle the decay and corruption eating out the heart of Christendom."

"Make our people righteous again before going forth to spread His Word," Francesco finished for him. He could scarce believe how he had refused to set foot in the tavern. Yet deep among the sin it begat, he had found inspiration.

"We've spent too much time behind the walls of the Temple," Francesco said.

"Paris is the star of Europe," Andre began, " His Holiness the Pope has all but named King Philip as Defender of the Faith. Of all people, King Philip would set an example, fight the corruption here in the heart of Christendom."

Francesco sat back, overwhelmed by a second epiphany.

"I put a little bit away whenever I can," Lisette told William. "In another ten years, I can have a house in the Latin Quarter, hire a couple of girls, and take good care of them while they take care of the men."

"A whore monger, to ruin more girls' lives?"

Lisette flushed. "I said I'd take care of them."

William pressed her. "There's the Order of St. Mary Magdalene, reformed women who—"

"The white ladies!" Lisette laughed. "The life of a nun doesn't suit me."

"Neither does the life of a whore and thief." He looked away.

She glared. This man William was nothing like the men she knew from the streets.

"Etienne," William called firmly.

Distracted at the sudden sound of his name, Etienne spun the cup nearly off the table's edge. He caught it as it slid to the brink and placed it squarely at the middle of the table before hurrying to William's side.

"Yes, Brother?"

William placed his hand on the boy's shoulder, affectionately, Lisette thought. Not the harsh hand she'd seen so many craftsmen lay on an apprentice, and not the hand of the men who brought boys here.

William stayed seated, keeping his eyes level with the boy's. "I need you to tend the fire," he directed. "Stoke it up well, to help the others get dry so we'll be ready to move out when the time comes."

The boy's head bobbed eagerly. "Yes, Brother. Right away." He hastened to the fireside, gathering sticks and split wood from a short pile behind Armande. The fire glowed brighter, roaring, as the boy arranged and fed it.

"You watch over him," Lisette said to William.

"He's a boy. Surrounded constantly by grown men. Soldiers. Our life can be too harsh for a child."

William shook his head as Etienne patted out a spark that had leapt from the fire onto his cloak, proud the boy neither panicked nor jumped but handled the problem easily.

"Is he yours?" Lisette asked William. The Templar's brow knit. Before he could respond, Francesco stole between them and whispered to William.

"Brother, sanctuary is a mistake. The more I consider it, the more dangerous I realize it is."

CHAPTER XV

"Enough!" Jacques De Molay roared, tearing his arms free of the guards. "I have borne this insult too long." His finger stabbed at the inquisitor, a slight shadow in the dark before him. "You have wholly overstepped your bounds, Imbert."

"Sit," Imbert ordered in a soft voice, firmly.

"I am Grandmaster of God's Army on Earth, and you haven't the authority—"

The two soldiers struggled to again control the Templar Grandmaster. His thick silver hair whipped around his head.

"Sit," Imbert commanded.

"I will not," De Molay thrashed in the middle of the dark room. The men guarding him were strong, but basically untrained, the type that rely on their size and physical power to overcome their opponents. De Molay relaxed his struggles as he felt the soldiers' hands clamp down on him. After another considered moment, he stopped struggling and was rewarded by their relaxing their hold slightly.

"We answer only to the Pope," he bellowed at Imbert. "You have no authority over me or this Order."

Imbert bared his teeth, for the first time flashing emotion in De Molay's presence. Perhaps, De Molay considered, this was the opening he sought, a mistake provoked by his fighting and refusal to heed the inquisitor.

In the gloom, in his dark habit and robes, Imbert was a ghost. De Molay watched him pull open a pouch, wraith's fingers tearing from it something De Molay could not make out.

Imbert lunged from the dark, the broad, rattling item clenched in his hand.

"This," he said, shoving the parchment into the light, "This gives me every authority."

De Molay could find no words. Squinting in the gloom, his mind raced. His eyes traced over the Latin phrases of the document, settling on the dull gray *bullum* attached to it and the papal seal stamped upon the leaden disk.

Imbert let it hang before the embattled Grandmaster. "The Papal Bull *Vox in Excelso*. A decree from His Holiness the Pope himself, released in secret, soon to be made public."

Cold horror swept up De Molay's spine as icy fingers clenched his stomach.

Imbert continued. "It commands that your Order be hereby dissolved, suppressed, and made subject to interrogation by the Order of the Holy Inquisition."

De Molay was ashen. His limbs went numb, his knees no longer able to support him. He felt faint even as his heart hammered in his chest. Words failed him as he tried to tear his eyes from the signet. He had misunderstood and miscalculated.

The Order was done for.

"Now," Imbert began. His voice was surprisingly soft, De Molay's shocked silence lending him confidence. "You will answer my questions."

De Molay roared. His arm was like a writhing snake in the guard's grip, twisting over the soldier's arm and reversing his hold. The guard screamed as his hand was twisted back where it shouldn't be and his knees buckled.

The second guard faltered. His companion's shriek snapped him from his fog and he clamped his hands on De Molay's other arm, torquing it up behind the elderly Grandmaster to force him to the floor, but De Molay's foot lashed out, smashing the second guard's knee, freeing him as the man collapsed, clutching at his leg. De Molay whirled, his freed forearm crashing across the first guard's face, driving him to the floor, too.

Horrified, Imbert stumbled back, pitching over the brazier. The metal bowl crashed loudly, sparks erupting from it as the tiny fire was scattered across the floor, plunging the room into deeper darkness. The Inquisitor retreated into the deep shadows, away from the flame he'd lit. Lungs heaving, he pressed himself into the corner, clutching at his golden crucifix, the jewels cold and smooth under his fingers.

"Guards!" he cried over the chaos. "To me, Guards!"

The chamber's heavy door flew open and two more guards burst in, rushing the Grandmaster. One crashed across his shoulders, brawny arms wrapping around De Molay to pin his arms at his sides. The Templar squared himself and threw his head back, shattering the guard's nose with a spray of blood. The guard fell away, hands clasped over his flattened, bleeding face and what was once his nose. The other guard that had burst in with him hammered a vicious punch into De Molay's kidney. The Grandmaster's back arched and he howled in pain and rage as another who'd rushed in followed the blow with a hook to the old Grandmaster's ear.

De Molay counterpunched the man but missed, stunned and off balance from the blows he'd taken. The guard with the shattered nose reached for De Molay from behind, but the Grandmaster slipped him and hurled him off balance into one of the other guards. Backpedaling, he kept to the edge of the fight, the wall at his back. Like a dog herding sheep, he turned and cut their attacks at tangents, keeping them in front of him. He knew it could not go well. He was too outnumbered, and even if he escaped the room, he would face the hundreds more marching the corridors of the Temple. He banished the distraction of those thoughts the moment they entered his mind.

His legs were taken out from under him as guard charged and tackled him low. De Molay crashed to the floor, driving the air from his lungs. The guard with the broken nose rushed him, kicking him sharply in the ribs. Once. Twice.

Another guard was on him now. They all wrestled, De Molay wheezing to recover his breath as more hands clamped on him, snaring his limbs and pounding his body into compliance, keeping him pinned to the floor.

With all quiet, Imbert stepped forward from the shadows, peering at the trapped Grandmaster. Satisfied he was held fast, Imbert righted the brazier, tossing a handful of tinder upon it. He straightened his robe, adjusted the cord at his waist, and stalked closer toward De Molay.

"There's much evil you must answer to God for," he said, his tone chastising. "Much evil your Order must answer for."

Despite the hand that had him by his silver hair, De Molay shook his head slowly, unbelieving. His mistake. He led them all to this.

Imbert continued, going back to the brazier and feeding the fire some more.

"Confession will be good for you all."

CHAPTER XVI

Brother Odo and Brother Armande had gathered close around William and Francesco. Francesco looked at the stained planking of the floor as he spoke, his voice a penitent's confession.

"I assumed wrongly that the Church and the Pope would shield us."

"Sanctuary's a right anyone can claim," Odo said.

"And the Temple is sovereign territory," Francesco reminded. "Under no one's direction but ours and the Pope's. Yet the king brazenly marched his army in and took our brothers into custody."

"Foolishness," said Armande, "You're talking foolishness to consider such complicity could exist."

Francesco ignored the animadversion. He directed himself to Brother William, pulling his white gloves taut on his hands. "We must effect a new plan. Chance this weather. There's no doubt we need to leave Paris."

Andre looked up at him, recognizing opportunity.

Armande continued, "It makes no sense he'd move against the Church's own."

"No," Odo disagreed, folding his massive arms over his broad chest. "He's right. Only a king with Philip's resources would possibly dare such a thing."

William liked it all less with each moment. "If you're right, we must escape not just Paris but all of France."

"There must be another explanation," blurted Armande.

"It's the only thing that makes any sense so far," Odo pointed out.

"It still doesn't explain *why* he would act against us."

"No, it doesn't," William agreed, "but it indicates the scale of the attack." His words trailed off. He looked over each of his men and added, "We may not be safe anywhere in Christendom."

CHAPTER XVII

Jacques De Molay groaned as he slumped against the door to his office. The smooth, heavy wood was cold on the raw skin of his back. His face bruised and swollen, his head brushed the door's top edge. Bleeding welts striped his naked body. On trembling toes he stood, balanced unsteadily upon the stool where his interrogation had begun. Weakened by the inquisitor's abuse, it was all he could do to keep from sagging as his arms were pulled up and away from his sides.

He couldn't stop from crying out as one of the guards hammered an iron spike through his wrist, nailing his arm to the door. He writhed against the pain, his body going rigid, his other arm held fast by the other guards. Only discipline kept his choking gutturals from becoming a sobbing scream as another spike drove through his other wrist. Arms outspread, one pinned to the door and one to its frame, he was stretched across the opening between.

As the guard climbed down from his work, De Molay's head slumped forward, long, silver hair spilling over his eyes. Gulping air, he panted in agony, gathering all the strength he had left to keep up on his toes and prevent his weight from pulling at his tortured wrists.

From the darkness of the corner, Imbert watched him silently, waiting for the worst of De Molay's pain to abate. The minutes passed. He watched calmly as his captive's ragged breathing deepened, becoming more regular.

"Confess to your sins, Jacques De Molay," the inquisitor called out as he stepped from the deep shadows of the room. "Let God welcome you again to His love."

De Molay fought to raise his head, squinting through his disheveled hair. "I have done nothing. We have done nothing."

"So claim the most guilty." Imbert glanced at the guard who'd hammered in the spikes. His nose was swollen and irregular, discolored and still bleeding from the Grandmaster's shattering blow. He laid down his hammer and kicked the stool out from under De Molay.

The stool skidded and tumbled off, and the Grandmaster dropped. De Molay screamed as his own weight tore at the spikes in his wrists. His feet stopped inches from the floor. For a long moment, he dangled there, fighting the torment, hands twisted above the iron spikes in his wrists, fingers flexing slowly. His breath came in short heaves, and the only other sound that escaped him was a dry mewling from the back of his throat.

Imbert waited to speak again, watching.

At last, the inquisitor unrolled the parchment again. Holding it before him, as if reading it aloud in the dark, he quoted the document, eyes covertly on De Molay.

"You and your Order have denied the Saints and Christ as the savior."

"No—" De Molay choked.

"Defiled the cross by trampling, spitting, and urination—"

"No," De Molay's strength redoubled to deny the lie.

Imbert nodded to the guard with the broken nose. The soldier placed a hand on the thick, wooden door and pushed it open just slightly. It creaked as De Molay strangled a cry, the iron spikes grating against the small bones in his wrists.

"Held highly secret, heavily guarded meetings," Imbert continued.

De Molay fought to push away the pain that burned in his wrists and shot through his arms into his chest. Forcing his lungs to expand in proper rhythm, he shook his head in denial and looked up.

"Untrue," he managed to gasp. The sound of his own words encouraged him to go on. "All of it. Allow me to contact His Holiness, the Pope."

Imbert ignored him and quoted on, "Renounced the Holy sacraments. Altered the ceremony of the mass—"

"Let me write to him," De Molay pleaded. "Let us summon the Church's leaders."

"Confess now!" Imbert shouted.

"We serve only God."

Imbert laid the parchment on the Grandmaster's desk and began to pace. Back and forth, from the dim light of the brazier to the deep shadows and back again, his steps were slow, measured.

He stopped before De Molay. "You practiced adoration of an unholy idol, known by names such as 'Baphomet' and 'Head 58.'" His dark eyes were bright with certainty.

De Molay could but squint at him. Realization lit his eyes, followed by confusion.

"Yes," Imbert said. "We know. From the report of former Brother Esquin De Florian."

De Molay remembered Brother Esquin. Commander of the Templar facility at Montfaucon a few years ago, Brother Esquin had been brought up on charges of apostasy. When they had proven true, he was expelled from the Order and stripped of his title. In his outrage at the dishonor, Esquin killed the assistant prior of Mont Carmel, and for that, he was imprisoned in Toulouse. Even with the agony gnawing at his thoughts, the Grandmaster knew a man—a criminal—so discredited was an enemy, and any accusations he might make would be dubious and suspect. At least in a just inquiry.

"His report," Imbert continued, "was then verified in the confessions of Brother Jean Taillefer De Genay and Brother Pierre d'Arbley."

Fools, De Molay thought. They would agree to say anything when the inquisitors no doubt threatened them with torture. They must have answered any way to end the threat, for the truth to be warped into support for the charges he—and they all—now faced.

Imbert's words snapped him from his desperate musings. "Your denials," said the inquisitor, "and your lies condemn you to eternal damnation. Confess your sins, salvage your immortal soul."

"This is not—"

Imbert cut him off. "Tell me of this bearded demon head and how you worshipped it."

"It's—" he started. The pain attacked his reason, clouding his response as he tried desperately to craft it. The facts were twisted and woven into the lies, lending credence to the untruths. "There is no demon," he said.

Imbert cut the air sharply with his finger. The door slammed, wrenching De Molay's arms straight back behind him. His broad shoulders collapsed behind his spine as the door and frame came together with his wrists pinned upon them. The spikes tore in the flesh below his hands. He screamed. He squeezed his eyes shut, fought the agony, unable to catch his breath.

Impassionate, Imbert watched the Grandmaster sag from the door, arms straight out behind him, almost weeping openly from the torment.

"We're God's loyal servants," De Molay moaned. "We've done no such evils."

While he was gulping at the air, Imbert stood over him, resolute and unmoved. "You obtained wealth," he continued with the charges, "through unlawful methods and hoarded the money instead of putting it to good use." His tone was even, no longer accusing, as if making a reasonable appeal. "To this, surely, you can confess."

"Resources," De Molay managed to cough out. "To mount crusades. To ready another—" The pain was unraveling his thoughts. Imbert had facts, pieces of the truth. He distorted them as he brought them forth, twisted the pious toiling and achievement into sins. "No Order gives more charity than we." A pins-and-needles numbness crept into his fingers. He flexed them to stave it off, shooting white hot blades of pain from his wrists through his arms.

"Lies. You placed yourselves in league with the infidel, working to put the Holy Land back in the hands of the Saracens." He was cold in his certainty, precise and without doubt.

"We *protected* the Holy Land." Strength rose up in him to deny the charge and the ignominy it cast on his brothers' sacrifices in the far-off lands of the Crusades. Dry, croaking, his voice rose. "No Order has shed their blood more readily in defense of the faith than we."

Imbert nodded, unmoved. The door swung open, twisting De Molay's wounds over the spikes, again stretching his arms out, again stealing his breath.

"Please," De Molay wheezed, "allow me just to send word to—" The pain made it impossible to think and focus. He managed a moan. His chest heaved, and his head sagged to one side.

Imbert watched in the darkness of the office silent. He waited, studying the De Molay, his body shining with sweat, his chest heaving shallowly, silver hair swaying before his face.

The inquisitor moved nearer. His lips close, his breath was hot in the Grandmaster's ear. "You'll confess, Jacques De Molay. You'll gladly admit your evil."

He stepped away, allowing his voice to rise.

"Everyone does, eventually."

CHAPTER XVIII

Brother Nicolas remained at the door, on watch as always. He lent an ear to his brothers' concerned whispering.

The other knights closed tight around them. Etienne knelt before the hearth, stacking wood in the fire. Lisette stood over the boy, eyeing the Templars suspiciously as she downed another cup of ale.

"So, we leave France?" Andre asked William.

"Brother Francesco's right," William answered. Why had it taken him so long to see it? "Sanctuary's no option."

Ramon shook his head. "To escape all of France—"

"It will be easier the farther we go," Odo interrupted. "The farther they have to cast their nets, the less chance they have of catching us."

"Assuming they're looking for us," added Francesco. "They may believe they have arrested the entire Order back at the Temple."

Armande snorted. "We should be so lucky."

Ramon turned back to William. "Even if we escape the borders, what then?"

"We will rally with whatever Templar forces we can."

"But we're the Church's soldiers," said Andre. "King Philip wouldn't—"

"He's your king." Francesco pointed out. "It's difficult for you to see..." his voice trailed off as his gaze drifted toward the low, rough entrance to the room. His neck tensed, and he stared wordlessly. In the doorway stood two royal officers.

One was a man of middle age, with a full head of thick, silver hair that made him appear at first to be much older than he was, his skin by contrast tanned and tight. With him was much younger noble no older than Brother Andre. He was pretty, with long, blond hair and dark eyes that offset his otherwise angelic appearance. In matching blue cloaks, they stood at the threshold, taking in the room, seeming unconcerned by the cloaked strangers gathered at the end of the near table.

Nicolas' cold eyes locked on them. His hand slipped his long dagger from beneath his cloak.

He glanced to William. A terse shake of his head, a quick tightening and relaxing of his neck muscles, ordered Nicolas to stand down. He sheathed the knife.

Andre leaned close to William, his eyes cold on Lisette. "The whore betrayed us," he hissed through clenched teeth.

"Wait," William breathed.

By the fire, Lisette felt a chill as she recognized their' sudden unease and the reason for it. She hurried to William's side.

"The serving wench," Armande said under his breath. "She realized I'm in armor." He scanned the room for Felicité. Her absence confirmed his suspicion for him.

Odo's thoughts traced back to their passage through the tavern, to the dice knocking against his boot and the tired eyes of the old gambler with the syphilitic scars. "He saw my mail coat, and my sword," he recalled quietly.

Armande's hand snaked into his cloak. Before he could draw, he found William grasping his forearm, staying his hand.

Lisette pushed into their circle, close to William.

"I've seen them here before." She said in a desperate whisper. "Many times. They're regulars here: Captain Renier De Ronsoi, and his nephew, Captain Érard De Valery—"

"You're lying," Andre accused through clenched teeth. He reached to seize her, but William blocked the young knight's arm.

"Andre, stop," he ordered.

"I'm telling you the truth," Lisette whispered "If they were after you, they'd have their weapons out, wouldn't they?"

"Yes, they would." Francesco agreed.

"And more men?"

None of the Templars answered.

"They're probably just getting out of the storm," she explained. "Like you all."

Armande was unconvinced. "They could be reconnoitering."

"Not in plain view, wearing the king's colors," Odo disagreed.

William nodded toward the door. "They're dodging work."

A slim, gloved hand slipped over the silver-haired De Ronsoi's shoulder, caressing his neck as a young woman in only her chemise pressed herself tight against him, her other hand slipping confidently down the front of his cloak as her bare legs rubbed against his. Two more young women slid into view behind the young De Valery. Dressed only in sheer chemises as well, their flimsy underdresses left little unseen, even in the flickering light of the candles and lanterns. With one hand, De Valery stroked the long blonde hair of the taller girl absently, like a familiar pet. With his other hand, he held close another girl, smaller and darker than the others, nuzzling her without affection as he groped at her.

Without even a glance at the disguised Templars, the two officers strolled in and made their way toward the warmth of the fire, the half-undressed prostitutes attached to them like leeches.

"Regulars." Lisette stated to Armande and Andre with a vindicated glare.

Etienne scurried away from the fire as the two officers took Odo's and Armande's seats by the hearth. Before settling, De Ronsoi reached across to the table, pouring drinks for himself and his nephew from the pitcher set there.

"Storm or no," said William, "we go. Now."

Armande started up from the bench. Andre and Ramon started after him. But William caught Andre's arm.

"Not all at once." His face was immobile as a mask. Ramon took his seat again. After he realized Brother William was not going to release his arm, Andre sat again as well. "Odo, Armande, you leave now. We'll join you outside, in small parties."

Odo nodded, lifting his great frame from the bench. Pulling his dark cloak tighter about him, he left the room. His exit went unnoticed by the officers, William observed. They were too taken by the overeager attentions of the girls cozying close, teasing and fondling, spilling clay cups and quickly refilling them.

"Francesco, you and Ramon take Etienne out shortly," William rasped under his breath. His eyes lingered too long on the other party. "Andre, you go with Nicolas after that. I'll follow up the rear."

By the fire, De Valery and De Ronsoi continued their carousing. Their drunken laughter was loud. The laughter of the girls was louder, coming in squealing or giggling peals that erupted too quickly and sounded forced perhaps only to those with senses undulled by drink. The blonde stood behind De Valery as he sat, head back. Leaning forward over him, she shook her long, pale hair in the aristocrat's face, a teasing game as it tickled his nose and lips. They roared in delight.

William watched, wanting to be less obvious. He forced his eyes to meet Francesco's, finding his brother pensive, and then to Lisette's, finding the girl uneasy. Her eyes darted from Andre to Ramon to William. She jumped, startled, as a crash behind them left a shattered cup on the floor, foamy ale running off into the floorboards. The officers burst into boisterous laughter.

"Excuse me," came a small voice behind William. Francesco looked to the floor as William and Lisette turned to see the shortest of the girls who'd come in with the officers.

A pitcher was in her hand.

Up close, William could see more her thick, black hair, her slim form, and her delicate features. She was no older than Etienne, perhaps a year or two younger. She held out the clay pitcher, offering it to William.

"Captain Renier and his nephew send this and their compliments," the girl said. Her voice was tired, William noticed, weary and worn. The voice of a laborer, not a child.

Lisette accepted the ale jug with one of her dazzling smiles. "Thank you, Caresse," she said to the little girl.

Caresse held her dark gaze on William's pale eyes. "You're so still," she said flatly. "It's making him anxious. He says it's like sitting in a room full of monks."

William started to reply, but the girl's comment was like a blow to ribs and he stumbled on the words.

"Caresse, thank the darlings for us," Lisette covered quickly for him, all charm. "Assure the *comte* and his nephew that my friends are *spent* from their evening with Solange." She rolled her eyes dramatically drumming her fingertips on her breast.

"Captain De Valery *did* ask about you," the little girl confided.

"Tell him perhaps another night." She looked past her to the young, blonde officer, pouting apologetically.

Caresse shrugged and turned. William watched her cross the room, appearing more lively with each step, becoming like Lisette, all charm with her clients.

"Francesco," William whispered, "fill your cup, and Ramon's. Etienne, when Brother Ramon stands, support him. Help him walk as if he can't balance."

Francesco nodded. Taking up the pitcher awkwardly, he made it a point to slosh some over its spout before crashing it against one cup and the other. He filled both cups sloppily, spilling the flat alee in big puddles that dripped over the table's edge to the dirty floor.

Etienne hesitated.

"Do it," William reassured the boy. "Meet Broth—Meet *Odo*—outside."

Without giving the boy a chance to respond, Francesco stood up. As more laughter erupted from the officers' party, Ramon started to his feet, wobbling unconvincingly, doing his best to mimic the drunken exits he could recall from his parents' feasts.

Etienne darted to his side, propping him up on his shoulder. He shuffled clumsily beside Ramon, trying to keep up with his unpersuasive stagger, lurching with the knight until he stumbled himself. He bumped against Ramon's injured arm. In sudden pain, Ramon tensed, and Etienne fell against his hip, nearly knocking him from his feet as they made it through the door. Francesco managed to catch him, and he steadied them both, rendering their exit, perhaps, believable.

As he sipped from his cup, De Ronsoi happened to spy the exiting men. Worry flashed on Lisette's face as she saw his eyes narrow. Heart pounding in her chest, she knew he had to be distracted or, better, convinced. She glanced at William and instantly straddled his lap, pressing her lips to his. William stiffened, and started to pull away, but then went along.

Andre could but stare at the two, shocked into silence.

Lisette kissed William deeply, hungrily. Grabbing his rough hands in hers, she positioned them on her breasts, then on her hips. She pulled him closer, grinding against him and moaning theatrically, loud, aching.

It was enough to draw De Ronsoi's attention.

Tossing back her head with a professional's practice, Lisette glimpsed the officer as he stared at her, watching her straddle the man for a long measure before allowing a thin smile to cut across his face. At last he looked away, grabbing the girl he'd paid for and pulling her near. He knocked back another drink and laughed with his own party.

Lisette eyed De Ronsoi as she kissed William, watching the officer as he lost himself in the women and drink. She broke away, her lips lingering on William's, their faces close.

He was not what she was used to. Any other man she'd known would have taken advantage of the moment's ruse. Yet when she stopped, she looked into his eyes, gray and intense, hard but somehow still kind. She searched his face, desperate for the reaction, the connection, she longed for, that she needed from him.

He locked his eyes on her, questioning.

"The captain was growing suspicious of your friend's terrible playacting," she whispered, leaning closer in again. William noticed her breath sweet, smelling faintly of pear. She stroked his hair, put her cheek against his, speaking in his ear. "I had to draw his attention."

"Did you?"

She hesitated, unsure of how to take his response. "He was watching us. He seems convinced."

"Of what?"

"That you and your friends belong here."

William nodded. She let her eyes almost close and drew closer. "Then we go now," William said.

Lisette stopped. She slid from his lap, and he stood up, watching the two officers. Lisette took William's hand with an affected giggle, leading him away like a playful little girl. William tapped Andre's shoulder as he passed him, the younger knight on his feet instantly and right behind him.

Nicolas slid out the door before they reached it. Once clear of the room and the officers' eyes, Lisette's pace quickened. In spite of the hour or perhaps because of it, the tavern was more crowded. Lisette glided effortlessly through the crowds, navigating the knots of patrons that collected in the dim, narrow passageways.

Without her practice or her hand to hold, Andre began to fall behind in the winding gloom. He had to squeeze hurriedly to get past people. He paused at an intersection to see which way the girl went. He spied her only as she rounded a distant, smoky corner. Blocking his way, a pair of *cocettes* were negotiating a rate with a well-dressed youth. His face hidden behind a simple kerchief, he claimed he had no more money after the night's celebrations, maintaining he would gladly bring more the next night. Laughing, the working girls accused him of being the servant of one of the aristocratic patrons. They giggled until Andre pushed past the three of them, earning a flurry of disparagements from the girls.

Hurrying, he collided with a gangling, long-limbed drunk who staggered into his path. The drunk bounced off the wall and crashed to the floor in a heap of spidery limbs atop the Templar initiate.

Andre shoved him off of him, the drunk confused and mewling about his head. Andre scrambled to his feet, looking about.

He'd lost sight of the others.

His heart raced. In the dimness, he couldn't distinguish one hallway from the next, one roughed out arch from another. He was lost.

He dashed to the next corridor. Peering to his right, he glimpsed in the shadows a small crowd gathered in a loose circle, waving hands and cheering. He moved closer to see in their midst a small man—a dwarf—wearing only a loincloth and a crude mask that resembled the face of a cat. They urged the cat-masked man on as he locked his arms around the neck of an enormous dog, nearly the size of a small pony, pushing with squat, powerful legs until the dog tipped over to one side.

He turned and went the other way, stumbling into a small chamber.

Andre turned back to the corridor, his heart in his throat. He saw no sign of any of his brothers. As his eyes were sweeping the corridor again, he was slammed into the wall. His head crashed on the rough plaster, raking open the skin of his forehead, as rough hands seized his arms and turned him, shoving him into a corner. Andre froze at the cold of a dagger against his throat.

"Who are you?" Captain De Ronsoi demanded. Holding him pinned, he patted at Andre's body, at his shoulders and chest. "You *are* wearing armor. I thought as much when I saw you and the others."

Andre struggled, but De Ronsoi held him firm.

"Unhand me!" Andre cried.

De Ronsoi let his knife answer for him. He pressed the blade so it bit into Andre's neck. The Templar froze as he felt the warm trickle of blood on his throat.

"Answer me," De Ronsoi ordered. "You men are hiding something."

Squirming, Andre managed to get hold of the captain's knife hand, twisting the edge away from himself. De Ronsoi smashed his other hand across Andre's face, dazing him and bloodying his nose. As they wrestled, their struggle pulled open Andre's cloak, revealing his white habit and the red cross over his heart. De Ronsoi hesitated, staring down at the Templar emblem.

"It's true," he breathed. His forearm now choked across Andre's throat. "They said some escaped."

Andre struggled. His heartbeat pounded in his ears. His vision started going white at the edges. He remembered his charge, realized he couldn't allow himself to be captured, yet he couldn't break the choke hold. Fumbling behind him, one hand found his hidden pack. He squeezed his eyes shut in desperate prayer.

A long, cold dagger slipped beneath De Ronsoi's ear and across this throat, slicing open his neck as the weapon's point sank behind his collarbone. Blood sprayed hot, splattering Andre's face. His eyes snapped open in time to see De Ronsoi arch backward and go limp in Nicolas' arms.

Andre watched Nicolas lower De Ronsoi's gurgling body to the floor with one arm, deftly sheathing his bloody dagger with the other. With a terrible expertise Andre did not want to consider, Nicolas maneuvered the fresh corpse into a dark corner, sitting him up like a passed-out drunk. Doubled over, Andre wheezed, forcing a deep, long breath. Staring at the floor, he saw another pair of boots race toward him.

Brother William stood over him, Lisette at his side. She spied Nicolas' grisly work. Her hand went to her mouth to smother the scream. William looked his two men over, taking in the scene. His eyes burned angrily.

"Make haste," the whisper hissed through his teeth.

"You," a voice rose through the corridor, louder than any had dared in this place. "Don't move!"

Andre saw William glance over his shoulder at a confused Captain De Valery. From the far end of the corridor, the captain strode toward them, agitated, drawing his knife. Patrons before him scattered, scurrying back into the corridors and the holes along them.

As he neared, De Valery paused as he noticed his uncle's unmoving form on the floor behind the cloaked men. He rushed for them, something cold tightening in his belly.

"Uncle?" he called.

William glared at Nicolas. "Wait for it," he said, voice low.

De Valery was too focused on his unmoving kin. "Uncle Renier?" he called, expecting an answer.

William whirled on De Valery, his fist driving into the young officer's belly, doubling him over as he seized the officer's knife hand and twisted his arm over painfully.

De Valery fought the hold. William torqued the officer's arm around the opposite way, forcing De Valery's blade to slash across his own cheek. He cried out as William's fist followed and cracked across his face.

Nicolas hustled Andre away, Lisette right on their heels.

With a shove, William sent the reeling De Valery to the floor. He hit it hard, wrist throbbing, the cut on his cheek stinging. Stunned, wheezing, he struggled to get back on his feet. The corridor seemed to tilt now, stealing his balance. The dark, hooded figure loomed over him, unmoving even as the passageway's walls swayed around it.

"Stay down," the figure warned before disappearing into the gloom.

CHAPTER XIX

Grandmaster Guillaume De Beaujeu summoned around him his knights who could stand. His word was grim.

"The Mameluks have seized St. Anthony's Gate."

The fighting wasn't visible from the Templar's keep by the sea. The roar of combat had dwindled to a low rumble that William felt as much as he heard. Grandmaster De Beaujeu squinted out over the crowded courtyard, the deep creases around his eyes deepening further. "With the gate open, the attacking forces are streaming freely into the city."

Gasps breathed from those who overheard. Scurries and whispers followed as the news fanned out among the refugees and the injured throughout the fort like fire on the wind. Panicked crowds pressed nearer to hear the Grandmaster's news. The Templars took the report silently, looking to their Grandmaster only for his next order.

William noticed a stain of red at the edge of the Grandmaster's *kafiyya*, spotty, as if it had soaked through from the back of the fabric. He looked closer and saw the long head cloth hid a seeping gash along the Grandmaster's neck. Slashing from the side of this windpipe to under his right ear, it was a close cut that could have easily severed his artery and vein.

"We have but one choice," Grandmaster De Beaujeu continued. "We must recapture the tower and retake control of the gate."

"That would be foolhardy," a voice rang over the crowd. "Foolhardy and suicidal."

William recognized the voice of Tomasso Di Anselmo and glanced backward to see him shouldering his way past the crowded refugees, flanked by his two chief cronies, Corrado and Fazio. All in their dark armor, their surcoats torn and bloodied, they shoved through the crowd, helmets in hand. They were brawny men, older than William, with closely cropped hair and a sweaty, oily sheen to their skin that never seemed to fade. Not knights, barely soldiers, Tomasso and the rest of his crew were hired and brought from the north of Italy by some of the middle-ranking barony, a gesture to augment the fighting forces protecting the city. More often, the city needed protection from them, William thought. Tomasso and his mercenaries were undisciplined villains. They cared only for coin, their ranks made up of murderers, rapists, the self-serving, and the excommunicated. Creating more problems than they were meant to solve, for months they'd pressured the city's fragile peace.

Grandmaster De Beaujeu glared. The freebooter went on.

"We should get out. Put all who are capable into the boats in the harbor and leave the city to the Saracens."

"Give up now, and we lose our last hold in the East." De Beaujeu stated.

"As if there's any chance of holding onto it?"

"The harbor holds too few craft for everyone to escape," William interjected. "Besides, the people here require protection." The Grandmaster cast the young Templar a curious glance, remarkably unoffended by his impropriety.

"Try and re-take the tower, and you'll get yourself killed," the mercenary said.

"Re-taking the tower will slow them." William countered.

"Slow them? They're pouring in through the breach!"

"Forcing them to keep to the breach restricts their numbers. The gate gives them access to the road, and with the road, they're free to enter and bring whatever siege engines they please inside the city walls. If we retake the gate, we limit them and their advantage."

The mercenary smiled without mirth, baring his teeth and shaking his head. "And how many sieges have you fought, boy?"

"How many have you run from?"

The joyless smile dropped from Tomasso's face. His hand went to his hilt, but he paused, noticing the cold-eyed Templar brothers flanking William and the Grandmaster behind him. He let go of his blade and pointed threateningly at the young knight before whirling away, his men disappearing with him into the masses that crowded behind the Templar walls.

William turned to find Grandmaster De Beaujeu glaring at him. "We face enough enemies at St. Anthony's Gate, Brother William. Let's not make more."

William lowered his head. "Grandmaster, even with a common enemy at our door, those men are not our allies."

The Grandmaster nodded, his eyes twinkling in the only form of a smile he ever allowed himself before his men. He bade William and the other Templars closer.

"You were at the harbor?" he asked William.

"Yes, Grandmaster." William reported the scene, sinking boats and floating bodies choking the path to the sea. He recounted the struggle against the horsemen. The Grandmaster's expression grew dark. "We could do little for the chaos at the harbor. So I returned, bringing Brother Odo back for attention."

"How is he?" De Beaujeu asked without changing his gaze.

"Resting now, in the care of the Hospitallers."

"Then he's in the best hands possible short of God's own," came a voice from behind them.

William turned with Grandmaster De Beaujeu to face another knight. The man was tall and gaunt, his garb bloody and dusty like the Templars', but he wore a surcoat of black instead of white, emblazoned with a white cross that marked him as of the Order of St. John—a Knight Hospitaller.

"We'll keep him in ours," the Hospitaller finished, offering his hand to Grandmaster De Beaujeu. William recognized he was standing before Jean De Villiers, Grandmaster of the Knights Hospitaller.

De Villiers' expression turned serious. "We've much planning, Brother."

De Beaujeu took his hand, "And almost no time," he replied. They led the two bands of knights inside the Templar barracks.

William paused, searching the crowded, sun-beaten compound for the Hospitallers and Brother Odo. He saw merchants and citizens, women and children and pilgrims. Some huddled, like scared birds. Some paced anxiously. Others sat, still and tense, while a few were praying in fevered murmurs or desperate wails. They were here under his Order's protection, William recalled with regret. He worried how he could still meet their obligation.

He started after his brothers. Chancing to look up, he spied the Templar banner, the *Bueasaint*, flying high above the fortress walls. Quartered in black and white squares, a red cross at its center, it had torn free at one corner. He would have to alert the Temple Marshal who would want to know the flag was sagging, dying in the failing winds.

CHAPTER XX

Outside Le Basilisk et Chalice, the rain had nearly stopped, heavy drops falling irregularly and splashing loud on the ground. The muddied streets oozed, pocked with shiny puddles, shallow and dirty.

Nicolas burst through the tavern door, bloodied Andre in tow. Immediately behind them, Lisette appeared, William at her back, hustling her into the night. Leaping from the low steps, they splashed into the avenue. They ran through the muck, harried glances over their shoulders expecting pursuit, eyes searching the surrounding darkness for a trap.

"Brother William," a small, hushed voice called out.

They slid to a stop. William spied Etienne at the mouth of an alley, pressed against the wall. The boy's eyes darted nervously as they approached him.

The door to the tavern stood open. Jean-Marie craned his head out, cautious. He'd left his post at the door to check on the ale casks one of the serving girls claimed was empty, and he was more than perturbed to find the door to his establishment wide open, inviting anyone in from the night. He was able to learn from the drunks and gamblers that men in dark hoods rushed past.

"A girl was with them, too, no?" the one explaining asked hazily of the gambler at his side. The second gambler shrugged and looked over the faces of the dice on the table. Angry, he threw down more coins.

"It was Solange," a scrawny, emaciated woman with black ribbons at her shoulders said, tugging on her gloves. She blew a kiss across the room, its target unseen by Jean-Marie. "Some fellow was hustling her out."

The ones she brought in, Jean-Marie deduced angrily. He distrusted them the moment he saw them, but Solange had vouched for them. He ran the place on confidence and silence. If something came back on him from this, he'd find the girl, and take it out of her.

He was getting ahead of himself. He went to the door and craned his neck out.

"Solange?" he called out to the empty street.

No answer.

"Dear?" he called, predator's eyes searching the wet streets. The rain had stopped, and the loud drips from the buildings were a constant background drone, like crickets' song in summer.

"Dear Solange?" he called louder.

No answer. Casting one more glance at the muddy streets, he considered the mess it would become in the day, once the muck was churned by the feet of horses and men. He shrugged to himself. Whistling a tune he'd heard earlier in the evening, he returned to the tavern's darkness and shut the door.

✝ ✝ ✝

At a dark, trash-strewn street corner, Nicolas and Andre caught up with Etienne, William and Lisette right behind. The other Templars were waiting.

"We need to move," William said, heading for the next dark intersection. He strode right past the group, assuming the point. The knights fell in behind him, marching to match his pace. At the rear, Lisette hurried to keep up.

As they marched, Odo noticed Andre dabbing at his bleeding nose. He then saw the blood spattered over him. Odo closed in, looking closer in the gloom.

"You're injured."

Nicolas cut him off. "He's fine."

Odo's one-eyed stare ordered explanation.

"One of the officers," Andre stammered, collecting himself before the elder brother. "He became suspicious of us. He cornered me as we left, demanding answers."

"And?" A gap grew between Odo and the group, his stride slowing as he questioned the two.

"I handled him," Nicolas stated.

Lisette spoke up. "You killed him. Stabbed him in the back."

"Keep your voice down," Armande ordered.

Odo doubled his pace, making his way to the front of the party. "William, is this true?"

William kept his eyes forward. "One's dead. Yes."

"Two would have bought us more time," Nicolas added.

William glared. "Don't."

Nicolas turned back to Lisette, eyes cold. "I did not stab him in the back."

"We shouldn't have been there in the first place," Armande said.

William kept walking. "We can't correct it now."

Lisette stayed behind Nicolas. "The captain wasn't a cruel man," she accused. "To take his life like that—"

"He held a knife on one of my brothers," Nicolas stated. "That's all I needed to see."

William stopped and turned on Nicolas. "Our task and the Order's survival rely on stealth. On our ability to move undetected, unnoticed. You drew attention to us." His stride quickened and he resumed his place at the point. "Attention we don't need."

✟ ✟ ✟

In the darkened hallway outside the Grandmaster's offices, King Philip waited, crushing his fine leather gloves in his bare hand, silently twisting and knotting them as he paced. Guillaume De Nogaret noted his king's agitation, uncharacteristic in a man accustomed to seeing his will done instantly.

The Inquisition's monk wouldn't allow him to be present for De Molay's interrogation. Instead, he listened to the Grandmaster's cries from a distance down the hall, concerned over the lack of pleas and genuine screams he heard among De Molay's outbursts. Much was riding on these plans.

The heavy door swung in with a creak. Imbert squeezed through the narrow crack between door and frame, closing it with a hush behind him.

"Well?" the king demanded.

"*Confessionem esse veram, non factam vi tormentorum.*" Imbert declared. "The confession was true and free. I've ordered him taken down and his wounds tended."

"What has he told you?"

Imbert paused. *Less than was required,* De Nogaret read in the hesitation.

"He's willful—" Imbert began

"That we knew," De Nogaret cut him off.

"But he has confessed."

The king stepped forward. "He's confessed to all of it?"

"Only to idol worship and un-Christian hoarding of wealth."

"That's not enough," said the king.

"We drew up the charges specifically," the chancellor reminded the confessor. "To gain leverage—"

"This is enough," Imbert argued, "for the leader of a Holy Order. He'll be required to step down, renounce his position. He'll never stand with such authority again."

"Discrediting one man isn't enough," insisted King Philip. "The entire Order has to be implicated."

"The entire Order cannot be guilty," Imbert said. "They are perhaps unpopular, but a blanket condemnation will stand neither the eyes of the public nor the Church."

De Nogaret glared at him.

The king waved him off. "Of course not. Not all will confess." He cocked his head, his feigned concern practiced. "If some among them are innocent, it's expedient they should be assayed like gold in the furnace," he paused looking at his nails, "and purged, by proper judicial examination."

The inquisitor nodded. "We have extracted confessions from others," he assured.

"What others?"

"No one else has been questioned, my king," De Nogaret said. He was certain of his facts and suspicious of the inquisitor.

"No one else has been interrogated thusly," Imbert corrected, indicating the door behind him. "But a number of the Templars were ordered isolated from their brethren. Under the mere suggestion of what was in store if they did not cooperate and answer questions fully, several confessed."

"Who?" the king asked.

"Servants," Imbert told him. "And some of the retired brothers."

"Stable boys and old men," King Philip derided, pacing away.

"It will take time," Imbert said. "The knight brothers are as defiant as their Grandmaster. Most are younger, stronger."

De Nogaret went to King Philip's side. "Dawn is hours away, Majesty," he reminded. "We hold their temple, and reports should begin arriving on the morrow as to our success with their other installations throughout France."

"Delays will cost us. You know the plans."

Imbert slid back so he was outside the heavy door. Hands folded in his robes, he watching the exchange between king and chancellor.

"I know we cannot hurry certain legal maneuverings," De Nogaret said, voice hushed. "The pieces are in place, and their positions favor you. We have to play the game out as planned." The king nodded, unhappy with the answer but reconciled to it.

De Nogaret turned back to Imbert, pointing at the door. "He must aver to all the charges. He has to be broken."

"Spare no means," the king added solemnly.

"He'll confess the rest," Imbert's eyes shone with cold confidence. "I have faith."

King Philip came up behind De Nogaret. "Search the Grandmaster's papers," he spoke into his ear. "Find their records, rites, treaties, and charters. They may hold something we can use."

De Nogaret nodded. "At once."

On the stair at the end of the corridor, a soldier appeared and waited. Seeing him, De Nogaret bowed deferentially to the king, his eyes asking leave. The king dismissed him with an impatient wave without turning from Imbert.

De Nogaret backed into the hall. After a few respectful paces, he turned, motioning the soldier to him while walking quickly to meet him. As De Nogaret neared, the soldier stopped, standing at attention. Uncomfortably close, De Nogaret leaned in.

"Report," he ordered.

"Lord De Nogaret," the soldier began, "we believe we've found the room, but the door—"

"Break it down."

"It will not yield," the soldier explained. "These Templars have mastered arcane architectures. The door—"

"I did not ask for a description of it."

"The door will not yield," the soldier summarized. "I've sent for smiths and tools."

"Have them work quickly. The sooner the king has his treasures, the better off we'll all be."

"Yes, lord." The soldier held his eyes forward.

"I'll advise the King," De Nogaret said, dismissing the soldier. As he turned, he found this king lost in thought, with his face, stern and unreadable. Beyond him, he saw Imbert slip back into the Grandmaster's office, closing the door behind him with a thud.

✝ ✝ ✝

Lisette struggled to keep up with the Templars' march, her thin slippers less certain in the muck than the knights' heavy boots. Etienne fared little better, his sandals giving him only slightly better footing in the slick ooze.

Keeping an eye on the two stragglers, Brother Francesco hung back from the rest. He lagged behind Brother Andre, keeping the group in sight as he made sure the boy and the woman kept pace.

In a cart rut, Lisette's foot sank into the mud past her ankle. She wobbled, nearly losing her balance, her foot trapped, and tugged at her buried foot as her other slid in the muck. Her hem dragged the ground as she sank, dirty water leaching into her dress, staining its edges a ragged brown.

Francesco took Lisette by the elbow and steadied her so she could draw her foot free. She growled deep in her throat and cursed under her breath as she looked ahead to see the others moving steadily on.

She yanked her elbow from Francesco. Bunching up the sides of her dress in her hands, she hiked up her skirts almost to her knees, lifting the hem so it wouldn't drag in the filth. Francesco watched as she tramped past Etienne and past Andre.

The initiate was scandalized by her immodesty as she made her way bare-legged to the middle of the small company.

Francesco found Etienne with his foot mired. Before he could reach him, the boy had freed his foot, and was reaching down to pluck the sandal from the mud where it had been snared. Francesco passed him by as he replaced it on his foot.

"You believe the king himself is behind all this?" Etienne asked him. He hopped after his elder until his shoe was in place.

Ahead of them, William turned a corner, the others close behind. Francesco picked up his gait, waving for Etienne to follow close.

"I do."

"They say he's readying another crusade," Etienne said as they caught up to the pack. "He'll need the Knights Templar to mount it."

"I fear he needs other things more," Francesco answered without looking at the boy.

"More?" Brother Andre asked, overhearing. "We held the Holy Land for two centuries. The Order knows the region and its fighting strategies better than anyone. Any action without us would be doomed."

"We're loyal servants of the Church," Brother Armande added without glancing back at them. "The king has no cause to move against us."

"Let's reason this," Francesco exhaled slowly, almost a long sigh. "The way they teach in the seminary."

CHAPTER XXI

"Four years ago," Francesco began, "King Philip ended a ten-year war for control of Gascony. The fighting with the English was constant and the war costly. It exhausted the royal coffers early, and he had to borrow monies from the bankers of Lombard and the Jews to sustain it. Raising taxes wasn't enough to pay for the fighting and maintain the loans. You'll remember he recalled and re-minted all the currency in France."

Armande remembered. He'd been part of a number of escorts for the coins as they made their way back to the king's hands.

"Reducing its value while lining his reserves with what little surplus it provided could not generate enough funds," Francesco continued. "So, when the wars in Gascony ended, and his daughter Isabella was betrothed to the English Prince Edward, he expelled the Jewish and Lombard bankers to whom he owed monies, seizing their properties while dissolving his debts to them."

"They were expelled for their wrongdoing," Andre argued.

"They were expelled by being arrested *en masse*. Then each had one eye plucked out and was ordered to leave France and never return under threat of losing the other."

Francesco paused, letting his words sink in as if delivering a homily.

"Two years after that, King Philip annexed Lyon and Lorraine after another costly war. To refill his coffers then, he taxed all clergy in France in direct defiance of the instructions of the Church, going so far as to publicly destroy the Papal Bull *Unam Sanctam*. When the Pope objected, the king used his influence to remove him and put on the Papal Throne a French bishop who was more agreeable to his views."

"Pope Boniface was an old man," Armande pointed out. "He died—"

"He died right after the king's right-hand, Chancellor De Nogaret, paid him a visit with three hundred troops of the royal army in tow."

Andre slowed, Etienne passing him. He picked up his stride, anxious, and moved alongside Francesco. "Go on."

✝ ✝ ✝

Odo hastened to William's side. "Where are we headed?" Odo asked.

"The west wall of the city."

"The west wall?"

"They know our nearest preceptories are north and east," William explained. "They'll expect us to head that direction and will position themselves in between."

"So we go another direction," Odo concluded for him.

"They won't leave this path unguarded," said William. "But it should be sparse, as they direct their numbers elsewhere."

Odo looked at William. Quietly, he said, "We won't make it, Brother. Not like this."

William narrowed his eyes on him.

Odo's voice was low, barely a deep whisper. "These men are running when everything in them tells them to fight."

"We can't—"

"They're Templars, William," Odo little more than exhaled. "Warriors. *Soldiers.* They need a clear enemy—"

"The royal army of France isn't enough?"

"They need a clear goal."

"Survival seems an obvious one at this point."

"They need better than that."

"Better?"

"You expect that to be enough for them when it wasn't enough for you at Acre?"

"That was the Crusades."

"They're Templars, William, same as you. These men have given themselves to God. Their lives are as the arrow is to the archer. They don't fight for survival. They let Him decide it. You know this. They need a cause—"

"Saving the Order isn't enough?" William spat the words.

"They all look to you," Odo pressed. "Even Brother Armande. Regardless of their words, they trust you and your leadership. But their doubts make them wary, cause them to stumble in their trust and their faith. They doubt because you hold yourself apart from them."

William kept his eyes on the darkness ahead. "With good reason."

Odo's voice dropped further, and he leaned in close. "They know nothing of your resignation, but they sense your ambivalence. Because of their faith in you, and knowing nothing more, they interpret it as doubt. This is leading them to doubt themselves, doubt their purpose. Even the Order itself."

"I'm still fighting to save it," William said, eyes forward. He felt Odo's heavy hand on his shoulder.

"Because at your heart, you're a Templar," Odo said. "Because you see these men, your brothers, as the soldiers of God they are. Because you can see past the missteps the Order has taken, see what it represents, and can represent again. It's the fire in your blood, the thunder in your soul. Lead with that, William, and they will fight beside you through the gates of Hell and back."

William let his gaze meet his old friend's, and they marched on.

✛ ✛ ✛

Francesco realized that for the first time, he had an open mind in Brother Andre. Brother Armande's heart was hard to turn, so invested he was in what he understood as right. Still, he was neither blind nor simple.

"Recently," Francesco continued, "more costly fighting's broken out to the north. The king has never had an opportunity to rebuild his reserves and has found himself mired in debt. So, what does he do?"

Armande marched on, listening half-heartedly. Andre felt a cold fist squeeze the pit of his stomach.

"He once more acts against his creditors," Francesco concluded. "Us."

Ramon broke his silence. "But the Order has long been the French monarchy's financial agent, even before King Philip."

"You talk as if this were some insolvent merchant," Armande growled. "He's the king of France."

"I'm sure," Francesco said, "at this point, his debts are considerable."

Andre spoke again. "But we're not some foreign bankers. We're God's army."

"To act against the Order would be to act against the Church," Etienne pointed out.

"You forget his influence over the Pope." Francesco cast his eyes toward Armande and Andre. "He bullied the convened cardinals into putting his pope on the Papal Throne, a pope who spends as much time in France as in Rome."

"Which is why he could so brazenly lay siege to the Temple," Armande said. His jaw tightened.

"Perhaps why the Grandmaster stood down without a fight," Andre added. "That's why sanctuary isn't safe for us."

They stopped as William's raised hand signaling a halt.

William spied two dark, whispering figures in the gloom ahead. Hunched down near a wall leading to the mouth of an alley, they worked hastily over something low to the ground before going motionless at the sound of the Templars' approach. Stock still, they waited, ears like rodents' and straining at the darkness. Looking in the direction of the oncoming Templars, a quick, whisper hissed between the two, and they darted away, disappearing among the shadows of the alleyway.

Leaving something on the ground.

William drew his sword, the blade flashing in the dark. At his side, Odo, too, drew steel. Cautiously, the two approached the corner the dark forms had fled from. The remaining Templars eyed their backs, hands on hilts.

As they neared, William and Odo heard the splashing and slapping of running footsteps on the wet streets fading into the distance. Odo shook his head at the sight they found. Crossing himself, he began whispering a prayer. William turned away in disgust, sheathing his weapon and signaling for the others to approach.

Andre checked the pack hidden at his back, grateful for its weight in his hand. As he and the others neared, they could make out on the ground a human form, unmoving. Drawing closer, Andre looked down and saw a dead man.

Open eyes slitted and unseeing, the corpse lay on the ground, one limp cheek in the mud. Beneath his chin, a terrible gash marked his throat, open but no longer bleeding. In life, the man had been around forty, with tired circles under his eyes and narrow shoulders. His clothing marked him a common man, perhaps a tradesman. The long tail of his pale hood snaked away from his head, wicking up the dirty water that puddled nearby. Tied over his right shoulder, the short cloak he wore had been pushed open, revealing a simple shirt of wool belted over muddied leather stockings.

"Robbers," William pronounced with scorn.

Andre felt the weight on his back grow heavier as he looked to the dead man's feet. Jutting palely from his stockings, he noticed they were bare and clean. He looked to his own muddy boots.

Odo put his sword away, shaking his head. "They killed him and took his shoes."

Andre found his teeth grinding. He felt himself shaking, the rage swelling hot and bitter in his gut.

"What are we doing?" he nearly shouted.

"Brother," Odo warned in a harsh whisper.

"These people—" he said, his voice almost a yell. Lisette backed away from him as his eyes darted over her and then past her. "They care only for themselves. For their own base needs."

William stepped in front of him. "Brother Andre—"

"They care nothing for God. They strive for nothing higher, worshipping their own lusts and greed, idolizing dishonesty."

Lisette looked away.

"This is a city of criminals and cowards," Andre cried. "Why do we even try—"

William seized him, cutting him off. Taking him by the face with one hand and torquing his arm painfully with the other, William hauled Andre away, forcing him into the alley nearby.

Stunned by Andre's outburst as much as by William's response, the others stood by and watched.

William dragged the initiate for a dozen paces before he released him with a shove. Andre stumbled back, crashing against the rough wall.

"What's going on?" William demanded, his voice low.

"Nothing," Andre answered. His seething eyes met William's cold gaze.

"Don't lie to me."

"I'm not lying."

William strode close. "You're hiding something," he said. "You've been hiding something since we left the Temple."

"Why—" Andre stopped. "Why do you say that?"

William jabbed his thumb back toward the mouth of the alley. "That scene. You're a man burdened by a secret."

Something cold quivered in Andre. "It's the events that besiege us, Brother."

William shook his head. "We're all besieged."

"The things I've seen tonight of this city." Andre admitted. "These people don't deserve—"

"Deserve what?"

Andre turned away. "I can't. A Templar knight shouldn't—"

"You keep saying what a Templar should and shouldn't do." William stepped back, giving the initiate space. "How long have you *been* a Templar?"

Andre drew himself up. "I was initiated in L'Ormteau four days ago."

William found no words. He couldn't decide whether to laugh or to rap the initiate's skull.

"Since *Tuesday*?"

"First thing Tuesday," Andre added.

William's surprise faded, and he considered what he knew of this initiate. When he'd chanced upon him in the dark Temple corridor as the arrests began, Andre told him he was arrived from La Rochelle. Why would he be dispatched to Paris so soon after his initiation?

"Wait," said William. "You were initiated in L'Ormteau."

Andre nodded uncertainly.

"That's over eighty leagues away. And you were in La Rochelle *before* coming here?"

Andre hemmed, staring at the ground.

"That's what you told me back at the Temple," William reminded.

Andre said nothing.

"The harbor at La Rochelle is nowhere on the route from L'Ormteau to Paris. It's days out of the way."

Andre didn't answer.

William continued. "You had to have ridden without stopping to cover that much ground and reach Paris in so short a time. Why would you be sent here so soon after initiation?"

"No younger brothers are presently assigned to the preceptory at L'Ormteau. All there are aged. The House Commander felt no one else could ride the route as quickly."

"The route to the port," William asked, certain of the answer.

Andre nodded.

"You're a courier," William recalled.

Andre lowered his head, nodding.

"A courier who missed the ship he was to meet. That's why the commander at La Rochelle sent you to Paris."

Andre drew himself up. Squaring his shoulders, he looked straight ahead. "Yes, Brother."

Orders sent to a ship would be directed to its next port or held for the next vessel leaving for the same destination. He wondered what would be so important.

"What were you carrying?"

Andre said nothing.

William recalled his first encounter with the initiate. *I was instructed by Grandmaster De Molay to find Brother William.*

"You were given orders before the arrests began, weren't you?"

Andre didn't respond.

"Orders from the Grandmaster himself," William continued. "Orders you now fear you can't carry out."

"Why would you believe—"

"Your burden. You were cast into all this unprepared."

Andre turned to him, meeting William's even gaze. "No, I was told—"

"Start with why the Grandmaster ordered you to find me."

Outside the alley, the knights took up positions, waiting for William and Andre. Establishing a perimeter, they watched the darkness for signs of pursuit. Etienne crept up beside Brother Ramon.

"Brother, what if this is God's will for us?" he asked.

The Templar's eyes stayed locked forward. The wound in his arm was burning, and he felt feverish. "All we're presented with is God's will."

"No." Etienne said. His voice shook. "I mean, what if God's given up on us? On the Order?"

"You can't know that," Ramon answered, peering into the darkness. Etienne noted his voice, not lecturing, like so many of the other brothers when he asked questions, but quiet and clarifying as Brother William's usually was. "No one can know it. We're not to decide God's will, Etienne. We're to be moved by it." He glanced at the boy, who stood with his arms over his chest, clutching at his sides as if he were cold. "Do you believe He wants our Order eradicated?"

The boy nodded slowly.

"With all His power? If God wanted us destroyed, don't you think we'd be so much dust?" He glanced at Etienne, finding his expression serious. Ramon turned back to his watch. "Perhaps, Etienne, what we face is a trial, something put in our path as a test. An opportunity to prove for God our faith and our worthiness."

Nearby, Odo watched Etienne nod, more from habit and respect than agreement. He admired Brother Ramon's confidence and optimism. As the boy seemed to sense and Odo's years had shown him, God's plans were seldom clear. The Crusades had taught him that faith and a strong sword arm sometimes weren't enough to carry the day. He'd seen the holiest fall to the wickedest, seen the most innocent grow to become the most vile. He found himself praying for something more to help them prevail.

CHAPTER XXII

Brother Andre cast his eyes back to the ground. "Grandmaster De Molay instructed me to find you because he believed you were the best choice to guide me in my mission."

"What mission?"

Andre shook his head. His mouth tightened to a taut, pale line. "He ordered me to tell no one."

"Your brothers have risked their lives," William reminded him. "One has given his up. Secrets have no place among us."

"Grandmaster De Molay was clear about this."

"Your orders were incomplete," said William. "Had you brought me back to his office, I would have had more details. Be certain: if I were to conduct you for any mission, the Grandmaster would have briefed me before we set out."

William watched the conflict play out over the young initiate's face. Tense, Andre's hand went to his belt, halting there before reaching across his chest to his shoulder, throwing off his dark cloak and his white mantle.

William spied the strap of Andre's hidden pack as it slid from his shoulder.

"You were to take that from Paris?"

Andre nodded as he hefted the small sack in his hands, carefully opening it and unwrapping its contents. "He thought you're being English would help me." He slid the item from a flaxen sack and began unwinding a dark, worn silk from around it. "We have to get this someplace safe. Out of France if the entire Order is threatened as we fear."

William saw a small box in Andre's hand, decorated in carvings he couldn't make out in the gloom. Andre opened the box, held it out for William.

"With all I've seen tonight, though, I don't believe the world deserves it."

At the mouth of the alley, Odo squinted at the darkness, his eye able to make out William and Andre. William blocked Odo's view of the initiate, and he could see Andre was presenting something to William.

Odo squinted against the dark as he saw William drop to one knee and lower his head reverently before Andre. His mind raced for a reason, a cause, and as his gaze darted over the surrounding darkness, he saw that Brother Ramon, too, witnessed what transpired in the alley.

Ramon had started toward them when Odo stopped him, hooking a huge hand under his arm. Together, they watched William stand up again, once more blocking Andre from their view.

"What does this mean?" Ramon breathed.

"It means our circumstances have changed," Odo answered.

William turned, and strode from the alley toward them, purposeful. Behind him, Andre raced to catch up, adjusting the strap at his shoulder, hastily replacing his mantle and cloak.

"William?" Odo called as he marched past.

"We have a new plan," William announced.

"New? How?" asked Ramon.

William stopped at the center of the group. As the other Templars drew near, curious about the sudden change in Brother William, Lisette hung back, uncertain. She felt herself a hair's breadth from being ousted from the group, with only William insisting she stay with them. Untrusted by the old sour one, scorned by the others for what she did to survive, even the one-eyed one tolerated her only because of William. She could see a change in him. He stood taller now, and no longer seemed so tired.

"There's a ship, anchored on the Seine, not far from here," William said as they gathered close.

"The Seine's full of boats," Armande said.

"It's one of ours," said William. "A Templar galley."

"How did you learn of this?" asked Francesco.

"Brother Andre."

Armande turned on Andre. "You didn't tell us this before?"

"He was under orders not to," William explained. "From the Grandmaster."

Francesco's eyes narrowed. "What reason is this vessel awaiting us?"

"It doesn't await us," said William. "The crew knows nothing of us, which is why we must haste. We can, however, make use of it."

"The boat may have been seized when the arrests started," Odo began.

Armande agreed. "It could be a trap."

"Unlikely," said William. "She's unmarked, and she docked after sunset."

A chill chased up Odo's spine. "If we can set sail by dawn—"

"We can make our way to the sea, escape the king, and join up with our brothers outside France," William finished.

The knights considered the plan as Etienne spoke up. "Then we'll be safe?" he asked.

"We'll have the entire Order behind us," said Nicolas.

"All of God's army," added Ramon.

William glanced back at Andre. "And we can start righting what we've seen wrong."

Odo nodded to the others, inhaled sharply, excited. In another time, they would have marched on, singing the *Non nobis*. This was the Order he remembered.

Lisette slipped between Ramon and Etienne, drawn to William. Even in the gloom, his gray eyes shone with purpose.

Andre looked to each of his brothers, skeptical, confused. "We're besieged by a world that's turned on us, that's denied what we stand for."

"Perhaps it has lost sight of itself," added Francesco.

Ramon smiled.

William looked to each of his men. "We can make it through this. With our faith and with our skill, we'll fight for God's glory and heal His creation." He glanced at Brother Andre. "We possess what we need to prevail even against the impossible."

At his side, Lisette looked at him proudly, composing her finale to the fairy tale she was authoring in her head.

CHAPTER XXIII

The river was near. The sounds of the Seine carried through the darkness, the rushing of the river, the lapping of the water upon the shore, and the soft knocking of the boats anchored and tied off at the docks.

The sounds were heartening to the fugitive Templars, a sign that they were nearing their goal. Led by Brother William, with Brother Odo at his side, they bore south through the Paris streets. They hiked with purpose, careful and quiet, yet for the first time since fleeing the Temple, certain of their course. Rather than hanging back, Lisette walked in the midst of the party, keeping a few paces behind William.

Odo glanced at Andre before turning to William. "It's anchored on the Left Bank?" he asked, voice low.

William nodded. "We can cross the Seine at the *Pointe*—"

"It will be guarded there," Odo reminded. "It always is."

"It won't matter. They won't be prepared." William stepped up his pace. "They won't be expecting *us*."

Lisette slowed and paused, listening to the air. The others marched past her. Something, a sound above the noises of the river, caught her ear. Following up the rear, Ramon stopped to help the girl keep up. Her eyes met his quizzically.

"What is that?" she whispered, listening to the gloom.

Ramon's ears pricked up, and he listened, too, brow knit. His heart sank, and he realized their trial was to resume as he recognized the clopping of horse's hooves and the footfall of marching boots.

"Not now," he breathed.

He scrambled to the point. William and Odo had stopped, signalling the others and listening over the river's sounds themselves.

"Take cover," William ordered. The Templars all darted for the deep shadows, ducking between buildings, pressing against walls, disappearing around corners. Confused, Lisette started in one direction, then another as she watched them melt into the darkest recesses of the avenue. William took her wrist and hustled her out of the street. Wrapping his dark cloak over her to hide the colors of her dress, he crushed her against himself and squeezed into a doorframe.

The hoofbeats and marching grew louder. They could hear over it the quiet orders and hushed reports. In the intersection ahead of them, bearing from the west, royal soldiers appeared. Some with torches, others with spears, they marched slowly, surveying the cross streets as they passed.

More soldiers followed through the intersection, the clopping hoofbeats growing louder until a mounted officer appeared. Surrounded by soldiers, he rode slowly, cold eyes searching the gloom.

William immediately recognized the long blond hair of the young officer from the tavern, the one he'd had to incapacitate as they escaped. The captain Lisette called De Valery.

Captain De Valery pushed his long hair from his face. His lips were tight. His eyes were narrowed. The fresh slash on his cheek was open and swollen. He looked down the street in the Templars' direction.

Against his chest, William could feel Lisette's heart beating rapidly as a bird's. Cool and soft, her arms slipped around him, pulling her still tighter to him. This mere touch, he knew, violated so many rules of the Order, yet in these circumstances, it would have been foolish, dangerous, to push her away.

Andre checked his hidden pack. Armande's hand slipped over his pommel. Nicolas watched with unworried eyes. With no view of the intersection, Ramon and Francesco listened to the night, waiting for the sounds of the officer and his company to fade and disappear. Unable to see from his vantage, Etienne froze, like a rabbit that's caught the scent of a hunter nearby. Odo shut his eye, praying before looking out over the avenue.

In desperate silence, they waited as De Valery passed. Seeing nothing out of the ordinary in the muddy street, he continued on, troops trailing behind him. William watched. Ten more men went by. Twenty more, then thirty. A full company.

William and the others stayed in hiding. The clopping of the horse's hooves faded. Only the sounds of the river were in the air.

William listened to the night, waiting. When he at last heard nothing more, he unwrapped Lisette from his cloak and stepped back into the street, signaling for the others to rally.

"This works in our favor," he whispered once they'd assembled. "We wait and stay to the places they've searched."

"But the galley," Andre interrupted.

"They've passed us." William explained. "We can cross the river behind them while they're searching ahead of us."

Andre nodded, a smile spreading on his face.

William turned and started back the way they came. His men fell in behind him, Lisette in their midst. He led them to the intersection where De Valery's troops had passed. They could stalk the royal company and then break off at the point they needed. William knew De Valery would have no reason to have his troops double-back. If he and the others could maintain their distance, they could keep De Valery's company in sight and watch the troops as they hunted them.

They rounded the next corner and faced four royal soldiers.

Coming from the north, they were stragglers, William realized, probably left behind to tend to some bodily functions and ordered to catch up as they could. Two carried spears; another an axe. Only the first of the group, the one at the front, wore a sword.

The first of the soldiers looked up at William, more surprised than the Templar to see anyone on the street at that hour.

"You there," the soldier managed to call out. "Halt!" Behind this stranger, the soldier saw more cloaked forms prowl up. He drew his sword and shouted, "Captain!"

In the next block, Captain De Valery ignored the soldier's call out of habit, but when the distant voice cried out again, insistent, De Valery yanked back hard on his reins, spinning his horse around, scattering his men as they scrambled out of the animal's way. He stared up the dark street and made out a knot of figures standing in the intersection.

William's men spread out behind him as the soldiers readied their lances, the one with the axe swaying, uncertain. The soldier at the lead pointed his sword at William.

"In the name of His Majesty, King Philip—"

No way to resolve this quietly, William decided to settle it quickly.

"Take them," he ordered, hoping De Valery had ridden too far ahead to hear the soldier's cries.

With a menacing metal hiss, the Templars drew their swords at once. Facing so many blades, it occurred to the straggling soldiers they were outnumbered. They ran, scattering in the darkness.

The Templars paused, weapons drawn. From behind them, the night air carried the sound of furious hoofbeats growing louder, racing nearer.

Andre looked to William. "Do we stand and fight?"

William spun to see what was coming. "Only if we must." He spied Lisette, standing, confused, unarmed. "Etienne," he shouted, "get her aside!"

The boy darted to Lisette, snagging her arm and pulling her around the corner, away from the fight to come.

Returning his gaze to the street, William saw De Valery charging at them, sword high. As the others fanned out, William pushed past them to face the officer, yanking back his hood and raising his own sword.

De Valery set his jaw as he saw the lone, cloaked figure square off at him. He spurred the horse on, and glanced to his side. He looked to his other side and backward.

He'd left his men far behind.

On foot, they rushed to catch up with him on his horse. Even with the mount, he didn't like the numbers.

He heaved his reins, twisting the horse's head back in a sudden stop. He stared coldly at the scattered fugitives.

William stared back, noting De Valery's racing company in the distant gloom beyond.

His weapon low and ready, Odo glanced aside to William. "God must've bestowed a revelation upon that captain."

"Whatever buys us time," William replied. He watched the captain glare at them. His eyes locked tensely on the hesitant officer, waiting for his company to catch up. William lowered his sword.

"We move," he ordered, waving the others on.

From his saddle, Captain De Valery watched as the fugitives fled, disappearing into the darkness of the narrow avenues. The last one, bareheaded, waited, watching him guardedly. His blade vanished beneath his dark cloak, and the last of the fugitives escaped from the captain's sight.

De Valery slammed his fist into his saddle, bellowing as his men neared. He recognized the brazen one who had faced him with the sword. He knew he was at *Le Basilisk et Chalice*, the one who assaulted him after killing his Uncle Renier. Armed as he'd seen the man and his cohorts, he had no doubt who they were.

The Templars that escaped past Le Brun.

The young captain didn't relish the thought of carrying the news of his uncle's demise to his aunt and his mother, his uncle's beloved sister, for the wailing and questioning and whispering. As his men rallied around him, he was planning how to deflect the accusations that would come, having no doubt he would make these last Templars pay.

Through the darkness of the wet, winding street, the Templars ran, some with weapons drawn. Their blades flashed as their arms pumped in their mad sprint. Their boots sloshed in the mud, splashing through the puddles. Each turn, each duck to one side or jog to another they prayed would throw their pursuers from their trail.

The streets changed to wet cobblestone. Etienne slipped, his feet flying out from under him as he rounded a muddy corner that started them up a steep hill. Lisette looked back and slowed as she saw the boy crash hard on the ground and slide to a stop. She turned back to see to him when Ramon took her by the arm.

While he kept her moving up the hill, Brother Odo scooped the spindly boy up in his arms and climbed the hill. Huffing, he deposited Etienne on his feet near the top, and the boy hit the ground running.

"We'll never outdistance them," Andre said to the others near him as they ran. "Not if they have horses."

"I saw only one," Armande spat out. "And the officer on it didn't look too keen on facing us without his entire company."

"We can lose them," Ramon said. The girl's wrist was in his hand as he ran. "Perhaps double-back as they search."

Nicolas sprinted ahead, disappearing down a dark alley. The others started after him until they heard William order, "Stay to the streets."

"We can lose them in the alleyways," said Francesco. William caught up.

"The alleyways are winding, but might lead to a cul-de-sac. We could end up cornered."

Andre recalled soldiers he and his brothers had led to one when their flight began. He shuddered.

Nicolas was silently padding back to join the others. "Still, they'll have more trouble following us this way."

Odo huffed, catching his breath. "Better to be caught in the open than trapped at a dead end."

William nodded. "Let's keep moving," he said, leading them off at a run.

The next street ended at the steep banks of a canal. On either side, it dropped off, almost vertically, to the shallow, black ribbon of water below. A lone footbridge was the only way across as far as they could see upstream and down.

Made of stone, the bridge arched gently upward at its middle. The path across was lined in a row of weathered rock forming a low wall perhaps as high as a man's hip. It was ancient, the arches it rested upon perhaps standing since the time of the Romans.

The path down its center was narrow, not wide enough for two to cross at once. Single file, the Templars dashed over the dark, slick stones, slowing as they reached the far side to look back for signs of pursuit.

The last across were Ramon and Lisette, the girl again falling to the back of the pack and Brother Ramon making sure she kept up. As the two stepped off the bridge, Odo suddenly spun, heel high. His boot crashed loud into the stone balustrade and a spray of water erupted from its surface. The masonry held.

"Too solid," Odo said under his breath. His single eye narrowed over the bridge's gentle slope.

"It won't burn, either," William added.

Winded, the others gathered near.

"Our lead slips," Nicolas reminded William.

William nodded. They had to hasten. Looking at the narrow bridge, it seemed to him there had to be a way to stop the captain and his troops here.

"Even standing," Francesco spoke up, "it will delay them. It's too narrow for them all to cross at once."

William's musings stopped. The words were familiar,

Eyes darting from side to side, they all listened to the dark. Over their own panting and huffing, they heard hoofbeats and distant, shuffling boots. The marching became louder, the captain and his company nearer.

William saw Etienne's eyes grow red. Lisette was like a horse caught in a burning stable, no idea where to go but desperate to get away. His brothers looked to him, chests rising and falling slowly, controlled, as each readied himself.

William looked to the bridge again, studying it and the dark street beyond.

"We'd best get moving, before they catch up," Odo advised.

"They won't," William said.

Odo studied him quizzically. "Can't you hear?" The distant, approaching marching was plain in the air. "We haven't lost them."

"I know," said William. "Take the others, and go on ahead."

Odo could only stare at him. "William, they're on their way."

"The bridge is narrow," William said. "It eliminates the advantage of their numbers." He stared back at Odo, nothing but certainty in his eyes. "I can hold them here."

"No, William!" Lisette cried. She flung herself at him, arms out, hands grasping. William stepped away.

"Go on with the others," he told her firmly. He looked up at his brothers. "Safeguard her as one of our own."

"No," Lisette repeated. She and Odo drew closer to William, as the others, save Etienne, distanced themselves.

Jaw set, William refused to meet their eyes.

"There's another way," Lisette pleaded. "Don't do this."

"Go on," William ordered without lifting his eyes.

Welling tears blinded the girl. "There's too many of them, William."

"Go," he repeated.

"You can't. There are *too many*—"

"This isn't a discussion," William said, eyes meeting hers coldly.

"Come, William, please."

William stopped himself before he could answer her, looking up into the starless sky as he listened to the air. Relentless, the hoofbeats and marching were louder, the royal troops closing in, slowed for their searching, a few streets away.

"Leave," William told the girl and his brothers. "Now."

"Brother." Etienne, spoke up, uncertain.

"You help the others prevail, Etienne," he instructed the boy.

"You'll be all alone," Etienne said simply.

"I have God with me," William told him, forcing his face to remain a mask. "I'm counting on you to help the elder brothers." Etienne nodded as William looked up toward the others. He met each man's eyes, Ramon and Francesco, Nicolas and Armande. "The Order must go on." He fixed his eyes upon Andre. "What we hold must go on."

Andre averted his gaze, staring at the wet ground.

"Don't do this," Lisette pleaded once more. She reached for him. "You can't face that many by yourself! They'll—"

His glare stopped her. His voice low, so only she could hear, he said, "Don't make me have one of my brothers carry you."

"Come with *me*," she begged. Neither sobbing nor hysterical as she pleaded with him, William saw the strength and spirit he glimpsed in her the first time they spoke back in the alley. She reached out for him no more.

Only the marching could be heard in the silence. All eyes but Andre's were on William as he stood before the bridge. Odo stepped in close to him.

"William," he began.

William stared into his old friend's gaze. "This is my reason," he told Odo quietly, so only he could hear. "I'll catch up when I can."

Brave Horatius, Odo thought, *you'll let none pass.*

Understanding struck him suddenly and hard. No, not Horatius, he realized, grasping his brother's intent.

Leonidas.

For a long moment, Odo studied him, mournful and proud. His throat suddenly raw, Odo could barely rasp the words out, commendation and command:

"Be *glorious*, Brother."

Odo whirled, composed himself, and strode past the others, taking the point.

"Let's move," he commanded, marching into the dark street.

Once by one, the Templars fell in behind him. Lisette hesitated, glancing over her shoulder at the bridge. She felt a gentle hand and turned to find Ramon taking her by the arm, leading her away.

William turned back to the bridge. With his right hand, he crossed himself before drawing his blade with a slow hiss of metal and a gleam of bright steel. Praying quietly, he mounted the bridge as he shrugged off his dark cloak, sword in hand.

CHAPTER XXIV

William brought his sword down hard on the Mameluk's skull, splitting and crushing bone beneath the warrior's white turban. The young Templar gathered himself behind his shield, boots digging in as the line slowly slipped back. Shoulder to shoulder with his brothers he fought. But the assault on St. Anthony's Gate had been fruitless, costing the crusaders too many brave men as they pressed for the gate's controls.

The Accursed Tower, as the knights had named it since planning the assault, remained in Saracen hands.

English knights, led by Otho De Grandison, attacked north of the gate, drawing scores of Saracen fighters from the tower to the northeast wall. The distraction wasn't enough. Even with the Templars, the Hospitallers, the Teutonic Knights and the Knights of the Order of St. Lazarus marshalled together with the remnants of the city garrison, the Mameluks were too fierce, too terrible, and most importantly, too numerous to drive back. Thousands of their forces stormed screaming through the gates and the breach into the city, trumpets blaring victory.

William knew this would be the end, his last fight— Templars didn't retreat, didn't surrender, and were never, ever ransomed. They would fight until the last man, the force here at the wall giving themselves up to buy more time for those at their tower overlooking the sea.

His shield was beaten almost to scrap, edges folding, surface caving and splintering, hammered by the unyielding attacks. He stabbed out with his sword, feeling the blade sink into flesh and glance off bone. The battle roared in his ears. Screams and drums drowned out the screech of the arrow volley as it hailed down, a horrifying surprise. Shafts bounced off helmet and shield, and some punctured flesh. Beside him, Grandmaster De Beaujeu lifted his sword high and an arrow buried itself under his arm.

The Grandmaster fell. William scrabbled backward, the other Templars closing ranks to seal the line. Kneeling in the gore, he tore away the Grandmaster's helm. The old Templar's eyes fluttered open.

"I'll get you back to our keep," William told him.

Before De Beaujeu could instruct them otherwise, three more Templars broke off from the fighting. Grasping the corners of the Grandmaster's white cloak as a makeshift litter, they lifted him and carried him off.

As they shuffled over the streets, the Grandmaster fought to sit up. His face contorted, grimacing teeth bright through his beard. He cried out once before sagging back, demanding his knights put him down.

Rounding the first bend in the avenue, they found Amalric, brother of the king of Cyprus, and several of the lesser nobles, on groomed horses with flowers and ribbons braided into their manes. They sat, talking amongst themselves as if at court rather than defending a city besieged. In full and spotless armor, they'd gathered more than a thousand paces down the narrow, winding street, far behind the fighting, a contingent of knights from the Cypriot garrison before them—between the nobles and the battle.

"I pray God forgives you your cowardice," a voice shouted out at De Beaujeu from among them as the Templars passed. William stopped, and so did his brothers, stunned by the curses and jeers that followed the insult. Royal brother of the king of Cyprus or no, if they hadn't been conducting the Grandmaster to the Hospitallers—

"Put me down," Grandmaster De Beaujeu demanded in an angry groan. "I said stop and put me down!"

Hesitant, the Templars complied. They lowered his feet and he stood on unsteady legs. The Grandmaster drew himself up as he turned to the nobles.

"What more would you have of me?" he shouted back at Amalric and his men. His tired eyes locked on them, the nobles grew silent. A few looked away as if distracted.

The Grandmaster raised his arm. The jutting shaft was plain in his side, a stain of vivid red running bright and wet well past his waist.

"See the wound? I am dead."

If Amalric and the others felt any horror or sympathy, William saw it not at all. After staring long at the wounded Grandmaster, the nobles closed in close amongst themselves.

Grandmaster De Beaujeu winced. His breath hissed through his teeth as he lowered his arm. Turning his back on the nobles, he marched slowly back to his men and walked past them.

William and the other brothers followed. "Grandmaster, please let us—"

He shook his head, commanding silence with an impatient hand. William watched the Grandmaster press on. His expression distant, his features set, Grandmaster De Beaujeu hobbled down the steep street that led to the harbor gate and the sea.

CHAPTER XXV

So far, they'd found nothing.

Curfew, along with the night's storms, left the streets deserted. Captain De Valery slouched in his saddle as his horse plodded along. Infantry was always slower than cavalry, but fanning out through the streets, his foot soldiers searched each intersection and each alleyway. They were advancing at less than a crawl.

He worried the fugitives might give up stealth for speed. At an all-out run, they could improve their lead on his inching to where they'd have no real chance of ensnaring them. Silently, he cursed the accounting that left him the only horseman in the company for the night.

His cheek pained him. The swelling and the burning of the slash, and the scar it would leave, kept at the front of his thoughts. One more thing, he thought, to take out of the monks' hides when he caught up with them.

"Captain!" one of the men called from ahead. The man who called out stood at the end of the street, waving his arm for the captain to see him. De Valery spurred his horse into a trot.

The avenue they were on ended at the steep banks of a canal. De Valery slowed his horse. Before him, a lone, narrow footbridge spanned the channel. De Valery stopped, and waved his men to him. The signal was passed and relayed, and after a few moments, his entire company had formed around him at the end of the bridge.

Ahead, on the bridge, stood one man.

De Valery peered into the darkness, discerning at first nothing more than a silhouette in the shadows. As he stared, he came to recognize the figure: the one who had so brazenly faced him, sword raised, in the street minutes ago. The man from *Le Basilisk et Chalice* who'd murdered his uncle and dealt him the slash on his face.

The man stood alone. His weapon low but ready, his head was bowed prayerfully. Free from his disguise, his armor was plainly in view, the iron rings of his mail hauberk and chausses dark, the polished ailettes upon his shoulders glinting, catching what little light there was. No longer concealed by the dark cloak, the white of his mantle and the bright crimson of the cross over his heart were unmistakable.

As De Valery had suspected. The fugitives were Templars.

He eyed the one on the bridge coldly and wheeled his horse about to look over his troops.

"You," he barked at one young soldier whose name he hadn't cared to put to memory.

The young soldier snapped to attention. Dressed better than the other troops, he had a sword buckled at his hip. De Valery dimly recalled from when his uncle first assigned him to his company that the man was the bastard of some lower noble, a place in His Majesty's Army bought so he could perhaps earn some status through service to the king.

Tonight would be his chance. De Valery leaned from his horse. "You go and arrest that arrogant Templar bastard."

The young man squared his shoulders and made for the bridge, walking past De Valery's sergeant. The two fingers Sergeant Luc Caym lost in the Crusades began to itch. The veteran cursed through clenched teeth the phantom digits he could do nothing to scratch as he watched the young soldier step on the bridge and draw his sword.

The Templar stood, unmoving. Several paces away from him, the young soldier slowed to an uncertain stop. "In the name of His Royal Majesty, King Philip," he began, finding his own voice loud in the silence. "You are hereby—"

"Go." William cut him off.

Incredulous, the young man's voice trailed off. He stared at the Templar.

William's voice was little more than a whisper only the young man before him could hear. "Stand down. Turn back. Just go. This road now passes through me."

The young soldier's cheeks burned. He'd suffered enough humiliation for his birth, and only his unacknowledged father's generosity had gotten him this far from the taunts and abuse he'd suffered in his mother's countryside village.

He raised his sword, and with an outraged cry, charged at William.

William shifted almost casually. His foot slid back and his sword flashed out, cutting the young soldier down mid-stride.

The young man's body dropped to the deck of the bridge with a heavy thump. De Valery sat in his saddle and stared. His belly went tight and something in his chest stung. The troops beneath him gaped in stunned silence as the fugitive retreated behind the fallen body lowering his weapon and withdrawing to his original stance.

"Insolent—" De Valery rasped. He spun and looked over his company. His eyes fell across three standing together—broad-shouldered brothers, Briand Le Sarrasin and Michel Le Tristram, and their friend Daniel, christened in jest "Le Petite" by the company. De Valery remembered the three. The first day of his command, they impressed him at melee training, the three fighting back-to-back with wooden and blunted weapons, nearly defeating the rest of the company by themselves.

"You three," he called. He stabbed a finger at the bridge. "Bring him here."

Michel and Daniel drew swords. Briand handed away his torch and tugged an axe from his belt. The three pushed their way through the assembled troops, and made their way for the bridge.

William stood alone as they stalked near. Briand at the lead, Daniel and Michel squeezed almost side-by-side behind him on the narrow footbridge. With a sudden howl, Briand leapt at William over the fallen soldier's body, the heavy axe head high. Michel and Daniel closed in behind him, blades flashing.

Before the axe could fall, William burst forward. His blade trailing behind him, he dashed past Daniel, hamstringing him with a slash across his thigh. The soldier toppled, blade clattering on the stone deck while he clutched at his nearly severed leg.

William's sword flashed high, parrying Michel's attack and riposting with a blow across the soldier's throat. Blood spraying from his awful wound, Michel fell back.

The Templar's weapon spun in his hand. The point reversed, the blade slipping under his own arm, between elbow and ribs, aimed straight behind. Both hands on the hilt, he thrust it back into the axe-wielding Briand, halting him as he had begun to turn.

William yanked his sword from Briand's body, and his lifeless form crumpled. He turned on Daniel.

The last of the three soldiers had pulled himself almost standing against the bridge's low wall. His sword on the ground where he dropped it, he clawed for the weapon, struggled to reach it, one leg useless and bleeding. He froze as William turned on him.

"Stay down," William rasped as he neared.

Daniel's mouth moved but produced no words. He strained again, desperate to reach his fallen sword.

William stepped in on him. Clutching the terrified soldier by the tunic, he shoved him over the wall. The soldier screamed a long moment, followed by a loud splash and more cries, softer and pained.

William resumed his position on the bridge, three corpses scattered before him.

De Valery stared in disbelief, shamed and chagrined. Four men, and the Templar stood as before. If it took all the men he had...

Angrily, he waved his troops forward, ordering more onto the bridge.

"Alive or dead, you bring him to me!" he shouted, flecks of foam spraying from his mouth.

A half-dozen more soldiers rushed the bridge. But they slowed as they mounted it, unable to proceed on the narrow span more than two across.

Impassive, William watched them race for him. In his right hand, he held his bloodied sword loose and ready. His free hand reached purposefully to his hip and drew his long dagger.

CHAPTER XXVI

Odo at the point, the Templars fled through the night at all but a full run.

Brother Ramon tended to Lisette, doing his best to keep them from being left behind. The girl was like a sleepwalker, empty-eyed and almost limp. Ramon was almost dragging her and considered hoisting the girl over his shoulder and carrying her.

A shambling flight of rough-cut stairs led them down a steep hillside, the muddied, wet stones treacherous under their hasty feet. More then once, one of them slipped, a brother's hand steadying a tumble.

At the bottom, they found the stairs led into another alley. Dark and narrow, it was no more than a slim space between two houses, rocky and uneven and strewn with garbage from the dwellers on either side. Odo led them quickly through the slogging mess, emerging on the next street in the middle of a wide, open intersection. Staying close to the buildings, he halted them. They waited, so intent on what lay ahead and what might still ensnare them from behind, none noticed Etienne's small hands wiping tears from his red-rimmed eyes.

Odo moved into the street, scouting cautiously ahead.

"This running grows tiresome," Armande whispered to Francesco.

"It's not our way," Francesco agreed, pressed to the wall beside him." But outnumbered, what choice have we?

"We're soldiers," said Armande. "Warriors. And we're hiding like rabbits."

Francesco began to answer when Odo signalled for them to follow. Francesco stalked into the dark after him. Armande, then

Nicolas followed, with Andre and Etienne close behind. But as Ramon took after them, Lisette dug her heels into the ground, pulling back on Ramon's arm.

"No!" she shrieked.

Odo and the others whirled.

+ + +

At the center of the footbridge over the canal, William whirled, the heart of a maelstrom of weapons and soldiers.

The entire company was upon him.

The Templar was a blur of sharpened steel. He parried and dodged. Deadly thrusts and crippling slashes swept and crashed, one move leading into the next.

The bridge kept them to no more than two at a time before him. Any who mounted the low walls had their legs quickly cut out from under them, some lucky to only be shoved off to a long fall into the canal.

William's white tabard was streaked in wet red. His rustling mail coat was split below his right shoulder, and the tearing pain he felt when he moved his sword told him he was cut, though not deeply. He wished he'd thought of a way to conceal and carry his shield when they'd first fled. When he took the bridge, he'd tugged up his mail coif to cover his head, only to find that the pack carrying his helmet was gone, lost no doubt in the hasty flight from the tavern. The hooded coif would protect him from a blade's edge but not its impact. Without a helmet, he knew, any blow that landed would hit like a hammer to his skull.

So, he decided, he'd have to keep them back.

From his horse, De Valery glowered at the fight on the bridge. Casualties were mounting and his company was being held off by a single man. He inhaled sharply and let the air go as sharply. His lips tight, the wound on his cheek began to bleed. The drops turned cold as they ran down his face. With a gloved finger he flicked them, smearing the blood on his cheek.

His sergeant stood beside him, fixed on the fight ahead. Watching the Templar brought back memories for Sergeant Luc, memories of the Crusades. Some good, some glorious, others were little better than nightmares he knew he'd been awake for. He watched and his concern deepened.

"Sir," he addressed De Valery. He chafed at serving the officer—not because he was reporting to a man younger than some of his own sons, but because he'd merely bought his way to command. "You didn't fight in the Crusades, did you?"

The captain made it obvious he was offended. "No." The answer was bratty even for an aristocrat who'd been handed a commission he could never have earned. "I was too young."

The sergeant kept his eyes on the bridge, on the fight.

"At Antioch," he recalled, "I went into battle alongside a company of Templars, and was glad of it. They were terrifying. Fought like God's own avenging angels."

William could feel the fight chipping away at him. His wounded shoulder felt as if it was on fire, and his lungs ached for respite. He swerved, casting a soldier aside, slashing the trooper below his ear as he went by. One movement led to the next and the next, their assault on him unceasing, each fallen man replaced by another. He thrust and blocked. Drove his pommel into one man's mouth, shattering teeth. Slammed his foot into another's knee, the crunch of sinew and bone snapping followed by an agonized scream. He lashed open another's hand, his blade immediately flashing aside to parry yet another blade.

Somehow, he was holding his own.

De Valery turned angrily to his sergeant. "If you think you owe them some old war debt—"

The sergeant rubbed his left hand against his belt, trying to stop the cursed itching of his long-missing fingers. "Sir, they never broke ranks. No matter the odds, no matter the casualties. I saw them fight outnumbered two-to-one, three-to-one, sometimes five-to-one—"

"I'm sure they were brave," De Valery mocked. Feeling a cold drop run along his cheek, he dabbed at the blood, watching his men fall to the Templar.

The sergeant watched, too. They were getting closer, tighter on the Templar, some clipping his armor before he dispatched them or slipped past. He saw one man trip over one of the fallen, another trying to push past a screaming man with a severed hand. As in the Crusades, their own dead and injured were becoming obstacles, hindering the soldiers' attacks. He knew the Templar knew this.

"Sir," Luc spoke up, his words careful to reflect the respect his tone did not. "As long as he's on that bridge, *sir*, you haven't enough men here to take him."

De Valery felt a chill at his sergeant's words. He looked back to the bridge, at his men crowding its entrance. Almost a third of his company had fallen, and the Templar still held his ground.

The captain turned to the next man nearest him, who had not yet been herded into the melee.

"You," he said, and the soldier turned. "Captain Le Brun and his company were searching one of the next blocks. Find him. Apprise him. Bring him."

The soldier nodded and ran back into the dark and tangled avenues. De Valery leaned forward in his saddle, watching the fight on the footbridge with slitted eyes.

✦ ✦ ✦

Lisette tore her arm free of Ramon's grasp, stumbling back. "We can't leave William behind," she screamed.

Etienne looked to the ground, wiping his eyes and cheeks. "Quiet, girl," Armande retorted.

"I will not," she shouted back. "We have to go back."

Andre turned to Odo. "The galley sets sail at dawn, Brother. We haven't time."

"Cut her loose," Armande said. "She's dead weight only slowing us down."

Ramon reached for her arm. "Come, Lisette. We're losing time."

"But what of William?" she asked, yanking her hand away.

"You heard his orders," Armande said through clenched teeth.

"When did his orders begin to concern you?" Lisette's lip curled.

Armande started at her, his hand coming up. Odo caught him, hooking his elbow with a thick hand.

"She's a woman," Odo said into Armande's ear. "And it proves nothing. You'll only waste our time."

Armande shrugged free Odo's hold and backed off. The girl did not.

"He's your friend," she cried to Odo. He turned his eye upon her as she looked to Etienne. "And for you," she said to the boy, "for you he's like a—"

"Enough," Odo ordered as he closed in on her.

Lisette's voice shook as she looked up at Odo. "We have to go back for him. All those soldiers—"

Odo's voice was little more than a whisper. "That was his decision."

"We have to help William," she said. The corners of her mouth turned down as she stared into Odo's one dark eye. "They'll kill him."

Towering over her, he returned her gaze in silence.

"He's your friend," she repeated almost under her breath.

Odo leaned close. "Don't make my brother's sacrifice an empty one."

Her eyes darted over his thick beard, the eye patch and the scar it failed to hide, his dark, deep-set eye. Then she realized what he'd told her.

She fell back a step and another. Her eyes leapt to each of the Templars, cold and accusing.

"You're all cowards," she cried and spun around. She raced into the dark back the way they'd come.

Ramon started after her, but Francesco caught him, palm flat on his chest.

"She's in God's hands now," he told Ramon. "We still have our own trial to finish."

✝ ✝ ✝

His dagger shattered, William discarded the broken blade, plunging it into the shoulder of his nearest attacker. He tore his mace from his belt. Its spiked head whistled up, blocking yet another sword before lashing out at the soldier holding it.

William fought to keep focused. He'd thinned his attackers' ranks considerably. They knew it, too, and they'd become more wary, certainty fading as the advantage of their numbers slipped.

William was battered, sore, cut in a half-dozen places and bruised in many more. But as he looked at his attackers, at the dead and injured stacked on the bridge, a light sparked for him.

He saw a chance.

Perhaps, *perhaps*, he could do this, defeat the troops here and rejoin the others. Still, the remaining soldiers were fresh, sitting out most of the fight waiting to get at him.

He drove the thoughts from his mind, clearing it as for meditation. If he had any hope of success, he could afford no distraction. He couldn't impose himself in the fight let his own inclinations cloud pure response. He had to be removed, open as in prayer, a conduit for God's will and strength.

Then he heard it, behind him. Footfalls. The rattle of weapons. Hoofbeats.

He deflected an axe head, winding the soldier's arm painfully in his own and trapping the man between himself and another soldier. As the one he'd caught went slack from the blow of his fellow's war hammer, William chanced a glance at his back.

Another full company of men neared.

Led by the officer they'd escaped when fleeing the Temple, they raced for the bridge behind him.

William parried another blade and cracked its wielder's elbow, then tossed him under the feet of the next attacker. Behind him he heard wooden bows creak, strings pulled taut. He steeled himself.

With a shriek, four arrows ripped through his body. The fresh company followed, crashing over him in a great wave. William was swallowed in a surge of men and weapons.

From the street, De Valery watched as the Templar was swept under. He could hear the sounds of flesh and bone, iron and steel, rending, yielding. Blood flew.

The soldiers were all around the Templar, on top of him. Bloodied blades and fists stabbed and slashed, pounding and beating, blow after punishing blow. Captain Le Brun angled for a better view but could see only his soldiers, their weapons thrusting and cleaving, their fists and boots pummelling. He glanced across the bridge at De Valery. The young captain smiled slightly and gave the other officer a grateful nod.

A horrible cry split the air, startling the officers as William exploded from the fight. Streaked with gore, he threw the soldiers aside, and for a moment seemed to tear free of them all...

...only to be dragged back into their midst and disappear, swallowed into the violence.

CHAPTER XXVII

Odo flattened himself against the alley wall and waited. His brothers did the same, all praying they hadn't been seen. A pair of men passed at the mouth of the alley ahead. One with a staff, the other carrying a pike, each wore a dark cap and a dark cloak pulled close against the weather.

The city's Night Watch.

Patrolling the streets at night, they enforced the city's curfew, challenging any they found and taking them into custody if need be.

Odo had failed to see the two as they approached from his right, his blind side, as he crept from the alley. Only their low conversation, carried on the still air of the night's rain, warned him of their approach. He shrank back into the alley, hiding among its shadows.

Behind him, Nicolas fell back into the shadows as well, signaling for the others to do the same. They waited, hearts pounding. Etienne and Brother Andre held their breath, afraid even that sound might give them away.

The watchmen passed, walking deliberately. Their eyes shifted from one side to the other, searching for anything out of the ordinary. The one with the walking staff paused near the alley's mouth. The other kept on and peered into the dark alley.

Armande's hand slipped to his hilt. Nicolas' was upon his. Odo readied to reach out and take the watchman by the face, drag him into the darkness the instant he showed any sign of recognizing any of their group among the shadows. The watchman leaned closer.

His companion called to him. The watchman at the alley looked away, up the street, where his cohort demanded loudly that he keep up so they could finish their rounds. He hurried after him.

Odo's ears strained to hear as the watchmen's footsteps receded and faded away. He looked across the alley at Nicolas, who was slowly returning his dagger to its scabbard. Odo went to his side.

"That was too close," he whispered. "William was right. One eye does make me a bad lookout." He nodded toward the street. "You take point."

Nicolas glided silently ahead. Making his way from the alley into the street, he signed for Odo and the others to stay before disappearing among the shadows.

Looking back, Odo saw all in position in the alley, waiting, watching the street, impassive. All but Etienne.

Behind all the others, the boy was against the wall. Anxious veins and tendons stood out on his thin neck, and his hands were tight, bloodless fists.

Odo slipped back past them and slid alongside the boy. He crouched low, as if concealing his giant frame.

"You're afraid," he whispered.

The boy didn't respond, as if he didn't hear. On the verge of tears, he slowly nodded his head.

"Good," Odo said. "It shows you understand how deadly our situation has become."

"You're not afraid," Etienne said, staring into Brother Odo's dark eye.

"My soul's been tempered in the fires of battle."

The corners of the boy's mouth dropped.

"It's no failure of yours," Odo told him. "Fear springs from uncertainty. The Crusades taught me my faults. And strengths."

"You've lived through worse."

"I'm more certain than a less-tested man."

With the end of his sleeve, Etienne wiped his eyes. He nodded, unrelieved.

"You're unconvinced," Odo said.

"No brother. I believe you've been tested more than I."

"Unconvinced about our situation."

Etienne looked at him, confused. "Brother?"

"I overheard you and Brother Ramon."

The boy bit his lip and waited a long time before he spoke. "I'm afraid God's turned His back on us." Etienne's voice trembled as he finished. Tears welled in his eyes, but he fought them back. "First Brother Bernard, then Brother William. I fear this is God's will for all of us."

"Oh?"

"The king is against us. The Church is against us. Even the girl left us."

Odo leaned close to the boy, face level with his. "Times such as these are meant to test us. Harden our spirits. Polish our souls. Pray for strength, Etienne, and sometimes, God places something like this before you so you can become stronger in meeting it." Odo cast his gaze at the ground. "God does not require our success; He requires only that we struggle for it. Have you given up this fight?"

He hesitated. "No, Brother."

"Have you turned your back on God?"

"No, Brother."

"Then He would never turn on you." Odo stood back up to his full height. Before finishing his first step, he added. "In these dark moments, you must reach out with your faith. You'll feel God's hands holding you, supporting you."

Etienne nodded.

"At the bridge, you showed great courage facing Brother William's choice, and you helped him. You can be strong, boy. Like steel. We need that now."

Etienne sniffled. "Yes, Brother."

"William was counting on you. I'm counting on you, too."

Etienne again wiped his eyes on his sleeve, and then his lip. Odo had decided to step away when the boy whispered, "Brother, what Lisette said when she left—"

"What about it?"

"She barely *knows* Brother William. Why—?" He didn't have the words to finish his question.

Odo stepped back, sank on his haunches again. He kept his voice low. Etienne had to lean forward to hear him.

"She's a girl," Odo said. "One who's been shown little kindness in her life. Never consider any act of kindness insignificant. Remember this, and mark what the slightest good will can mean to some."

Etienne's brow furrowed, and he neither answered nor nodded. Odo stood and returned to the mouth of the alley. Leaning, he saw Nicolas reappear in the street, signaling for the others to follow him. Odo passed on the signal, waving for the other Templars to follow. Single file, they forged on into the night.

The brazier burned in a corner of Grandmaster Jacques De Molay's offices. Imbert stared at the fire, the flames flickering and dancing as the inquisitor fed it scraps of wood and straw. He sniffed, the scent of blood light in the air, and glanced up at the empty door. Gouges from the iron spikes marred the wood above dark, wet streaks. But the man was gone.

He'd ordered De Molay taken down and removed to recover. The thorniest part of the inquisitor's work was deciding how far the interrogated could be driven. For fear of obtaining anything less than a full confession, he could hold nothing back. But excess, at the same time, risked death, wasting time and requiring penance. The Church forbade the taking of a life, even by a chosen inquisitor. Only a king or his justices could assign and carry out a death sentence. Often, though, he worked closely with the court to ensure the proper verdict was found.

Scuffling echoed through the corridors, growing louder as it neared. Imbert placed a few more scraps to the fire, brightening the flames as the edges of the coals glowed orange. His fingers seared as he hurriedly fed in the last of his kindling.

Creaking loudly on iron hinges, the heavy door swung open. Four guards carried in a lifeless prisoner. Stripped naked save for bloody bandages binding his most awful wounds, his body bore marks of terrible abuse, covered over in bruises and bleeding gashes.

Imbert chose not to look up. Instead he stared at the flames, the thinnest bits in the fire blackening and curling.

The guards lurched as their prisoner came to life. Though weak, he wrestled one arm free. The guard he tore away from kicked viciously behind his knee, collapsing the man before driving a fist into his temple.

The prisoner crumpled. Together, the four guards hoisted him onto the Grandmaster's heavy wooden desk. The guard who struck him jabbed an elbow into the prisoner's gut, driving a gasp from him. The guards spread his limbs, stretching and binding them to the table. The prisoner gasped as his arms were bent painfully back and tied in place. His legs were pulled tight, strapped to the table, and his feet jutted over its edge.

The guards lingered, parting as Imbert approached. The prisoner watched them, noting their positions as they melted into the surrounding dark. Imbert studied the beaten and bloody man. His breath rattled dryly over cracked lips. His teeth were ragged and broken, blood collecting at the corners of his mouth and flecking his beard. Darkening to a blotchy purple, his left eye was swollen shut.

Imbert's eyes drilled into him. "In the presence of these witnesses, you will identify yourself and answer to the charges brought against you."

The prisoner's lips parted and a croaking sound issued. He coughed and swallowed, working his tongue around his mouth before answering.

"William of Barking," he rasped, voice grating in his throat. "Brother of the Poor Fellow Knights of Christ and the Temple of Solomon."

Imbert reflected on the Grandmaster's interrogation. The old Templar had been strong, stronger than they'd anticipated, and had not given up as readily as he had estimated.

This William of Barking was younger than the Grandmaster, and one glance over his lean, battered muscles was enough to apprise Imbert of his strength and resolve. The beating had perhaps softened him. But in his years, Imbert had found that beatings also had a way of making some men more resolute.

Particularly fighting men.

Yet he was a servant of God, a monk, and Imbert thought it best to approach him as a figure of authority. "William of Barking," he intoned as if beginning a mass, "you and your Order are accused of the most vile and obscene heresies, including denial of our Lord, desecration of His presence, worship of false idols, sodomy—"

"I am William of Barking," William repeated from the table, eyes closed. "Brother of the Poor Fellow Knights of Christ and the Temple of Solomon."

Disorientation, Imbert decided. But confusion might help things proceed. "You will describe what you have done," he ordered. "You will describe what you have witnessed others do."

"I am William of Barking—" the words were stronger. "Brother of the Poor Fellow Knights of Christ and the Temple of Solomon."

Imbert understood. "You are not a prisoner of war!" he nearly shouted.

"I'm a soldier in God's army," William explained quietly. "And..." He glanced over the restraints binding him to the table before looking back to the inquisitor conclusively.

"And *we* are God's hammer against evil," Imbert insisted. "You *will* answer these questions."

William stared at him with his one good eye. He inhaled, wincing, and let the breath go. "I have witnessed no such things."

"A lie," said Imbert. "Evil goes on behind the walls of your Order's temple. We have statements. Confessions." He stalked away, letting the silence of the dark room fill the air. William closed his eyes, breathing slowly. He felt a sharp dig in his side each time he inhaled.

Imbert continued. "You will tell me, William of Barking. Describe for me the Templar Order's obscene rituals, and the four-faced demon head your Order worships."

William's concentration broke. He looked at Imbert, the swollen knots on his face and head pressing on him painfully. His cracked lips parted, and recognition sparked faintly in his eye.

Imbert knew he'd found something.

"There's no demon head," William met his gaze.

Imbert began circling the table, slowly, his dark eyes locked his heretic prisoner. William watched him as best he could, losing sight of the inquisitor when the pain of craning his neck to follow became too great. So, he laid his head back and listened, tracking the Dominican by the sounds of his soft footfalls and the rustling of his habit.

The inquisitor had stopped at the head of the table, directly behind William, above his head. William heard more footsteps, boots on the polished floor, walking away. He heard a scrape of iron on stone, and the booted footsteps returned. Even through his closed eyelids, the room grew lighter.

Letting his eyes fall open, William saw one of the guards carrying the brazier from the corner of the room to the desk where he was tied down. The brazier sat low. William couldn't see it over the edge of the desk. He didn't recognize the thing, and he knew it hadn't been in the Grandmaster's office when he'd spoken with him there last.

The guard stepped from sight. After a moment, the inquisitor paced into view. Wordlessly, he looked William over again.

"You speak French well," Imbert said finally. "For an Englishman."

William put his head back again. *"Latina mea melior est,"* he breathed.

Imbert refused to react. *My Latin is better.* The Templar's enunciation and diction was perfect. He was challenging him, baiting him, showing that he was learned. This Brother William was not just one of the bodies, one of the disaffected nobles or excommunicated mercenaries the military Orders recruited to fill out their ranks and feed battles.

"So it is," Imbert acknowledged, still in French.

"Kaif Arabi?" William asked.

Imbert fought to keep his face from contorting, but his mouth puckered, and one of his eyes narrowed. *How is your Arabic?* William had asked, probing at the inquisitor. In the Crusades, it was a matter of course that a knight and his retainers learned Arabic so each could understand and make himself understood to the people of the Mediterranean. Knowledge of the language was essential to conduct business with local merchants, and especially when negotiating with sultans and their generals. William knew it was unlikely, to the point of impossible, that this Dominican had ever learned it. He was surprised he recognized it.

"You will not speak that devil tongue in my presence," Imbert threatened.

"It's the language of trade and parley in the Holy Land." William said. "But then, you've never been to the Holy Land or visited the lands of our Lord's birth and ministry, have you?"

Imbert's cheeks flushed. "You are here to answer *my* questions."

"I have answered them."

Imbert stared into his prisoner's eyes, one purple and black and swollen almost shut, the other clear. He waved one of the guard's closer and again began circling the table slowly.

"We will arrive at the truth." He indicated the foot of the table to the guard, who William saw was carrying a small bucket.

William lifted his head, straining to look down his length. The guard produced a creased, greasy cloth and scooped it into the bucket, drawing out a handful of thick, lardy fat. He began smearing it on William's left foot. Cold and slippery, it clung to his skin, clogging between his toes, smelling faint and rancid.

Imbert slowly stalked to the foot of the table as the guard strode off, lost again to William in the surrounding shadows. The Templar's cheek and eye throbbed as he watched the inquisitor inspect the guard's work.

"I'm confident you will share all your sins before morning," Imbert said.

CHAPTER XXVIII

Lisette crept alone through the empty streets. She picked her way among the puddles and muddied dung. Long-shuttered windows and dark doorways reminded her she was alone and that she shouldn't be in this quarter of the city alone.

She didn't care to be out alone at night. Even as streetwise as she was, it was dangerous, as her brush with the blacksmith and his friends back in the alley had proved. *If it hadn't been for William, the Templar...* She put the thought out of her mind. She'd had the situation in hand. A night of soreness and a few days of bruises would have been the worst of it. Maybe the men had no intention of paying her, but hadn't she taken her payment from them?

Nonetheless, William had helped her and expected nothing for it, to her surprise. And when she cornered him about the threat the men he'd run off still posed her, he offered to take her with him.

She stopped. At first she thought she heard distant voices, but decided it was a trick of the clear night air, perhaps the mumblings of a sleeping townsman carried and magnified. She started forth again, her foot sliding out from under her. Her toes slid beneath the mud, burying her foot before stopping sharply on a jagged rock concealed beneath the slop.

She cursed loudly and yanked her slipper from the muck. Shaking it clean, she spat, cursing in her mind the knights she'd left. The uncaring cowards. Dear William was their friend, and as certain as he'd seemed, he could never stand against an entire company of soldiers. Courage wasn't always enough when the odds were so overwhelming.

She stopped. What then, did she intend to do even if she could find her way back to him? She pictured him, wounded and bleeding, limping determinedly for the docks. She could help him, bind his wounds, and slip under his arm to support him.

Lisette heard the voices again, and she realized it was no drowsy mumbling, no trick of the air. Someone was near. Low moans and pained gasps drifted to her ears, too distant to make out. Heart pounding, she replaced her shoe and slithered cautiously, peering around the corner.

The footbridge where they'd left William was ahead. Planted upright where the thick mud would hold them, a few scattered torches flickered, throwing shifting light over the street.

Injured royal soldiers sat in the muck, gasping and grinding their teeth. Some minded their own bloody wounds, and others tended the gaping slashes and broken bones of others. Lisette gasped as she saw blood fountain from a reclining man's shoulder below his neck. He cried out even as the soldier tending him pressed down on the terrible wound with a handful of his wadded tunic. Beyond the two, she saw more just as bloody but unmoving, lain out in the street's cold mud, eyes blank and unblinking.

Lisette's eyes sprang with hope. As she watched two soldiers drag a lifeless third and dump him among the deceased, her mind raced. So many injured, so many dead. Her heart leapt at the prospect. Perhaps, then, dear William yet lived.

Voices came, too closely. Startled, she stifled a cry of surprise as a large and burly soldier tramped from around the next building, a smaller, pinch-faced soldier on his heels, neither more than a few paces from her.

They whipped their gazes toward the abrupt movement in the building's shadows.

"You there," the big one shouted at her. "Halt!"

Her chest heaved with nervous panting, and with no further thought, she ran.

"Halt!" repeated the smaller soldier. His dark eyes were like a rat's. Lisette took only two steps when she felt a hand clamp down on her arm and drag her back. Slipping in the mud, she yanked back on her arm, but she couldn't break the big soldier's hold. He pulled her harder and spun her around, backhanding her and driving the girl from her feet. She crashed against the plastered wall she'd hid behind and fell.

Her face stung. She could feel her dress dampen, wicking the dirty mud. The two soldiers loomed over her.

"Curfew was hours ago," the big one said.

Lisette stared back saying nothing. The burly soldier clamped his big hand on her arm and yanked her roughly to her feet.

"What are you doing here?" he demanded. He closed on her. Lisette struggled, but the soldier's hand clamped harder, painfully, on her arm. Her eyes searched the street, and the soldier shook her for her silence.

The second soldier's black eyes fell over her battered face, lovely in spite of the injuries, and fell upon her ribboned shoulders. Lips parting, his eyes darted to her hands, and he saw the tattered gloves, stained dark from slips and falls in the mired street. His eyes narrowed, and his thin lips stretched into a flat smile.

"I know what she's doing here."

The big soldier looked at him, uncomprehending. The smaller one pushed between the two and seized the girl, his fingers digging into her arms. Lisette didn't like the glassy cold of his eyes as they traced up from her torn and muddy skirt to her neck until meeting hers.

"She's trying to earn a little silver," he said.

Lisette tensed as he pulled her close, kissed her hard. She stopped fighting him after a moment, and kissed him back. The rat-eyed soldier released her with a shove and turned to his friend.

"See?"

Lisette went along. Soldiers always wanted girls. She knew, from experience, that want made them careless. Perhaps she could earn a little silver from this.

The burly soldier yanked her to him. Clutching her close, he mashed his lips against hers, his breath heavy with onions and wine. Lisette, though, was a professional. She was accustomed to coarse handling and the less than pleasing tang her work oft required her to bear. She kissed him back, hard, lips gnawing hungrily on his. The soldier started to turn away, break the embrace, but she held him, stealing the very air from him until he could stand it no more and tore free. Lisette smiled at the burly soldier as he caught his breath. She eyed him eagerly as she'd learned to do from the more experienced girls. As the two looked her over, she tugged at the laces at the top of her dress with a professional's practice.

"What's going on here?" a new voice challenged behind her. Her heart jumped. But the two soldiers looked more irritated than concerned. She chanced a sly glance over her shoulder.

Two more soldiers had appeared from around the same corner as the first pair. One, though almost as tall as the burly soldier that found her, had the face of a child, with round, smooth cheeks, wide eyes, and a broad brow under a tangle of wavy hair. The other had a face that bothered her; with a mouth and eyes too small for his face, all tilted up at an angle that lent cruelness to his expression.

She beamed at them both, her smile a dazzling, inviting mask.

"I think," she heard the one with the cold, black eyes say, "we've found a more pleasing way to pass this watch."

She felt a groping hand tug at her skirts. She swiveled away, pulling back, feeling the skirt go tight before her knotted repairs began to pop. Lisette faked a squealing laugh and pulled her skirt from the soldier's grasp, careful to reveal a flash of her bare leg.

"Easy, boys," she breathed playfully. Confidence fueled her smile. She gathered her skirts to hide her flesh again. "As long as there's enough silver, there's plenty of this to go around." She knew the kind. They'd take turns, but not take long, and she could be on her way.

"Who said anything about silver?" the one with the boy's face said behind her, snatching at her skirt. She heard the fabric rip, and she whirled, lifting her professional facade in a sly, expectant smile.

Their hands were all over her, pulling and pawing. They all had the same smell of onions and wine. The boyish one squeezed in past the others. He pressed up close to her. His hard, groping hands were rough and calloused, scraping her skin beneath her dress. At her waist, the hands stumbled over her purse, and she felt the tiny sack slip away. Lisette clawed for it, but another soldier caught her by the wrist and whirled her around to him.

She tore herself away, frantic over the purse and her silver. She whirled, her facade slipping. Eyes darting over the men, she saw her purse in the hand of the one with the cruel, small features. He hefted it, pleased with its weight.

"That's mine!" she cried. She clawed for it again, but her fingers found empty air, the soldier snatching it back as the burly one yanked her to him.

He mashed into her, kissing her sloppily. Wide open, Lisette's eyes strayed to the purse, and the soldier weighing it in his hand. His lip jutted out and he nodded to himself.

She'd torn her mouth away from the burly soldier's when her arms were pulled behind her and her wrists pinned together. Pain shot up to her shoulders.

"Hey," she tried to tease, "you don't need to do that." Strain made her voice shrill.

The soldier with the boy's face leaned in close from behind. His cheek was as smooth and soft as a girl's on hers.

"I like to," he said in her ear.

The corners of her mouth twitched, and Lisette smiled, warm and carefree. She tried to shrug, agreeable and good-natured, but the boyish soldier pulled her arms tighter, crossing her wrists behind her. Her shoulders throbbed.

"You're hurting me," she said gently.

"Don't say you don't like it," the soldier said into her ear.

Her eyes flitted wildly over the soldiers and the street. The big, burly soldier was unfastening his belt. The one with the rat's eyes looked at her hungrily. The one with the features too small for his face stared expectantly down the street. Her eyes darted from one to the other, desperate for her money.

Lisette forced a smile. "I thought we were having fun."

"We are," the boyish one answered. With both her thin arms in one hand, he grabbed her hair with the other and jerked her head back. He covered her mouth with his in a suffocating kiss, like the blacksmith's, she realized with cold fear. Too late, she began to struggle.

The boyish soldier held her fast, fumbling at her skirts. Her hands trapped, she couldn't reach her hidden knife. Her eyes searched wildly for some way of escape.

Out of the corner of her eye, down the street where she'd spied all the casualties, she caught sight of a man on horseback. Head down, riding slowly, he surveyed the avenue. His uniform was the finery of an officer. Long blond hair glowed golden on his shoulders where the dancing torchlight fell upon it. Lisette recognized Captain Érard De Valery instantly. She knew he knew her.

She whipped her head to the side, tearing her mouth free from the soldier's.

"Captain!" she screamed.

The burly soldier's eyes were fearful. Clutching his belt to his waist with one hand, he punched the girl in the stomach to silence her. Lisette heaved and doubled over. De Valery's attention whipped in her direction. The boyish soldier slipped his hand from Lisette's hair, clamping it over her mouth.

The captain saw them. Bringing his mount about, he trotted toward them, squinting at the darkness. He saw the girl in the hands of his soldiers, one pressed tight behind her with a hand over her mouth, another clutching at his belt while the rest leered. He looked at the girl, met her gaze, uncaring. He sniffed, and turned his horse around, shaking his head.

Lisette saw the soldiers were scared, and she knew they'd become angry. They saw their captain cared not what they did with her. She squirmed harder and managed to twist her face free of the soldier's hand.

"Captain, I know where they are!"

De Valery whirled in his saddle and locked his eyes on the girl. She was familiar, and so he urged his horse forward.

"Desist," he ordered. Each soldier froze, uncertain now if the captain meant to punish them.

De Valery leaned toward Lisette. "What did you say?"

"I said I know where they are."

"Who?" he asked cautiously. He rode closer. Lisette saw how the captain cowed his men. She yanked her arms free of the boyish one's grip and cast him a venomous look before turning back to the captain.

"The ones you're searching for." Her voice was like a trader's. "The Templars."

"Release her," Captain De Valery ordered, and the soldiers skulked back. "Come here, girl."

Lisette lifted her chin, haughty, and drew nearer the officer. He could see the bruises on her face and recognized them. Not the solders' doing. He'd seen them before, earlier that night. He realized he knew the girl.

He slid down from his saddle and approached her.

"They call you Solange, don't they?"

CHAPTER XXIX

Imbert stood at the foot of the table where William was tied down. Before him, the brazier flickered. The flame swayed in its iron dish. With a long knife, he carefully prodded at the coals, studying the way the embers grew brighter and darker as he turned and arranged them with the dagger's point, the blade blackening where the flames touched it.

For a long time, he silently tended the fire, its crackle and pops all there was to hear. William lay back, for the moment giving up testing his bonds any further. His entire body pained him, sharply in his back where he'd been stabbed, stinging in his shoulders where he'd been cut. His face throbbed, his skull tender from jaw to crown from the blows he'd taken. He was certain of broken bones in his hands and ribs, and at the back of his throat, he could taste his own blood.

He was grateful for the respite. Keeping his breathing shallow for the pain in his side, he prayed, the words he pronounced in his heart focusing him, distracting from his sufferings.

"What do you know of pain, Brother William of Barking?" the inquisitor asked.

In his heart, William laughed at what he knew Brother Odo's response would be. He opened his eyes, and stared straight up at the dark above him.

"Only what the Crusades taught me."

"Yes." Imbert poked at the coals William could not see him clearly. "Your brethren all seem proud of what they've suffered."

"It was an honor. For God's glory."

Imbert had learned these men feared little after surviving those faraway wars. Nothing intimidated them. His pride still smarted over one arrogant Templar—the first he'd interrogated that night—who laughed at him outright when he intimated the suffering the Templar would face should he not confess. *I've marched and fought for days in full armor under sun so strong it heated helmets until they were like ovens, cooking men's brains in their own skulls,* he'd said, staring into Imbert's eyes. *I've watched a prisoner beaten, bound, and sewn into the steaming carcass of a dead pack mule. I've stood on city walls beside men impaled on pikes, lance points jutting out from inside their throats as they coughed pleas for death. I've seen my own brothers rent limb from limb at the hands of the Saracen, and what was left cut into still smaller pieces, all the while gasping for God's mercy. Torturer, you cannot threaten anything worse than I've lived.*

And I would live it all, bear it all over again for God's glory.

These Templars were a breed apart, hale and defiant. Imbert learned that night how must escalate his questioning.

"Fire is purifying, Brother William," he said, keeping his gaze on the flames. Isolated in their temples from the Church and society, the Templars were polluted by their heretic masters and their obscene, blasphemous practices. He jabbed his dagger into the embers again. "It burns away contamination and corruption, and brings forth Truth." Satisfied with the brazier and its coals, he slid it casually under William's greased foot.

The pain was immediate on his heel, scorching, blistering. William's body snapped taut, straining against the leather straps. The veins in his neck bulged and his teeth gritted as his foot failed to kick free of the bonds.

Imbert pushed the brazier away and watched his subject, as if from a distance. William sagged, panting. No other sound escaped his lips.

Imbert looked him over. The fat spread over the Templar's foot and ran, watery, dripping from his heel to the dark stone floor. "Now, admit the charges," Imbert commanded. "Confess your sins to me."

"I've done nothing you claim."

"Your brethren, then. I know every man in such a large association cannot be corrupted. Just as I know not every man could be pure. Tell me what *they* have done. If not all the accusations, then which ones? What have you witnessed, William?"

William put his head back.

"Most men confess at the mere suggestion of torture," the inquisitor continued. "But you and your kind don't respond to suggestion." The iron stand scraping on the floor as he again slipped the brazier under William's foot. "So I won't waste my time."

William went stiff, straining against the leather straps. His breath in short, clawing gasps, all the pain throughout his body drained and collected in his burning foot. He whipped his head from side to side as a sputtering sizzle began to fill the air.

Impassive, distant, Imbert waited.

Lisette faced the handsome young captain, her eyes needy and helpless.

Captain De Valery took her aside. Across the street, the four soldiers hung their heads and paced worriedly, casting long glances as the captain and the girl talked in the shadows of a tall house.

Captain De Valery stood too close to Lisette and she noticed, sliding closer to him. He whispered to her, eyes darting with interested over her. She thanked him, praised him, punctuating her gratitude and praises with her dazzling smile. This was the part of her work she enjoyed, the attention of men and the control her charm and beauty gave her over them. Nobles were always the easiest, she found. They understood the game of it as she did, appreciating the play more than the prize and paying the best.

She allowed her naked thigh to slip from the long rip in her skirts, kept her lips parted as she listened to him. De Valery noticed.

"You're sure the ship is docked there?" he asked her.

"That's where they think it is. Only the young one was given the instructions.

"The boy?"

"No, though he's not much older. The youngest of the knights."

"He'd have no reason to lie," De Valery thought aloud. "And they have no other plan?"

Lisette slipped a hand on his shoulder, her fingertips lingering. "They've no other means of escape."

"Those docks aren't far from here. Even with their lead, they may be moving slowly, fearful of capture."

"Oh very slowly. At least while I was with them." Lisette let her fingers drift up his neck, caressing him gently. Her touch had the effect she planned, and the captain turned back to her. He leaned in close, and she could feel his breath warm upon her cheek. She lifted her chin, pursed her lips.

The captain stopped.

His brow furrowed. And his eyes softened. "Poor Solange," he began, and the girl lowered her chin, seeing the cue. "They dragged you from *Le Basilisk et Chalice*, didn't they?"

Lisette put her lip out. Turning the corners of her mouth down sadly, she nodded like a hurt little girl. Her pale eyes were a child's, sad and watery.

She knew how freely the captain and his uncle spread their silver when they were at the tavern. The night would not be a loss.

De Valery lingered. "If they're tarrying as you say, we can make straight for their boat, cut them off there."

She pushed her bare knee against his leg. He looked deeply into her eyes and turned away.

"You're leaving?" she called after him.

"Duty, my precious jewel." He made for his horse, striding over the muck.

Lisette glanced nervously at the four soldiers. Seeing their officer coming toward them, their pacing had grown less nervous and more restless, hungry, like hounds waiting to be fed. She hurried after him.

He had his foot in the stirrup when she caught up with him, a few paces from the four soldiers. "Captain," she started.

"Another time, Solange."

She glanced past the horse's haunches. The boyish soldier was a pace closer.

"But—"

"Perhaps when I see you next at *Le Basilisk*. If what you've told me is true, I must move." His voice hardened at the end. Lisette glanced back at the soldiers, and saw the black-eyed one and the big one had crept nearer.

"But your soldiers," her voice was pleading.

Captain De Valery climbed into his saddle. He brought the horse around, forcing the girl to spring back to avoid its hooves. She almost lost her footing in the mud.

The captain and horse stood directly between Lisette and the four soldiers. He indicated them to her with a cock of his head. "They're like dogs." He looked to his other side, and called out, "Well done, men."

He turned back to Lisette.

"They're good dogs, and every now and again, you have to reward them with scraps."

Lisette felt her heart stop at his words. Her mouth fell open. He had believed her. She'd been sure he would let her go, perhaps pay her first, and she could continue looking, searching.

De Valery started away at a trot, leaving Lisette alone with the four soldiers.

"We move in five minutes," he called to his troops. "Be done with the whore by then."

"No!" Lisette screamed, tears burning in her eyes.

De Valery urged his horse to a gallop, headed back for the footbridge. Lisette turned back and was swallowed by the hungry gang.

✝ ✝ ✝

Tears squeezed from William's eyes, streaking his sweat-slicked face. The bitter stench of his own charring flesh filled the air along with the sizzling hiss of the burning oil. He thrashed on the table, his limbs pinned. His broken teeth gritted together as the sinews of his slashed and battered arms strained against the leather straps. His shoulders and neck quivered and shook, a scream fighting to tear itself from his throat.

Writhing on the table, he panted sharply, breathing faint words in a fevered whisper.

"Crux mihi certa salus. Crux est quam semper adoro—"

The murmurings drew the inquisitor. He listened, recognizing after a moment the Templar's words.

The Cross is my sure salvation. The Templar was praying. *The Cross I ever adore.* Imbert saw a weakness he could seize.

"Yes," he praised his agonized prisoner. He slid the brazier away from William's foot. The iron sounded hollow on the stone as the sizzling of the oil sputtered and died.

William groaned. The torment gave way to burning pain. The fire's crackle and the Templar's breathless whisperings were all Imbert heard in the dark office.

"Crux Domini mecum. Crux mihi refugium."

Imbert circled the table, keeping wide of its edges, hugging the shadows and out of William's sight. *The Cross of my Lord is with me. The Cross is my refuge.* The Sixth Psalm. The Templar had fallen back on prayer, a sure sign he'd given up hope of control in the interrogation and chosen to place his trust in God's power and intervention.

In that room, Imbert had become the instrument of His intervention. The Templar had ceded him authority. Confession would soon be at hand.

William continued, *"Domine, ne in furore tuo arguas me, neque in ira tua corripias me—"*

"Yes," Imbert urged him. *O Lord, do not reprove me in Thy wrath, nor in Thy anger chastise me.* "Yes, Brother William, pray. Pray for mercy."

"Miserere mei, Domine, quoniam infirmus sum; sana me, Domine—"

Imbert's mind raced back over the psalm. *Have mercy on me, Lord, for I am weak,* the Templar was saying, *heal me, Lord, for my body is in torment—*

"Quoniam conturbata sunt ossa mea," he finished the psalm with the knight. The pain, the pleading. Imbert knew how to direct this to confession.

"You can end this now, Brother William," he said lovingly, almost paternally.

William's voice did not waver as the inquisitor spoke over his hushed, desperate prayers. *"Et anima mea turbata est valde, sed tu, Domine, usquequo? Convertere, Domine, eripe animam meam; salvum me fac propter misericordiam tuam."*

Imbert smiled inwardly. *And my soul is greatly troubled, but thou, O Lord, how long? Turn to me, O Lord, and deliver my soul; save me on account of Thy mercy—* The Templar was pleading for release. "Your pain is the torment of your soul made flesh," Imbert explained. "Confess, Brother William. Confess your sins, here, now, and this will all be over."

William's eyes squeezed shut. *"Quoniam non est in morte, qui memor sit tui, in inferno autem quis confitebitur tibi."*

Imbert leaned in close at those words. *For who amongst the dead remembers Thee, who of the dead will tell of Thee.* "I can help you. You and I, we're not so different. We've dedicated out lives in service to God, to rooting out His enemies, saving His devoted. Confess, and you can again join the righteous in doing His work."

His eyes held closed, William paused, breathing deeply, wetting his lips with his tongue. Imbert kept at him.

"We can end this," he assured. "Recount the sins of your fellows. Say only what you've seen, and I can stop this for you, William. I can."

He bent down, placing his cheek close to the bound Templar's. His voice dropped to but a low sigh. "Confess for them. You need only whisper it, to me, and we can save their souls."

"Turbatus est a maerore oculus meus, inveteravi inter omnes inimicos meos."

Imbert saw the cracks. *My eyes are filled with grief, I have grown feeble in the midst of my enemies—* He had to now drive in the wedge, widen the fissure.

"You can speak with no fear of reprisal," he whispered, still closer. "Your Order is no more. You're under my protection. Beyond their reach."

William opened his eyes and turned to face Imbert. The inquisitor's eyes lit with a strange excitement. Imbert nodded his permissions to him, his own breathing short.

William's good eye narrowed to a slit almost as thin as his battered, swollen eye. *"Discedite a me omnes,"* he continued.

His voice cleared. *"Qui operamini iniquitatem, quoniam exaudivit Dominus vocem fletus mei."*

Imbert blinked at William's words. *Leave me, all you who do evil, for the Lord has heard the sound of my weeping*—Indeed, the psalm, but the words were not directed toward Heaven.

His face grew stern. "You're beyond your Order's help as well," Imbert reminded sternly.

William's lips pulled tight and he stared at Imbert. *"Erubescant et conturbentur vehementer omnes inimici mei; convertantur et erubescant valde velociter."*

The excited light in Imbert's eyes was snuffed. *May my enemies be put to shame and come to ruin. May they be turned away and be swiftly put to shame.*

"This is your chance to save your soul," Imbert warned. This was the psalm, he knew, but the Templar had managed to warp scripture into a weapon. Imbert's neck tensed and his head shook. "Your last chance—"

"Non nobis, Domine, non nobis," William cut him off, casting his eyes upward.

Not unto us, O Lord, not unto us. The Templars' motto and banner prayer. Only now, Imbert decided, the Templar spoke them as insult, as offense, insolent and prideful.

"Sed nomine," William continued, eyes turned to Heaven, voice more forceful with each word.

Imbert stormed back to the foot of the table, his own voice a low growl inarticulate in his throat. In a shower of sparks he heaved the brazier again under William's foot, the iron base screeching on the stones and nearly toppling.

William's body spasmed. His back arched, limbs straining, but pinned as he was, he could only endure it. Huffing, panting, he fought back a scream.

"Tuo da gloriam!" he roared instead, sincere and defiant.

Imbert watched him twist on the table. *But unto thy name give the glory*, he'd managed to finish. His prisoner howled, tearing against the straps, yet the leather bindings held, the grease upon his foot seething again to a rapid sizzle.

CHAPTER XXX

Tall, skinny freight houses of plaster and timber crowded one side of the stone wharf. At the other side was a steep and sudden drop to the inky, rushing waters of the River Seine. Wooden ships and other, smaller boats lined the wharf, rope lines tied off in sailor's knots to the upright pilings that dotted the wharf's edge. Narrow planks stretched down from many of the vessels' gangways to the shore, rising and falling and knocking occasionally on their hulls with the movement of the river. The air was cooler here, breezier, rife with the wet scent of mud, fish, and the city's waste. Dawn hung more than an hour away, the sky was dark, and the cobblestone was empty of sailors and dock wallopers.

Behind the freight houses stood two fortified stone buildings, an archway connecting the two as a gateway for carts and wagons to be inspected for duties and tariffs on the goods they carried. Across from the three huddling freight houses, a large, flat galley rocked on the water apart from the other vessels. A heavy line secured the galley's dark hull to the shore, where barrels and tightly wrapped bales were stacked high next to her gangplank, ready to load at sunrise.

Slowly stealing through the shadows of the stone archway, Brother Nicolas stopped when he spied the galley. He recognized it immediately. The ships of the Templar fleet were flatter and shallower than those sailed in Europe, their hulls patterned on the traders of the Mediterranean. He signaled for the brothers behind him to halt.

Seeing the galley rocking gently ahead, Brother Andre and Brother Ramon were visibly relieved. The younger sighed, and the elder murmured thanks to Heaven. Confused excitement played over Etienne's face. He'd only seen a ship once, and he'd never set foot upon one.

At the point, Nicolas remained cautious. He withdrew into the shadows, motioning the others to follow, eyes locked on the waterfront and the ship. Odo leaned forward from the shadows, turning his good eye ahead to see for himself. Their escape was close, but recklessness, he knew, had cost many victories. Nicolas had stopped for a reason, and Odo appreciated his caution and sharp eye, his skills honed well past his years.

He'd spied something.

After a few moments, Odo spied it, too. On the galley's deck, a head lifted up, peering over the rail and scanning the wharf, overlooking the Templars creeping in the archway's shadow before ducking back down. Shaven and wearing an arming cap, it was not the face of a Templar.

Etienne bit down on his lip and Andre stared. The others showed no reaction, accepting the turn as if expecting it. Nicolas continued glaring at the darkness.

"At least a full company of men await," he whispered over his shoulder. "Probably close to a company and a half."

Odo slipped up through their ranks to Nicolas's side. He stared at the shrouded wharf for himself. "Where?" he breathed.

Nicolas pointed at the galley and at the three freight houses. Odo could see an occasional shadow shifting in the windows of the nearest freight house.

"An ambush," Armande pronounced behind them.

Nicolas's voice was flat. "No doubt they meant to catch us on the wharf, move out from the freight houses to cut off our retreat, the river and the buildings penning us in."

Odo's head shook slightly. "What of our galley's crew?"

Nicolas shrugged.

"If there's no crew—" Francesco voiced quietly. "Can you sail, Brother Odo?" The sea was dangerous enough with seasoned sailors.

"By Jesu, I damn well better."

"How could they have known?" Andre thought aloud.

"Doesn't matter," said Armande. "They're here."

"Perhaps," Ramon suggested, "We should leave them here, lying in wait and depart the city on some other route."

While the others were whispering, Nicolas kept watch, noting each place he saw soldiers in wait.

"No," Odo said at last. "Running and creeping haven't worked. It's not our way. We'll solve this like Templars."

He drew his sword.

Armande nodded slowly. Relieved, unsmiling, he drew his sword, too. Ramon's blade slipped from its scabbard, followed by Francesco's. Andre looked to each brother, noting Nicolas' weapon in his hand even as he kept watch. Andre's hand went to his own hilt and drew his sword.

Odo dropped to one knee. Grasping his sword by the blade, he turned the point to the ground and pressed the cruciform hilt to his lips. Silently, the others did the same, Etienne kneeling on the muddied cobblestones just behind the brothers.

Odo lowered his head before the makeshift cross, shoulders square.

"*Non nobis, Domine,*" he began.

"*Non nobis,*" the others joined him.

✝ ✝ ✝

King Philip marched, agitated, through the dark Temple corridor, displeasure upon his face. Behind him chased De Nogaret, the chancellor hastening on short legs to keep pace with the long strides of his king.

"You found no records?" King Philip asked him once more.

"Merely empty shelves," De Nogaret reiterated. He knew the king's habits well. If Philip didn't care for an answer, he questioned it over and over until satisfied there was nothing of the response he sought.

"The patterns of dust indicate clearly that books and scrolls were kept on the tables and shelves until recently," the chancellor added.

"Papers, then?"

"Ashes." Searching the offices and quarters of the grandmaster and other masters of the Temple, De Nogaret had found only empty shelves and thick piles of cold ash. Room after room revealed the same evidence.

The king's countenance soured. "Your plan wasn't so perfect."

"How, my king?" De Nogaret shook his head. He'd planned for months. He'd prepared for six weeks in such secret that many involved did not know even where their orders led.

King Philip stopped and turned upon the Chancellor. "They were warned," he said darkly.

"By whom? If they knew the arrests were imminent, why stay?"

"Over a thousand of them were stationed here." King Philip proceeded down a winding staircase. "If the entire Order mobilized and withdrew, we would have seen."

De Nogaret conceded the point with a grudging nod. "Yet to stay here and allow all, including the Grandmaster, to be arrested serves no purpose."

"Except to keep our attention focused on the Temple."

De Nogaret caught his gasp, held back his reaction. "What could be so important that they would risk and would sacrifice so much?"

The stairs spilled into a squat passageway beneath the main floor of the Temple. The walls were of close-set stone, quarried and joined so well that the seams between the blocks were almost indistinguishable. The air was dry, strangely lacking the damp, subterranean feel of dungeons or catacombs. Torches and lanterns dotted the walls, their flickering light disappearing as the corridor twisted off into the distance.

At the bottom of the staircase, a lone soldier waited, anxious. As the king neared, the soldier drew himself up, inhaling loudly. Puffing his chest out, he lowered his gaze as the king and his chancellor neared.

"Sire," the soldier blurted.

The chancellor shot him a heated glance. This soldier was fortunate, De Nogaret thought, that His Majesty's time on the battlefields had lent him greater patience with his soldiers, especially toward such affronts to royal sensibilities.

"Speak," King Philip ordered impatiently.

"We've broken through to the Temple treasury."

King Philip exhaled sharply, his eyes revealing genuine surprise. "And?"

The soldier froze, glancing up from the ground at De Nogaret. "We—we await your command, sire," he stammered.

As much as he enjoyed watching the young soldier twist slowly, De Nogaret knew letting the king's mood blacken would make the night's work only harder.

"My instructions, highness." Fingers steepled before him, De Nogaret bowed slightly. "I was specific with them that only the king himself should first lay eyes on its contents."

"Why, then, do we stand here jawing?' King Philip asked. "Let us see the fruit our plans have borne us."

The soldier spun on his heel and marched through the flickering torchlight of the passageway, boots echoing hollowly on the stone floor. The king followed, De Nogaret a respectful pace behind him.

After a few steps, De Nogaret paused before a shattered door. The vault, he knew, was further on, but he had instructed the men to break in any door they found locked. He knew the Templars were clever. Versed in the arts of war, they understood distraction and misdirection, so he wanted to ensure the troops found everything of value the monks may have hidden in the open while the king's men were unsealing the vault. De Nogaret squinted, staring past the splintered timbers hanging in the doorway. Something glinted in the shifting, golden light. Weird shadows danced on the walls, thin and pointed. After another moment, he recognized the weapons.

The room was an armory. Lances were stacked neatly against the far wall. Maces, swords, and knives were strewn haphazard on the floor, spilled from overturned caskets that had held them. No doubt, he thought, this was the work of his own soldiers, claiming spoils for themselves as they could while they searched without oversight. The lances had remained untouched because they were too large to steal.

He was sure more armories were hidden throughout the Temple facility. With weapons so readily at hand, the Templars could have held them off for days, even fought to recapture their keep once the royal troops entered and took over. Yet, somehow, he had the Grandmaster of the Order in custody. De Nogaret decided he had much to be pleased about. He'd caught the mighty military force in their own headquarters, flat-footed and unprepared. His plan was a success, in spite of the king's reservations.

He saw the king and the soldier leading him disappear around a dark bend in the corridor ahead and he started after them. In the armory, torchlight glinted upon the spilled swords, drawing his eye. He paused, watching the reflected flame dance on the polished blades a moment longer before he hurried to catch up.

✝ ✝ ✝

The waters of the Seine were loud, rushing, the noise magnified by the still of the darkness. Boats thumped gently against the docks. The leaden clouds at last were rolling away, revealing a pale, waning moon that shone silver over the wrinkled, crawling river.

The Templar galley rocked gently. She tugged at her moorings, wooden hull creaking with each exertion. On her deck, De Valery and his sergeant hid behind the rail, flattened on the deck. Beside them, several more soldiers hid, pressed low and out of sight.

They strained to hear over the river. The rippling of the current and the knocking and groaning of the boats were constant. The occasional splash of a dace or goujon from beneath the water's surface startled and unsettled them as they listened.

Sergeant Luc Caym watched the others crouch, uneasily, on deck. His captain was impatient, the men anxious. Luc had learned patience in the Crusades, where the flat, featureless desert revealed an enemy army the moment it moved over the horizon, hours, even days, before they could be joined in battle. All a soldier could do was watch them advance, relentless, and wait until they were at last in range for archers on both sides and near enough to fight.

If anything, it was the boat itself that distressed the sergeant. He hated the smell of the river, the sea. Too much time away from water in the Holy Land had left him with a distaste for it. Most men couldn't get enough water once returned from the arid, sunbeaten sands of the Seljuk; somehow, he'd grown accustomed and acquired an aversion to the water.

Seated on his horse, Captain Le Brun hid with his company and the remainder of De Valery's in the freight house across from the galley. Two of the freight houses were stuffed with barrels, sacks, and crates. The third stood empty when they had arrived. Both companies of soldiers waited, crowded on the warehouse floor. From darkened doors and windows, they watched the galley and the stony wharf.

Le Brun cooed softly into his horse's ear, calming the beast. Nervous at the close quarters, it swayed, pawing at the wooden floor with its forehooves. Le Brun pulled on his reigns opposite the horse's swaying, checking its movement as it snorted disapproval of the crowded space. The soldiers were nearly as restless, fidgeting and weary of the silence and the wait.

In the far back corner of the room, a soldier leaned on the wall and drew back, surprised to find it warm against his wet shoulders, a welcome change to the cold and damp of the rainy night. A faint whorl of smoke drifted unnoticed, invisible in the dark. It took substance only when it snaked past a window and through a shaft of bone-colored moonlight. One soldier found himself coughing. The soldier next to him was coughing. He glanced at the wall and felt his stomach drop at the sight of flames lapping at the wall.

"Fire!" he shrieked. The cry was picked up, a dozen more men choking on the thickening smoke.

The flames licked at the timbers in the wall, rapidly blazing brighter. The room lit almost as bright as day as the blaze spread over the walls, scrabbling across the ceiling as it swallowed the old, dry timbers hungrily.

Captain Le Brun's horse wheeled about and crushed a pair of soldiers behind it. A soldier stationed near the door flung it open and fled into the cool, wet night air, a pair of his comrades at his heels. The men behind them crowded the door, bellowing curses as the others ahead of them stopped, blocking escape.

The first outside were dead on the ground, bleeding from terrible wounds.

Cut down.

Stepping over their warm corpses, the soldiers saw a massive, wild-maned figure. The blood of the fallen fresh on his blade, the fire blazed hellishly on the dock behind him, glinting on the dark mail of his armor. His surcoat glaring white, marked with a red cross, his great beard spilled dark over it. A black eye patch covered one of his eyes. The other eye burned black and cold.

He was coming for them.

CHAPTER XXXI

William thrashed on the table. Leather straps bit into his wrists and ankles, holding him tight. Pain stabbed white-hot up into his leg. He'd given up silence, embracing the agony and voicing it the only way he could mitigate it at all.

"Confess your sins, William!"

"*Non mortui laudabunt Dominum,*" William cried, unlistening.

"The others won't help you," Imbert shouted over the Templar's prayer. "They can't. Your Order is finished! Do you hear me? Finished. Speak now of its evil. Save your own soul!"

William tore at the leather straps, kicked against them again and again. He fought the pain and the impulse to surrender. "—*nec omnes qui descendunt in silentium.*"

"This can become worse, William!" Imbert threatened at the top of his lungs.

"*Sed nos benedicimus Domino*—" William shouted over him.

Imbert seized William by the hair. Never feeling the tearing in his scalp, William squeezed his eyes shut. His prayers choked in his throat as Imbert lifted his head, twisting it so he could see his own legs at the far end of the table.

"Worse than it already is."

Heaving, William let his eyes open. Blurred in his agony, he glimpsed in the flames the charred, blackened bones of what had been his foot.

And he felt nothing.

He sagged. "*Amodo et usque in aeternum alleluia,*" he finished quietly. His head lolled back, and he was lost to silence.

✝ ✝ ✝

At his Grandmaster's side, William stood on the docks of the Bay of Furor. Despite of the objections of the Hospitallers and the Templars, Grandmaster De Beaujeu was on his feet, directing the evacuation.

He kept his arm pressed tightly to his side. Even the slightest movement was excruciating, the arrow head burrowing into his flesh. The arrow could not be removed. The Hospitallers decided the shaft was the only thing stoppering his wound and holding his blood inside him, so they'd clipped the shaft off close to his ribs, even with his skin. The whole long march down the harbor road, Grandmaster De Beaujeu had held his arm close and rigid, making his tired limp more ragged.

William looked back up the hill to the immense and imposing harbor gate. Choking smoke billowed black over it. The fighting would be upon them soon. His brothers at the keep couldn't hold the line for long, and he was certain they'd soon be forced into the merchant's quarter. The battle would come down to a siege or, more likely, a stand.

He wasn't surprised to see Amalric and his Cypriot knights racing down the harbor road. Their heads high, they looked down with narrowed eyes upon the escaping pilgrims and injured. A few rushed the Cypriots arms open, pleading for safe passage on the royal ship. Amalric's men kicked them away. No room remained for refugees, with the nobles and treasure their servants bore. Trailing behind them were Tomasso and his mercenaries.

"We should keep watch on those freebooters," William said to the Grandmaster. "I wouldn't put it past them to start cutting throats for passage."

"They have passage with the Cypriot," Grandmaster De Beaujeu told him without glancing back. "They struck a deal, offering their swords to protect him and his retinue over the city." He turned back to the two remaining Templar galleys, the crowds surrounding them held back by the knight brothers. With their wounded loaded, he scanned the crowds, selecting joylessly who else would find a space on the ships' decks. They had only so much room, and as the corpses still bobbing on the water showed, a sunken boat did no one any good.

"We'll save those we can," the Grandmaster said to William, pointing out a mother clutching her two children. Two Templar brothers near her escorted her onto the galley. "Especially those who face a fate worse than death."

William looked to him.

"War reveals the worst in men, the most bestial and brutal, and we haven't the resources to protect those we brought here."

"We can hold them off, Grandmaster."

De Beaujeu raised an eyebrow.

"They're at the front wall of the city, and our keep is at the rear. Our brothers on the line are slowing them. If we can collapse some of the houses, the rubble will bog their march. Small skirmishing parties could harass them along the way. We know the city. Their resources and numbers mean less in its streets."

The Grandmaster's gaze strayed to their last galley. William followed it. Beside a French soldier with his jaw swaddled in bloody wrappings, William spotted Brother Odo. Dazed, he lay upon the deck, hair and beard thick with his own blood.

"*Hal tatalkam Arabi?*" the Grandmaster asked William almost under his breath.

"*Na am fahamt.*" William replied automatically, confused why the Grandmaster would care if he spoke Arabic.

"*Roah. Besorao,*" the Grandmaster ordered.

"Go where?"

"*Ela mohit. Inta fahamt?*"

He wasn't speaking too quickly, but William couldn't understand what he meant. *To the sea?* He worried Grandmaster De Beaujeu's injuries were impairing his reason. "I understand your words, Grandmaster. *Aewa*—"

The Grandmaster pointed at the galley where Brother Odo lay among the injured

"Those people require a Templar's protection," he told him. "Someone who can speak the language if there's bargaining to be done between here and Cyprus. Or if there's trouble, someone who's an able fighter."

"You need able fighters here to protect the city," William argued.

"I need able fighters to do as I order," The Grandmaster winced at the exertion.

William stepped away as he was ordered. Alone, he walked down the remainder of the pier.

CHAPTER XXXII

The soldiers were trapped, caught between the devil and his unpitying flames. They clung to the door frame, screaming, unable to choose between death in the fire and death by the sword.

More soldiers jammed the doorway, the pressure behind building, enormous and unyielding. Cries and curses were more desperate and panicked. Blinded by choking smoke and unreasoning fear, they pushed and heaved against the soldiers in the doorway until one man's grip tore loose.

He stumbled forward, crashing hard on the dock's stones. A half-dozen coughing soldiers rushed blindly out, trampling. Boots stomped across his back, face, and hands. Another soldier, eyes burning and blind, crashed on him, clawing at the ground and gulping the cool, clear air. More men wedged themselves in the doorway, jammed tight by their number in their panic.

Doubled over and wheezing, the first ones out never saw the sword that finished them. Odo waded in, blade flashing. He caught the first one above the nape, his sword slashing up enough to rip another below the jaw. His point stabbed into the next, finding space between his ribs before Odo kicked the dead man away to free the sword for the next soldier.

Soldiers continued jamming the doors. Fleeing the flames, they crushed against one another. At the back of the freight room, burning soldiers screamed. Their clothing on fire, their own armor became like branding irons on their skin.

Le Brun's horse screeched, terrified. Bucking, rearing back, it kicked at them wildly. Dying screams were lost in the roar of the blaze.

Ducked down on the galley, Captain De Valery heard the screams, recognized the crackling rumble of untamed fire. He looked to his sergeant, puzzled, and noticed the bright light quavering above on the ship's mast and rigging.

"Fire?" he questioned, and the two peered over the ship's rail.

The freight house where their troops lay in wait was engulfed in flame that swelled up past the building's third floor. It lapped at the roof, spreading fast. The freight houses on either side were burning, black smoke billowing thick from their windows. Yet it was the sight on the wharf that raised chills along their spines. In the windows and doors of the burning freight house, soldiers clawed over one another to escape.

Right into the blades of the Templars.

The giant, one-eyed Templar blocked the door. Three others manned the windows, felling soldier after soldier. The troops tore at the fallen blocking their way as the Templars waded through the chaos, hacking and stabbing, cutting men down left and right, trailing a gruesome wake. They were ruthless in their efficiency, terrifying in their discipline, unflinching and unyielding, just as Sergeant Luc remembered.

"They've ambushed *us*," he realized aloud.

A terrified shriek of a horse gone mad split the air. Fire lighting the freight house brilliantly inside, De Valery could make out Le Brun and his mount through the windows. Nearly thrown from the saddle, Le Brun yanked madly at the reins while the stallion was raging and bucking. It circled one way then the other, fighting his every effort to bring it under control. It crashed into soldiers, trampling them to cries lost in the roar of the flames.

Captain De Valery stared, the hellish sight overwhelming.

"Get them!" he managed to screech to the men around him. "Get them! Do you hear me?"

On his feet, the sergeant signaled the soldiers laying in wait on the deck to follow him. He sprang down the gangplank to the dock, the others trailing. Weapons high, they charged the freight houses and the Templars.

Out of sight, behind the barrels and bales and coiled ropes stacked upon the dock, Ramon, Andre, and Etienne watched the sergeant and the soldiers from the boat rush over the dock. Concealed in their dark cloaks, they slipped swords from their scabbards as the soldiers passed and started after them. Ramon paused, turning to Etienne.

"Stay here. Stay out of sight," he instructed. His forehead was damp, and to Etienne he looked pale, feverish, his eyes unfocused. The boy nodded gravely, and Ramon nodded back, winking. His eyes twinkled for a heartbeat, and he sprinted across the docks to join Andre.

Instantly, the two overtook the soldiers from the boat. The Templars' swords flashed, and two more of the royal troops fell dead behind the sergeant and the remaining pair.

Ramon took out the sergeant's knee with a kick and blocked the axe of the soldier beside him. Andre ducked the swoop of a sword, sidestepping and trapping his opponent's arm under his own, but the soldier was quick, and snapped a punch into Andre's face. His head jerked back, but he tore his dagger from his belt and plunged it into the soldier. The man's body slacked, and Andre let him slump to the ground.

Ramon slid to the side. The sharp axe head flew past and bit into the wet stones of the wharf, managing to throw sparks. Ramon stomped on its handle, ripping it from the soldier's grasp. Whirling, he drove his heavy pommel into the soldier's chin, feeling something give as he spun his blade high and brought it down over the man's shoulder and split him open.

Etienne gasped at it all. He understood what it meant to be a Templar, but nothing he'd ever seen in the Temple prepared him for the violence he saw the elder brothers dealing. He was repulsed and drawn, terrified and admiring.

A thump of boots landing heavily on the stony dock startled him. Glancing worriedly over his shoulder, Etienne saw Captain De Valery rise slowly after dropping from the deck of the galley, sword in hand. The boy shrank back, stumbling over one of the coiled ropes.

Among the flames, Le Brun struggled to rein his terrified horse. More men crashed into it, and the beast wheeled wildly. As it spun again, Le Brun glimpsed a shuttered window. Nearly consumed by the flames, it was crumbling, splinters dropping away and revealing the night sky. He spied a path, a momentary part in the fires and men. He pulled on the reins, forcing the horse about, and dug his spiked spurs deep into its sides. The horse bolted. Le Brun hooked his fingers in its bridle and ducked down, pressing his face to the side of the horse's neck as it charged for the wall and leapt.

It burst through the window, hooves skidding on the wet stones outside, jolting Le Brun almost out of his saddle. Away from the fire and turmoil, the horse regained its nerve and Le Brun brought it around.

The soldiers followed the horse's lead, bursting through the shuttered windows. Too many men escaping at too many points at once, the Templars could contain them no longer. Injured, angry, the soldiers drew their weapons and regrouped, hungry for reprisal. Out in the open, their numbers swelling, they could put forth a real fight.

Odo knew he and the others had lost the advantage of their ambush. He prayed they'd had time enough to whittle the numbers to their favor. A deadly cry snapped him from his reckoning and he turned. A soldier, face burnt and blistered, ran at Odo, an axe clenched high above his head. Before the weapon could come down, Odo stepped in on him. His hand shot out and he grabbed the axe by its handle and tore it from the burnt soldier's grasp, pitching him forward, pulling him off his feet. Odo pivoted and hacked into him with his sword as he buried the axe head between the shoulder blades of another soldier. The second soldier went stiff and sank to the wet stones of the wharf, clawing slowly at his spine.

Le Brun brought his horse about, scanning the scattered troops. They were gathering in small bands, some dragging off the crushed and burnt dead, others converging in ragged groups, weapons drawn. Le Brun stared past the men, perceiving in the shifting firelight the darting white forms his soldiers grouped to surround. His angry heart pounded. These Templar fugitives had become costly, and he decided he'd had enough of them. Le Brun watched his men as they fought. Against the Templars' blades, they were butchered and tossed aside as offal. Then he spied one Templar apart from the others.

Keeping the soldiers that fought to encircle him away from his back, the Templar had drifted to the edge of the melee and was almost clear of it. Le Brun's heavy longsword rang as it flashed high from his scabbard, and the captain spurred his horse into a charge.

Cut off from his brothers and surrounded, Francesco parried and dodged, laying into the men around him when he could. He fought to drive his skirmish back into the body of the battle. He parried an attack, countering from the right with a deadly thrust of his blade. A soldier fell at his feet and Francesco ducked to one side. The flanged mace in his left hand a crushed the next soldier's hip, crippling the trooper even as Francesco hooked the mace's spines behind another's knee and tore his feet from under him.

A stumbling soldier pulled a stunned and incoherent comrade from the fray, out of harm's way or so he thought until hoofbeats filled his ears like a burst of thunder. He looked up, and the two were trampled under the iron-shod hooves of his own captain's mount.

Le Brun leaned close upon his horse, its hooves beating triplet on the pavestones. Francesco whirled as he caught the sound, bringing up his sword and mace.

He'd heard too late. The captain's longsword slashed down with all the force of the charge behind it, splitting Francesco's mail and nearly severing his arm at the shoulder. His blood was a rapid, red slick on his mantle. The pain was too sudden and overwhelming for him to cry out. Spun by the impact, the battle around went silent and swirled. Francesco's sword fell from his unfeeling fingers. Weakly, he brought up his mace, praying aloud for strength as he saw the royal soldiers close on him. Francesco fell and the soldiers rushed him, stabbing and hacking.

Etienne hit the ground hard, landing again on his sprained arm. He cried out, clutching it tightly to his side as he scrabbled across the ragged, rutted stones. The wall of barrels and bales cut him off. Where they had hidden him before, they trapped him now.

De Valery kicked a barrel aside and lifted his sword high. His scorn was plain as he eyed the boy.

"They should know better than to leave the weakest one alone," he told Etienne. His sword arced down and stopped as the captain was tackled from behind.

Etienne saw him crash to the ground, hard. De Valery turned over, outrage burning in his cheeks as he struggled to his feet as Brother Andre rolled silently to his.

"A Templar's never alone."

Andre faced him, sword in a low guard. De Valery brought his blade around, its point slicing for Andre's neck. Andre bounded aside, bringing his own sword up, the metal crashing and the weapons ringing. He thrust out from the block only to find the captain's weapon encircling his, threatening to tear the weapon from his hands. Andre stepped forward, whipping his own point up and back, gambling offense for leverage as it forced De Valery's tip to his crossbar. Andre pivoted on his trailing foot and lifted his lead foot, slamming it into De Valery's ribs. But the captain turned with the blow, staying ahead of it, cutting its power. Andre saw then the captain was a skilled fighter. Though confident, worry squeezed his heart as another soldier lunged for him.

Brother Armande kept his back to the wall of the burning freight house, confident the flames would deter others from his back. With one flat slash, he cut down two men. The first fell dead upon the ground; the second writhed beside the other's corpse. Fighting so many at once, he had no time to consider his course, slashing at the next soldier while ducking a pointed hammer. He'd yet to draw a second weapon, trusting in the sword he fought with in the Crusades.

A whistling screech split the air and an arrow buried itself in his kidney. The impact pitched him forward. He staggered a step, head swimming as the combat tilted up at him.

Behind the freight house, Le Brun's archer notched another arrow, eyes white and round in his sooted face. He raised his bow, drawing back the string as he let his eye focus on the reeling Templar. His hand fell limp and the shaft flew over the battle, missing its mark and disappearing into the crawling river waters without even a splash.

The archer collapsed. Face down, the wet pavestones pressed into his cheek. A dagger stood in his back. From the shadows between the freight houses, Nicolas glided to the dead archer's side and collected his blade.

Etienne couldn't move. His limbs frozen in dread, he gasped in quick, short breaths as he pressed against the stacked bales. Before him, Andre fought off De Valery and two other soldiers. The officer was fast, skilled, and he pressed his attacks to keep Andre on the defensive. The initiate's sword flashed to parry one attack and block the next, dodging and turning to keep the soldiers' sharpened steel from finding any opening his blade left.

More soldiers were closing in on him from the edges of the main fight, spotting a skirmish where the numbers were in their favor. As a Templar, Andre would not, could not retreat. He was fast losing ground, and with the dark river rushing behind him, he'd soon be cornered. Etienne was desperate to help.

Armande forced his head clear. With a violent shake, he compelled his eyes to see straight, stopped the swaying of the fight around him. Soldiers were closing on Andre. Armande shoved back his nearest attackers with a grunt and reached behind himself. His hand found the arrow jutting from his back and snapped it off.

A soldier with a war hammer charged him. The arrow still in his hand, Armande whirled. Sidestepping the hammer, he tripped the running soldier and spun, driving the splintered missile into the neck of another blocking his way to Brother Andre.

He lunged after the young Templar. He could feel the arrow's head shift and scrape in his back with each step. Each dig cut his breath short. Ahead, he could see his young brother and Etienne, concealed among the barrels and bales. His eyes darted like a cornered mouse.

As he closed in, Armande gritted his teeth and raised his sword. Snapping the weapon forward in a flat slash, he caught the soldier nearest Andre between shoulder and jaw. The blade bit deep, severing artery and sinew with a dark spray. The soldier dropped.

Armande's sudden onslaught bought a startled pause to the assault on Andre. He took advantage of it, shifting and cutting down another soldier. Armande turned. The soldier nearest him started for the wall of barrels and bales. Armande drove his boot into the man's belly, doubling him over. He turned back to Andre and was caught full in the chest by De Valery's sword.

Armande froze. The pain hadn't registered, only the solid stop from the blow at the arch of his ribs. De Valery pulled his blade back, and Armande's limbs softened. Still standing, full of rage, the crusader thrust his sword out, a haggard guard to hold the captain off. His point started to sink, and his hand grew loose on the hilt. Cautious, curious, Captain De Valery lowered his own sword, and with a free hand, smacked the blade from Armande's failing grip.

Ramon watched as Francesco disappeared into the pummeling crowd of soldiers. He saw Le Brun slow his horse's charge and wheel it around. The beast cantered as the captain searched out a new target. Blood dripped from the officer's blade, the steel flashing in the flickering firelight. Ramon had no doubt that with the advantage of the horse, this captain could run them all down. Breaking free of his attackers, Ramon dashed across the pavestones of the wharf.

Le Brun spied the Templar out of the corner of his eye as he sprang at him, a ghastly figure shrouded in white and bloody red. Ramon crashed into him, slamming him from his saddle. The big officer hit the ground, something snapping in his shoulder as he struck. Clawing at its mane, Ramon stayed on the horse's back, taking Le Brun's place in the saddle. Even as Ramon clutched at its reins, it reared back, wheeling. Le Brun threw his arms up over his face, covering his head as the hooves smashed down on him, shattering his skull before the Templar could put the beast under control.

Odo's mace crushed in an iron helmet, the soldier under it staggering and collapsing. Odo caught the dazed soldier, slipping behind him and angling him as a shield, blocking the edge of an axe as it came down. The stunned soldier howled as the weapon chopped into his hip, hacking open muscle and splintering bone.

The roof of the freight house had almost been eaten through by the fire, the flames lapping unsatisfied at the dark sky. From deep inside the structure, Odo heard a low, shuddering moan. The remaining timbers were shifting and straining. He threw the crippled soldier at the feet of another, tripping the oncomer as the Odo distanced himself from the fires.

Armande's sword clattered on the pavestones as he faced the whelp of an officer. The young captain's eyes were bright, pleased, even mirthful. Angrily, Armande's left hand flashed to his belt, tearing free his long dagger and whipping it over his head to attack.

Before he could stab down, its point wavered. His arm sank, his limbs no longer obeying him. He discovered he couldn't breathe in. A slow, hissing gasp he couldn't stop escaped his lips instead. The pounding of his own heart in his ears went still. His rage swelled even as his knees buckled under him.

He was dead.

And his mind could no longer command his body otherwise.

His legs gave as his will faded. Rage draining away with his life, he crumpled to the ground. Only then his hand loosened on the hilt of the small blade. On the cold, wet stones, he was vexed, terrified that he could have done more. He prayed for God's mercy, that He would consider his service enough to absolve him of his excommunication.

De Valery stood over him. His nose wrinkled in disdain. Suddenly, he couldn't breathe. Gasping, he gulped at the cold air. His head felt light, and his legs weak, his knees watery. Realizing the sharp pain sprang from under his arm, he looked down and saw the boy he'd cornered moments before yanking a long and bloody dagger from his ribs.

Etienne watched the officer as he staggered back, clutching at his punctured side. The boy's eyes were cold, distant, as De Valery stumbled and crashed awkwardly on the ground. Blood spread slowly in a shallow pool around him.

At the galley's gangway, Andre dispatched another attacker. Glancing up, he started to call after Etienne, summon him to the ship so that they could make her ready, when he felt a sharp stab at his back, a point slipping past the ringlets of his mail.

Whirling, Andre slashed out with his sword, splitting open the gauntlet of a soldier behind him. The weapon flew from the man's hand, his thumb severed. As the soldier screamed out, Andre leapt at him, his sword flashing back the way it came and silencing the cry.

Clutching at his back, Andre called to Etienne. The boy didn't look up, his eyes fixed on the dead officer at his feet. Andre staggered to him.

Ramon steered the horse about. Like all Knights Templar, he was an expert on horseback. Templar cavalry were renowned on the battlefield, their *conrois* charge a formation so tight that light could scarce pass from behind the horsemen. They could punch through an enemy's lines, scattering them and driving them into their shattering second line of Templars that followed on foot. The stallion was spirited, trained but not as battle-hardened as the mounts in the Templar stables. The animal was flustered, unnerved, and any time Ramon directed it toward the fires and blazing walls of the freight houses, it reared back, anxious to bolt.

He put his heels to the horse's side, and sword high, spurred the beast into the thick of the fighting.

CHAPTER XXXIII

Lisette stumbled as she made her way on the dark street. One foot bare, her sole raked across a muddied rock.

She did not react. The pain was only the newest, the last after a litany dealt her by the soldiers at the bridge. The marks of their cruelty were throughout her body, which ached and smarted. Her wrists were raw. Her scalp was torn from where they'd held here by her raven hair, and her throbbing right eye now was bruised to match the left. She could feel the blood running cold upon the inside of her thighs.

In spite of it all, she made her way fairly quickly. If William's friends were proceeding slowly, maybe they hadn't yet reached the docks. Perhaps she could still catch up to them and warn them of the captain, his soldiers, and his plan. Even without William, they *had* looked after her. If they were warned of the forces laying in wait for them and they were but half the fighters the stories that came back from the Holy Land claimed, they'd make those soldiers pay dearly.

Accustomed to working the night, she knew dawn was some time off, yet the sky ahead of her was growing brighter above the rooftops. The glow was unsteady and flickering and she recognized it from so many times the cry of *Fire* rising and distracting her from her work in an alley or dark corner. The light danced on her battered cheek, and with a gasp she realized she was too late. Such a disaster had to be the Templars in a fight with their pursuers.

She lurched forward, rounding a corner to face two soldiers. Beaten and bleeding, their skin was burnt and their livery scorched black. With worried glances over their backs, she could see they were deserting.

Lisette recognized them from the bridge.

The one with the boy's face, who encouraged the others to hurt her as they had their way with her, was closest. His neck and cheek were red and blistered, in some spots charred black. His fair, wavy hair was burnt in irregular patches on one side of his head. His arm dangled limply, crushed badly, she surmised from the misshapen hand hanging from his sleeve. The other was the one with the dark rat's eyes. At first, he seemed better off than his fellow deserter, but she noticed he leaned heavily upon the handle of an axe, and she saw his leg on that side canted out at a horrible angle.

She started away, hoping they wouldn't notice her.

"You?" she heard the rat-eyed one say. She kept on.

The boyish soldier spun around, recognizing her too. "You warned them, didn't you?" he accused. He clutched at his wilted arm, useless at his side.

She would have expected seeing the soldiers' suffering to bring her some satisfaction. Instead, she wanted to escape.

"No. I've only just gotten here," Lisette blurted.

The boyish soldier trapped her arm, his good hand clamping tightly. She turned to tear away. The mad light in his eyes frightened her. And his burns made his face more terrible. Her hands this time were free, and she slipped her slim knife from her dress. The soldier with the rodent's eyes hobbled near, dagger in hand.

"I've spoken to no one," Lisette cried, and she stabbed out with her poniard. Its square blade gouged her captor's throat. The silver point wedged in an artery and blood gushed. The boyish soldier fell back, his weight tearing the dagger from her hand.

She turned to flee, but the other one was on her. The axe he held to prop him up fell away as he clawed at her with both hands. He pulled her near, black eyes burning with hatred. She pushed against him, feet suddenly finding purchase in the slick mud, and the two fell over.

They crashed hard onto the street. Lisette cried out in pain and outrage as his knife stabbed into her belly. The girl doubled over as the soldier flopped back. He groped for his axe, grunting as he pulled himself back on his feet. Without a glance back at the girl or his comrade, he resumed hobbling back into the city, soon lost in the shadows.

Lisette moaned and cried. She turned over, lifting herself from the muck of the street. At the end of the block, she could make out a dark arch and beyond it, intense firelight. They were there, she knew, and the wounded, fleeing soldiers proved the tide of the fighting. She got to her knees, hands pressing in the mud. Her delicate gloves were ruined. Tears streaked her face, hot on her cheeks. She struggled to get up. She was so near when he saw all her blood.

Crying as she had not cried in five years, she crumpled to the gutter.

✝ ✝ ✝

A torch in hand, King Philip ducked through the broken door and into the darkness of the Templar treasury. At last, *at last*, the months of planning and secret arrangements had come together. Once more, his beloved France's finances would be solvent.

Chancellor De Nogaret followed him, stepping though the door, the anxious young soldier that had led them a step behind. To the chancellor, the dark room had the empty sound of an old catacomb, their footsteps and voices echoing hollow out of the impenetrable dark.

Where the king stood with the torch, the gloom was dispelled. In the wall, he could see a dark alcove cut in the surface, lined by small, shadowy compartments. King Philip lowered the torch into it. Honeyed light spilled into the dark recesses.

"Their gold, Nogaret," he breathed.

He leaned close to the opening, almost trembling. Eyes weak in the dark, he could see nothing. He thrust the torch into the opening, a smile playing on his lips.

He saw nothing. The alcove was empty. No caskets of coins or chests of jewels. No palettes of ingots.

King Philip's eyes darted in confusion. He angled the torch, making sure it was no trick of the light, no fault of his eyes.

He remembered this room clearly, and the indignant surprise of the Templar bankers when he'd stumbled on them packing away the treasure, readying it for transfer. The vault was full then. Overflowing.

The king thrust the torch into another of the small compartments, finding nothing. He jammed the flame into each of the surrounding niches. All were empty.

He whirled, eyes racing over the rest of the large, dark room. Behind De Nogaret, the soldier shrank back, sliding into the passageway outside the door. De Nogaret watched his king. He let his eyes and face reveal nothing.

He hurried to the opposite corner of the chamber, torch wavering as he crossed. "They must have re-arranged it all," he muttered. Expecting the treasury to remain as he'd seen it a year before would be unreasonable, he told himself. He thrust the torch into another empty corner.

De Nogaret felt eyes upon his back. Glancing over his shoulder, he saw the nervous soldier who'd accompanied them to the vault. He was now flanked by a half-dozen more. All in the king's colors, each carried a torch or lantern. The king continued desperately, searching. De Nogaret eased aside and beckoned the soldiers in.

King Philip turned as the light began to fill the large, dark chamber, more brightly with each torch. Deferent and bowing, three of the soldiers fanned out and stalked cautiously past their king. The others took places nearer the door. Light shimmered on the walls of the vault, chasing away the shadows.

King Philip turned, taking it all in, his face unreadable. He quivered, his hands, his neck, and his head. His fists flashed upward as his eyes traced over every surface.

De Nogaret spoke, as he knew no one else could.

"Nothing is here, Highness."

The king threw his hands down, and from deep in his throat bubbled up a frustrated roar.

✝ ✝ ✝

Slowly, Odo backed his way to the galley. He hacked open the soldier nearest him and did the same to the next. He glanced and saw Andre on the gangplank with Etienne in tow. Ramon was on horseback, riding through the soldier's ranks, his sword raining down injury and destruction as he urged the steed and ran down any fleeing on foot. Their enemies' ranks were thinned, and Odo realized the night's gruesome work might nearly be done.

Brutally kicking the man nearest him, Odo brought his great sword up in a mighty heave.

"Be glorious!" he roared in rally and prayer. His sword cut a wide arc about him, scattering his attackers. He bounded across the wharf for the boat, his sword clearing his way where his shoulder could not. Ahead, he saw Andre hustle the boy onto the galley's deck.

Ramon maneuvered through the fight, sword flashing down like lightning from Heaven. Yet his breathing was ragged, his head light. His wounded arm burned and ached, pain stabbing as he bounced in the saddle. He could barely clutch the reins, direct the frightened horse through the retreating sea of enemies.

He brought the horse around again. As it spun, its hindquarters smashed into a pair of soldiers creeping from behind. The horse kicked and bucked. A hoof cracked against the nearest soldier's chin, flinging him into another. The two crashed unmoving on the hard stone wharf.

Soldiers scrambled away from the flailing horse. Ramon wrenched the reins, wheeling the beast around so sharply it almost lost its footing on the slick pavestones. More than once, the horse almost threw him from the saddle, the broad wooden cantle at the back of the saddle jamming into his tailbone. The horse's whirling made his head spin. His eyes lost focus. He found his arm weak, his wound burning. The leather reins slipped from his fingers. He let go his sword, dropping it to the ground and freeing his stronger hand for the reins.

Seeing him unarmed, Sergeant Luc rallied his soldiers. The horse backpedaled under Ramon as he maneuvered away from the attack. They were in too close, he saw, and he needed space. He wheeled the horse back, closer to the burning freight houses.

The soldiers were on him. Ramon tore his mace from his belt. He hammered its flanged head at their shoulders and skulls, raining down harm. He barely controlled the horse. He brought it around again, pushing back the men surrounding him. But Ramon's arm was wilting, his head sagging. Fever clouded his eyes and mind.

Almost at the galley, Odo looked up at the burning buildings to see roof beams pull slowly away from the structure. The roof collapsed in, the building swallowing itself as a section of flaming timbers broke free of the wall.

"Ramon!" he barked over the din.

At the heart of the turmoil, Ramon couldn't hear him. He brought his mace high as the sergeant's small band came at him, but before he could strike down, he heard the groan and roar of the collapse. He dug his heels into the horse, bowling over the nearest soldiers as the mount sprang in a charge straight out from the building. The fiery timbers crashed down on him, burying the knight and the attackers around him

Odo smacked away his nearest attacker and started back for the freight houses. His eye searched the rubble and flames for some sign of his brother.

He spied Ramon struggling in the wreckage, fires harrying close. One of his arms flailed loosely, the other strained against the beam that pinned him. But as Odo's blade gutted another soldier, he saw the sergeant had escaped the collapse and spotted Ramon, too.

Odo threw aside man after man as he saw the sergeant close in on Ramon and raise his sword. Ramon clawed for his mace, out of reach. The sergeant's blade came down. The fires surged, blinding. Odo had to avert his eye. He heard a shuddering moan of timbers, and another section of the wall crumbled and crashed down where he'd seen Ramon pinned. The surge of flame died down, and among the wreckage, Odo saw no more movement.

He had no time to look more. A soldier came at him with a broad, black axe. Feinting high, the soldier dropped suddenly. His leg shot out, and he pivoted, his outstretched leg sweeping at Odo's feet. Odo bounded up, ungraceful but clearing the soldier's leg, his boot soles brushing it as it slipped past. Odo landed lightly. The soldier lingered too long in the sweep and

Odo stomped down below the knee. He felt the man's shin crack under his heel and the soldier screamed.

The screeching soldier rolled, clutching his broken leg. Odo held off the remaining soldiers upon him, backing toward the gangplank, riding the fight, letting the press of it take him to the galley.

The soldiers, he realized were slowing. At first, he thought their resolve was flagging, but he noticed their darting eyes and the wary glances they shot to his blind side.

Odo turned to see what worried them. Among the bales stacked beside the galley loomed Nicolas. Sword in one hand, long dagger in the other, he stood half in the shadows, motionless.

Odo bounded to the gangplank.

"Nicolas, come on!"

Odo glanced back. Nicolas stood as before. Odo backed further up the gangplank, out of reach of his cowed attackers.

Motionless, Nicolas' gaze was distant, empty. The coiled tension in his body was absent. His weapons fell slowly, and he made no effort to raise them, even with the soldiers so close.

Nicolas swayed and fell forward, eyes expressionless and dead.

Odo sprang over the ship's rail and kicked away the gangplank. He caught sight of Andre and Etienne near the mast. The two were struggling with the sail and the riggings. Odo's mind raced back to the Crusades, to the crossings he made over the Mediterranean in ships like this one. He was no sailor, but he knew back then it would be foolish to ignore the boat's workings. Any attack or mishap could cost some portion of a crew. He observed what he could about piloting these galleys on every one of his voyages.

"Loose the sail!" he ordered the two as they wrestled at the bottom of the mast to unwrap it. "Let that rope out! Take up the slack on the other!"

Odo made a flat slash at a soldier who'd leapt from the dock and clambered up the low ship's rail. The man screamed and fell back onto the men behind him as Odo darted for the prow.

The Templar's blade flashed. He cut the heavy mooring line that tied the galley to the pier and turned his sword in a savage whirl that cowed the attackers still trying to board. The current's pull angled the bow from the dock and the ship drifted into the Seine and out of the soldiers' reach.

A faint line split the dark heavens above the horizon. Their chances of escape would fade with the sunrise. With the sky growing lighter, they had to get underway.

Andre and Etienne were sorting out the sail. Praying they would have it soon and he would not have to unfurl it himself, Odo made for the stern. His boots hit hard and hollow on the wooden deck planks, and he seized the rudder. The current dragged them farther from shore, slapping the galley's hull. She picked up speed as they were pulled farther out. Both hands on the tiller, he put his weight into it, shouldering he rudder against the current, pointing the ship midstream.

Far enough out that he feared no chance of boarders, he looked out from the Seine to its banks. Upon the docks, he saw no more soldiers, no more fighting. Only the dead. Corpses of friend and enemy littered the dark stone wharf. Sprawling limbs bent unnaturally, they all lay unmoving, too still with the fires raging so near.

The first of the freight houses was a blackened, crumbling skeleton, flames lapping at the remains of its walls and roof. The neighboring freight house swayed with the flames consuming it until the timbers midway up its side snapped. What looked to Odo like burning coals vomited from the broken wall. Beams, joists, and wall timbers hurled across the wharf with a burst of starry embers that faded to black ash. The way the fires were spreading out over the dock, the bodies wouldn't last long.

He thought of his fallen brothers, dying bravely and gloriously. He knew he'd left no one behind. He prayed for them all, asking mercy for each. He knew not what little sway an old soldier's prayers carried, but he owed them no less.

In particular, he prayed for Brother William. Odo knew he would never know his old friend's fate, He shut his eye. Days from leaving his vows, William's courage, his faith, his belief in the Order and its service to God delivered them all this far. He begged God to look over William, praying He show him the mercy and forgiveness Odo believed his sacrifice back at the footbridge merited.

"*Non nobis, Domine,*" he began chanting quietly, "*non nobis sed nomine...*"

✝ ✝ ✝

William could no longer feel the pain of his foot in the flames. Nor, he realized, did any part of his body pain him any more.

Imbert studied him. The Templar was bound supine before him. Restless, delirious, he strained weakly against the leather straps. His flushed face was streaked in tears. Perspiration lathered his body, soaked his hair. Feverishly, his lips traced soundless words.

"Speak, Brother," Imbert implored. "Speak."

William was on the deck of the galley escaping Acre. He'd settled the other injured refugees and casualties before returning to Brother Odo. He began checking the dressing over his eye and Odo waved him off impatiently, muttering a low grumble. The old Templar's color was returning.

"You look better, Brother" William said.

"Half-covering a face like this will do that."

William allowed himself a smile, slight and wan, before looking back at the receding docks.

The sun was blinding. The waters surrounding him were brilliant blue. But behind Grandmaster De Beaujeu, he could see the city burning. A low, black cloud billowed from it, spreading above the walls. William was about to speak, when the Grandmaster's hard stare cut him off. Grandmaster De Beaujeu signaled to the galley's crew and they pushed off. There would no more discussion.

"Be glorious, Brothers," the Grandmaster called to them. Grisly streaks from the fierce fighting in the streets striped his white surcoat. William realized that under his arm, the Grandmaster's tabard was soaked, thick with blood that was running freely down his side and over his leg. His face splashed in gore, his expression was calm, his eyes resolved and certain. On the rocking deck of the receding galley, William watched as the Grandmaster turned away, headed toward the city. He faltered and slowly closed his eyes.

Panic stabbed into Imbert's heart, cold and quivering as he saw Brother William cease his struggling. His face grew calm and William's eyes looked to an unknown distance, resolved and certain. He sagged.

"God lives, Grandmaster," William called out softly and breathed a last, rattled breath.

Imbert grabbed at the Templar's shoulders. But he had presided over too many inquiries, too many interrogations, to believe there was anything he could do or change.

The king would be displeased.

He crossed himself, and clapped his hands together in frustrated prayer.

CHAPTER XXXIV

The cold, gray waters of the sea roared in Odo's ears. The sun was bright. The chill winds were blessedly strong and gusting from astern so he had no need to tack the galley to keep her on course. He smelled salt strong on the air, and the cold, stinging spray the wind carried over his face was bracing.

God was with them, Odo decided. The voyage over the Seine was uneventful. The king's forces must have proceeded in the wrong direction, focusing their search to the north or west as predicted. Sailing downstream without stopping, he, Andre, and Etienne cleared Le Havre with ease. They were in the English Channel, and he was confident that as long as they could keep the shore in sight, he could pilot them to almost any port.

Uncoiling a line from its place at the stern, Odo wrapped it around the tiller, lashing the rudder. He stretched his arms, allowed himself to yawn for the first time since awakening before the king's raid on the Temple. He climbed down to the main deck, where Andre and Etienne waited.

The boy clutched the ship's rail. He stared awestruck and overwhelmed by his first sight of the boundless expanse of the sea surrounding them. An excited and nervous smile played over Etienne's lips, and he gripped the rail more tightly as a swell came up and lifted the galley. The flat-hulled boat rode across the wave before settling back to its gentler rocking. Odo patted the boy's bony shoulder as he made his way toward Brother Andre.

Sitting on the deck, Andre slumped sleepily against the mast. Odo squinted back at the shore fading behind them before lowering himself to Andre's side.

"Do you know where this vessel was headed?" Odo asked.

Hood drawn up over his face, Andre didn't answer.

Odo leaned in closer. "Andre, do you know where we are meant to be headed?"

In the bright light, he noted the pallor in the young knight's cheeks, the sharp, irregular breathing. He was less asleep than unconscious.

Andre's eyes fluttered open. "Scotland," he rasped. "To our Order's hold in Balantrodoch." He coughed.

Odo looked out over the bow of the ship. He'd journeyed to London once as part of an escort, but he knew of Balantrodoch only by name and its place on a map.

"That's a good distance. Perhaps even far-flung enough from Philip's influence to be safe, for a time. Assuming we avoid capture in the channel—"

"We have to" Andre pulled himself so he was seated upright against the mast.

"We don't know the scale of the assault on our Order," Odo reminded. "We don't know if it has survived."

"It must."

The initiate winced and shifted. Odo grew concerned. He'd focused only on reaching the sea. He'd paid little attention to the young man's languor, assuming it to be exhaustion and inexperience. He realized as Andre shifted his shoulders against the creaking mast that he couldn't stand.

In the bright sunlight, he could see that Andre's dark cloak was heavy and wet with his blood. Odo glanced aside at Etienne. The boy was looking out, enchanted by the unbounded sea.

Odo cradled the younger brother and leaned him forward. Blood dripped from the fabric as he gripped the cloak. Odo bit the inside of his cheek as he lifted the wrap and saw Andre's back. The white tabard was slick and red, clotted black in the gathered folds.

He spied Andre's hidden pack. The bag was small and leathern, hanging nearly square at the small of Andre's back. The leather was wet and stained dark where the sack rested against him. Andre reached around for it.

"Brother, I must give you this."

Odo tore open Andre's bloody tabard. He could see where the iron rings had split. The wound beneath was but a slit, but the color of the blood he saw oozing from it told him it went deep. Andre's breathing troubled him more for the injury to his lung it portended.

"We must bind your wounds," Odo stated flatly. He'd have to get Andre out of his hauberk, perhaps fashion his tabard into bandages. On their trip over the river, he'd found the galley's hold well stocked with water and rations. They wouldn't need to land for supplies.

"Brother!" Andre snapped.

Odo stopped and turned to him.

Andre fumbled with the bag, unlacing it with thick fingers.

"This is more important," he said. He leaned heavily on the mast. "Grandmaster De Molay entrusted it to me and ordered me to tell no one."

"You carried yourself like a man with a secret."

Andre laughed, wincing weakly.

Odo looked back to the rail. Etienne was watching him, unmoving.

From within the bag, Andre withdrew a bundled cloth. Odo could see it held something wrapped within.

"All has been arranged," Brother Andre explained, "through the Baron of Rosslyn, Sir Henry Saint-Clair."

Above, a gull shrieked to another. The roar of the ocean threatened to drown out the fading Templar's voice.

"All that is left to us is to deliver this to the safe hands of our brothers in Balantrodoch." He pressed the bundle into Odo's wide, bloody hands.

Carefully, Odo unwound the cloth. Beneath was an intricately carved box. Dark and polished, four sides were detailed with the images of a bearded man's face. They were, it seemed to Odo, like seeing the portrayed man in the flesh, so faithfully and sensitively carved was each. The first face depicted kindness and understanding, as only the patience of true forgiveness offers. The next image of the face was passionate, mad with anger and outrage. Not the face of a fighting man, though—the face of a man who can withstand no more affront. Odo turned the box over to a likeness of quiet happiness, the slight smile on this face that of a man among family or lifelong friends. Turning the box again, he found a portrait of pain, tortured agony borne in silent, noble suffering. The crown of thorns upon the subject's head made Odo certain of what he suspected.

These were images were carved with more love and skill than any of the work he had ever seen in the Temple. He turned it over again, marveling at the detail, when he lid caught his eye. Lacking any image or any sort of decoration, it bore an inscription: *LVIII*.

The top fitted to the box by a pair of grooves so the lid opened by sliding. Odo slipped the small panel away, tucking it under his arm. Inside the box, he found a small, chipped dish. Made of wood, it was shallow bowl setting atop a flat base. Its steep sides were stained dark by age and split along the grain.

Odo's fingers trembled as he connected the chalice he saw with the images upon the box that held it.

"Our greatest treasure," Andre breathed, smiling. "Found in the Holy Land two centuries ago, and protected by our Order ever since. The cup our Lord Christ held in His hands at the night of the Last Supper."

"The Holy Grail," Odo whispered.

Etienne said nothing, his eyes riveted upon him.

Andre's voice was tired, pleading. "Please, Brother Odo. The Grandmaster entrusted it to me, and I've only borne it this far. Ensure it makes it to safe hands. For when the world needs it."

Odo stared at the cup, memories of his lost brothers flooding over him. He looked to Andre, whose eyes were desperate, the initiate clinging to life until he could be sure his duty would be met.

Odo closed the box. He nodded. "You sleep, Brother."

Andre nodded back to him. He rested his head on the mast and closed his eyes, passing without sound.

"God requires only that we struggle..." Odo reminded softly. He called Etienne to his side, the boy stumbling on the rolling deck.

"Take this," Odo said, pressing the small, carved box into the boy's hands. "Keep it safe."

Fear lit Etienne's eyes. "Brother Odo, I can't. I'm just—I'm no knight."

"Not yet," Odo agreed, staring with his one eye at the gray sea to their north. "Which is why you must take it. The compromises the world demands of a man have left me too unpure."

He left Etienne with the box. Overcome, Etienne could only stare at it. He clutched it tightly to his heart as Odo climbed tiredly back to the rudder and unlashed it. Crossing the channel would be dangerous for one so inexperienced at sailing. Hugging the shore and working their way to a keep he knew only by name would be even more dangerous, especially if Philip's influence stretched over the gray channel waters. He took the rudder in hand and shut his eye, feeling the wind in his beard.

Etienne was terrified by the unknown ahead of them and by the responsibility put into his hands. When he looked up at Brother Odo's face, he found his fears calmed, for in it he saw only certainty.

Resolve.

CHAPTER XXXV

The hills were rolling and green, gliding past open meadows lined thick with trees turning bright with autumn's colors. Cautiously, from the brush beneath the trees, a hare crept into the open. Brown fur rippling, its nose wrinkled as it sniffed at the earth and wind before scampering for a thick tuft of grass where it could hide. A screech from on high split the air and an arrow suddenly buried itself in the ground beside it. The rabbit scrambled away, disappearing back to the cover of the tangled brush and trees.

King Philip IV lowered his bow, laying it across his saddle. He pulled his light furs closer against the chill.

"Blasted wind." His breath puffed before him, misty in the cold.

Behind him, his two massive bodyguards, Bertrant and Karles, shifted in their saddles. A glance passed between the two, and Karles relented. Putting his spurs to his horse, he rode ahead to where the arrow thrust from the ground as Bertrant kept watch.

De Nogaret maneuvered his horse nearer the king. Normally, His Highness enjoyed the hunting in the forest of Fountainebleu, but the sport had been poor. The game was sparse and wasn't readily chased from the woods. That the king loosed an arrow at a rabbit rather than a stag or a boar or another creature more worthy of his royal station was proof of the day's disappointment.

Ahead, Karles plucked the arrow from the earth. Wiping the mud from its head with his fingers, he turned and saw the king, hand raised high, an order for him to wait where he was.

The king urged his horse forward into a slow amble. De Nogaret matched his pace, riding closely yet behind. Today, the king seemed tired. The dark circles under his eyes had remained for weeks. The gray that streaked his fair hair brought out the ashen color of his cheeks, which had sunken hollow in the last few weeks.

"A poor hunting trip indeed," the king said to his chancellor without turning.

On foot, Karles trotted to his king's side, replacing the recovered shaft in the royal quiver before returning to his own horse, led by Bertrant.

"Your daughter awaits us," De Nogaret reminded. "Let us call this day ended and cut short the hunting."

King Philip nodded. Neglected by her husband, the English King Edward II, his daughter Isabella had returned to France along with his grandson almost two years ago. The king smiled thinking of his daughter and her toddler, a child who would one day rule and place his bloodline on the thrones of both England and France.

De Nogaret continued. "You're still recovering, highness. After all, when you took ill last—"

"Don't start with that curse nonsense, Nogaret."

De Nogaret paused. "One must admit, the timing following Grandmaster De Molay's final words at his execution—"

"De Molay was a fool. Before he spoke up at the sentencing, his punishment was the same as the other three Templars condemned that morning. He was to live out the rest of his days in prison." Perhaps it was the tribunal's setting on the steps of the Cathedral of Notre Dame, but something emboldened the old Grandmaster that March morning seven months ago. Shouting brazenly over the church's commissioners, he denied the confession Imbert had extracted from him seven years before. In withdrawing his confession, he invoked upon himself a sentence of death.

"Yes, sire, he was, as was the Preceptor of the Temple of Normandy for joining him in the recantation." Rushing to make an example of the defiant Templars before their actions heartened any of their surviving brethren, the king ordered a pyre built on the nearby Isle of Javiaux so the pair could be executed that evening. To discourage any others from following, he specified the pyre be constructed for a smokeless fire to roast the two prisoners slowly, without the choking black clouds that typically asphyxiated the guilty and spared them the worst agonies of burning.

Lashed to a stake among the coals, De Molay shouted challenges to the king and commissioners for an hour before clasping his hands in silent prayer and expiring. Even King Philip had to admire the final bravery the Grandmaster showed meeting his end.

But the Templar's last words before giving himself up to prayer troubled De Nogaret. "Let evil swiftly befall those who have wrongly condemned us!" he screamed. "God will avenge us!"

"He called for you and your Pope to join him before God in one year and account for your deeds against him," De Nogaret recalled.

"I was there," the king spat back. He squinted over the hills. He was glad to be out of doors again.

"So far, his curse has come true. Pope Clement is dead."

King Philip waved off his concerns. "It proves nothing. If De Molay had any true power, he wouldn't have rotted in my dungeons for seven years before I had him killed."

"Your recent illness—"

"Means nothing. A king has naught to fear from a man he's had executed and even less from his impotent words." The king's bravado was a good sign of his strength's return, but De Nogaret kept the royal physicians close because he knew how precarious King Philip's health had been for weeks and how uncertain the future of his rule had been.

The king spurred his horse to a trot. "Even if my illness was the doing of his curse, it failed."

De Nogaret rode to catch up. He was neither a superstitious man nor a religious one, preferring to trust results he worked with his own hands over prayer. Yet in the corridors of power where he strode at his king's side, he had learned a fine line existed between coincidence and evidence.

"I counsel only caution, majesty. The year's not out. And—"

"What?"

"There are reports. From the Bannockburn battle this past summer."

"Why does my son-in-law's latest failing concern you?" Any mention of Edward raised Philip's bile. King Edward II of England was weak in his estimation. He wasn't half the king his father, Longshanks, had been, and Edward had been losing the Scot Lands since ascending the throne.

"After nearly two days of victory," King Philip continued, "he was handed the worst defeat in his land's history by a ragged band of irregulars with neither cavalry nor archers. Little more than peasants with sharpened sticks." The entire matter was an embarrassment, for King Philip personally and for his daughter, who had to bear the humiliation of calling the milksop *husband*. "And that is from Edward's own account of the battle."

"Indeed, King Edward does maintain that's what took place," De Nogaret agreed. "But there are other accounts."

"Academically interesting, perhaps."

"Dispatches, sire. They relate that the English lines folded only after a phalanx of horsemen joined the battle on the Scots' side."

"Horsemen? The reports I saw said the Scots had no cavalry, no knights. That the English lines broke when they mistook a distant band of Scot servants as reinforcements for the Bruce." Philip tugged back on his reins, stopping his horse as he locked eyes on his chancellor.

"I have verified this as best I can any account of a foreign battle on foreign soil," De Nogaret prefaced. "I'm told these horsemen rode out from cover in the nearby hills of Coxtet. They're said to have smashed the English front line with a cavalry charge that scattered the forward forces, hurling them into a shattering second line of knights that followed on foot."

"The *conrois*," Philip breathed his thought aloud. It was classical, one of the tactics that had won the Holy Land generations before.

"This new contingent was reported to be unstoppable, flying banners of black and white, marked with a red cross."

"Ghost stories."

"Their cries of 'Be glorious' were said to drive the English columns to panicked collapse as the horsemen rode straight for

King Edward and his commanders. By these reports, it was *then* that Edward and his retinue withdrew, gathering their ranks about them for safety and fleeing for Stirling."

King Philip scowled. "This is first-hand?"

De Nogaret nodded. "From the Lancaster."

The king put no credence in curses. But assassination and revenge he understood.

An arrow's shriek split the air. Bertrant, riding behind the king, was hurled from his saddle.

The others whirled, bringing their horses about as the bodyguard crashed hard into the sod, the shaft of a long arrow lodged in his chest. Karles scanned the mottled colors of the tree line. He snapped straight upright before sinking into his saddle, an arrow jutting from his neck.

As the bodyguard sloughed from his horse, King Philip threw down his reins. He lifted his bow and snatched an arrow from the quiver at his side. De Nogaret froze, heart pounding loud in his ears. As the king notched the shaft to the bowstring, another arrow stabbed into his thigh, and then another into his back. He fell from his saddle, clawing slowly at the ground, trying to get up, while his horse cantered away uncertainly.

De Nogaret slid from his saddle to help his bloodied king. His mind raced for the identity of the assassins. The Flemish had been demanding further concessions in the treaties Philip had imposed on them. Perhaps some among their nobles thought a new king might be more accommodating to their desires.

As he neared the king, he heard behind him the crunch of dying grass under footsteps and the distinct rustle of chain mail. He turned and shrank away, horrified.

A big man, approached, wrapped in the dark robes of a monk. His stride rigid, purposeful, he carried himself like a soldier. Broad-shouldered and barrel-chested, his dark, wild hair was streaked in gray, as was his thick beard. An eye patch hid one of his eyes, while the other burned, black and angry. Coming from the trees, he marched straight for them.

De Nogaret started for the dagger at his belt, when beyond the one-eyed oncomer, he spied an archer. Perhaps a hundred paces back, he stepped clear of the tree line, another arrow leveled at the chancellor. De Nogaret stepped back. The one-eyed man passed him. His dark robes unfastened, they had fallen open to reveal the armor beneath and the sword at his hip.

Despite his terror, De Nogaret backed away, putting his horse between himself and the archer in the trees. His mind raced. The dispatches, the rumors from the English routing that summer. He saw the stranger grab the king and haul him to his feet.

Odo leaned close and gasped the arrow jutting from the king's leg. Defiant, Philip allowed himself only to wince as the sharpened arrowhead twisted in his thigh, scraping muscle and nerve.

"That was for the boy," Odo rasped. Back among the trees, Etienne kept his bow taut, an arrow notched and ready to fly. Now a young man, he was lean, his face marked with a faint scar that disappeared behind a thin, sandy beard. There was little left in him of the boy William looked after so many years before in the Paris Temple. The crucible of the years burned away all the extraneous in him. He was older, colder.

Steel.

Odo's jaw set.

"Who are you?" King Philip demanded. "How dare you!"

Odo shifted his grip to the king's throat, choking his words to a faint, gurgling wheeze.

"This is for the Order you betrayed."

Philip's eyes strayed to his captor's chest. His dark robes had come completely open, revealing the distinctive red cross emblazoned above the man's heart.

"And this is for my brothers you murdered."

He shoved King Philip back. The monarch staggered, off balance.

"I'll see you burn for this," the king raged, but his weight shifted to his leg pierced by the arrow jutting from it. The sudden, sharp pain cut off his voice and his knee gave out. He stumbled, and fell backward.

He crashed to the ground. The arrow in his back plunged through him, driven by his own weight. The steel point burst from his chest in a grisly blossom. King Philip went limp, air hissing over his lips and blood dribbling at the corners of his mouth. Odo watched, waited. King Philip lay unmoving.

De Nogaret was trying to stay still, holding his breath, hoping to remain unnoticed. The chancellor managed to keep from backing away as the big Templar turned on him, menacing. The scar, partly concealed by his eye patch, darkened.

"If you *ever* speak of this—" Odo jabbed a finger in the direction of the king's corpse, threatening. He started away again.

"There will be questions," De Nogaret called after him, stepping out from behind the horse. His arm swept over the arrow-riddled corpses behind him. "What would you have me say?"

"Tell them it was a hunting accident," Odo answered without turning.

"You have killed the king!" De Nogaret cried.

Odo marched back for the woods. "Kings die," he called over his shoulder. "Their kingdoms crumble."

Confusion and desperation somehow emboldened the chancellor. He started after the Templar but stopped and fell silent. Among the trees, he spied more Templars. Their faces grim, their robes open to reveal their scarlet crosses above their hearts, they stood. Watching. Waiting.

De Nogaret froze and gasped as Odo disappeared among the trees and his brothers.

The Templar's voice echoed to him:

"The Order will go on *always*."

✝ The End ✝

BIBLIOGRAPHY

God's Forge is a work of fiction, inspired by an account of the Templar arrests I stumbled across while researching another project. The image stuck with me, and the story kept nagging at the corners of my mind until I set aside the other project and wrote it. As far as I know, there is no record of any actual band of knights escaping from the Paris Temple in the early hours of October 13, 1307. First and foremost, it is a *story*. So, when lacking a needed detail, if I couldn't extrapolate something from known facts, I had to fabricate it. Please keep that in mind, and remember the old saw "never let the details get in the way of telling the story."

To convey a world like the 1307 of the Templars requires research. Outside their activities in war and their influence on the politics of the day, little is known of the Templars. Highly secretive before they were suppressed, few records survived the thorough destruction of their Order. Many aspects of their daily lives, their exact beliefs and rituals, their methods of training, and many of the secrets they discovered in the Holy Land and returned home with to Europe have been lost.

Still, some skilled and enterprising researchers have managed to piece together pictures of different aspects of the Order. An interested reader may learn more about the Knights Templar, their victories, defeats, and the world they fought and died in, through the same references I used in researching *God's Forge*:

Baigent, Michael and Richard Leigh. *The Temple and the Lodge.* New York: Arcade Books; 1991.

Barber, Malcolm. *The New Knighthood: A History of the Order of the Temple.* New York: Cambridge University Press; 1995.

Barber, Malcolm. *The Trial of the Templars.* New York: Cambridge University Press, 1993.

Burman, Edward. *Supremely Abominable Crimes: The Trial of the Knights Templar.* London: Alison & Busby, 1994.

Butler, Alan & Stephen Dafoe. *The Warriors and the Bankers: A History of the Knights Templar from 1307 to the Present.* Templar Books, 1998.

Haag, Michael. *The Templars: The History and the Myth: From Solomon's Temple to the Freemasons.* New York. William Morrow Paperbacks, 2009.

Howarth, Stephen. *The Knights Templar.* New York: Fromm Intl., 1991.

Partner, Peter. *The Murdered Magicians: The Templars and Their Myth.* Oxford, New York: Oxford University Press, 1982

Picknett, Lynn & Clive Price. *The Templar Revelation.* New York: Simon & Schuster, 1998.

Read, Piers Paul. *The Templars: The Dramatic History of the Knights Templar, the Most Powerful Military Order of the Crusades.* New York: DaCapo Press, 2001.

Robinson, John J. *Born in Blood: The Lost Secrets of Freemasonry.* New York: M. Evans & Co., 1989.

Robinson, John J. *Dungeon, Fire and Sword: The Knights Templar in the Crusades.* New York: M. Evans & Co., 1992.

Strayer, Joseph R. *The Reign of Philip the Fair.* Princeton, N.J.: Princeton University Press, 1980.

also from Legendary Planet